ALL
WE
COULD
STILL
HAVE

ALSO BY DIANE BARNES

More Than

Mixed Signals

Waiting for Ethan

ALL WE COULD STILL HAVE

a novel

DIANE BARNES

LAKE UNION
PUBLISHING

Published by Lake Union Publishing, Seattle

www.apub.com

Amazon, the Amazon logo, and Lake Union Publishing are trademarks of Amazon.com, Inc., or its affiliates.

ISBN-13: 9781662511813 (paperback)
ISBN-13: 9781662511820 (digital)

Cover design by Shasti O'Leary Soudant
Cover image: © Jean Ladzinski / ArcAngel; © Andrew Billington / ArcAngel

Printed in the United States of America

For Brittany, Robbie, and Ali: being part of your lives as you grew from newborns to the compassionate, kind, loving adults you are today has been one of the greatest honors of my life.

For Susan and Bobby: from Cape and Disney vacations to everyday and holiday meals to school plays and sporting events, thank you for always including me.

Chapter 1

Like a fairy godmother about to grant a wish, Dr. Evans positioned herself between the stirrups my feet rested in and lifted the wand. Across the room, my husband, Kyle, scrolled through his phone, probably looking at hockey scores. The first two times we'd done this, he stood beside me, his fingers laced through mine and his eyes fixed on the monitor Dr. Evans studied while she guided the catheter toward my uterus. When she'd reached the target and released the miracle potion, he squeezed my hand and smiled. Today, she discharged the embryos, and he yawned.

During our previous rounds, he'd kept me company after the procedure while I was required to lie still. We'd talked about our baby's future. Kyle wanted a little girl who took after me so he could see what I had been like as a kid. Honest to God, I'm not sure how I ended up with such a sweet husband. The baby's gender didn't matter to me. I only wanted to pass on a piece of my parents, keep the DeMarco bloodline going. I also prayed that the baby inherited Kyle's big heart and disposition. Compared to me, he was usually a lot less grumpy.

This afternoon after Dr. Evans finished the transplantation, Kyle said he needed air and followed her out of the room. I wished he'd stayed, because we needed to talk. I had to find out what was distracting him.

When I was finally allowed to get up, a nurse led me to Dr. Evans's office, where Kyle and the doctor were waiting. They stopped speaking when I entered, and I wondered if they had been talking about me. As soon as I sat down, Dr. Evans launched into the usual postprocedural instructions. My mind wandered as she spoke. I already knew this. *No rigorous activity; don't take a drugstore pregnancy test, because they often result in false negatives; come back on day eleven for a blood test.*

As if she knew I wasn't paying attention, Dr. Evans shifted her body so that she was angled toward me. "It's important that you both remain optimistic, emit positive energy." This was new, and I laughed, because positive energy, really? It was such bullshit. Dr. Evans didn't appreciate my laughter. I could tell by the way she pushed her glasses off her eyes into her long silver hair, the way she did when she told me something she didn't want to and couldn't bear to see my reaction. It was exactly what she'd done the two times she broke the news the IVF didn't work.

"I'm serious," she said. "Your mindset is important."

Sure Kyle would find this as funny as I did, I tried to catch his eye, but he was staring at the mauve-colored wall behind Dr. Evans's desk with his arms folded across his massive chest.

"Okay, then, I'll try." I was willing to try anything. In four months, I would be forty.

When we were ready to leave, Dr. Evans walked us to the door and placed her hand on my shoulder. "I have a good feeling about this time, Nicole," she said.

I didn't believe her, mostly because she usually called me Nikki and only used my full name when she was concerned about something.

On our way home, I clutched the overhead bar as Kyle dodged double-parked cars. At a red light, he lowered the window and stuck his arm out, reaching for the windshield wiper to clear it of the slush. In the city, the precipitation was a combination of rain and snow, but by the time we drove the two hours back up to Mount Stapleton, it would all be snow. They predicted eighteen inches. Kyle had suggested canceling our appointment so that we didn't have to travel in blizzard-like conditions. Of course, I'd told him we had to go today. It wasn't like we had a choice in the timing.

"I'm tired of doing this drive," he'd complained.

I didn't blame him. I was sick of the long ride myself. We could have chosen a clinic closer to Mount Stapleton, but the clinic we'd picked had the highest success rate in New England. When I'd met Dr. Evans, I felt an instant bond with her. While I still liked her, it turned out she wasn't such a great doctor. If she were, we would have had a baby by now, a little boy with Kyle's cleft chin and chocolate-brown hair or a girl with my bumpy nose and sinkhole-like dimples. Really, I wouldn't wish my nose on anyone, but Kyle's was worse.

"Do you think I'll be able to stay positive over the next couple of weeks?" I asked.

Kyle sighed as he raised the window. "I'm not doing this again."

When I turned to look at him, I saw hostility etched into his rugged profile. The furrow between his blue-gray eyes was more pronounced than usual, and his stubble-covered jaw was tightly clenched. "Doing what?"

"Jumping through hoops to have a baby."

My hands ached because they were balled into such tight fists. "You have the easy part." My voice cracked. "I'm the one who's the real-life voodoo doll." More than two hundred shots the past two years.

Kyle jabbed at the blinker. The ticking sound that echoed through the car reminded me of a bomb about to explode. "There is no easy part. It's bankrupting us, financially and emotionally." He jerked the car into the left lane. A horn blared, and he yanked it back, barely avoiding a collision.

"Well, let's hope it works this time so that we don't have to do it again."

His eyes moved from the road to me. "You're not listening. I'm not—"

"Watch out!" I reached for the dashboard as the car in front of us stopped for a red light. Kyle slammed on the brakes and muttered under his breath. The Jeep slid to a stop. "Let's talk about this when we get home," I said.

"I'm done talking about it. Whatever happens, this is the last time." He switched on the radio.

I punched the power switch to turn it off. "You don't get to decide that."

The light changed to green. Kyle inched the Jeep forward. "We can't pay for another round. We can't afford the ones we've done."

"You can't put a price on this."

"Where's the money going to come from, Nikki?"

So far, we had spent more than $57,000 on in vitro, emptying our bank account and maxing out our credit cards. Kyle was a carpenter, and I worked at a small magazine. We did better than most year-round residents in our tiny mountain town but were by no means wealthy. Adding in our mortgage and car loans, we would be paying off our debt until we were grandparents. The air in the car thickened so it became impossible to breathe. I lowered my window and stuck my head outside like our black Lab, Cole, used to do. Soggy snowflakes landed on my face and ran down my cheeks as they melted.

"Close that," Kyle said, using the switch on the driver's side door to raise the window himself. Strands of my curly dark hair got caught in it.

"I want it open." I pushed down on the button. Nothing happened. Kyle had engaged the childproof lock. "Lower it."

"Fine." All the windows zipped down. An icy wind ripped through the Jeep. "Happy now?"

"What's wrong with you?"

He sighed as he closed the windows. "I haven't had anything to eat all day." We drove in silence. Miles up the road, the Golden Arches came into view. We reached them, and Kyle turned in to the parking lot.

"Can we go someplace else?" I tried to eat healthy because I thought that might improve the odds.

"This will be quick, and the snow is starting to pile up."

Although Kyle said he was in a hurry, he refused to order at the drive-through because he was fastidious about his Jeep and didn't allow anyone to eat inside it. He parked, and I jumped out, slamming the car door and stalking toward the entrance without waiting for him. We stood in line, not speaking, staring up at the menu. By the time we reached the register, the smell of french fries had overpowered my will to eat clean. I ordered some with my salad.

For the first time that day, Kyle smiled. "I would have shared mine," he said.

I knew he would have, but I didn't want to eat his because I was mad at him.

Seated at a table in the back, Kyle devoured his burger while I pushed lettuce around my plate. "How many times are you willing to go through this?" he asked.

"As many as it takes."

"Why can't you be happy with our life the way it is? We have time to do things we enjoy. I play hockey with the guys. You do that painting thing. We ski all winter, vacation on the Cape every summer."

"I don't want paint night with my friends. I want a family."

"We are a family."

Two people made a couple. Could a couple be considered a family?

Kyle finished his fries and reached for a handful from my carton. "We can get another dog."

Cole had died fourteen months before. Kyle and I had agreed we weren't getting another because no dog could replace that sweet, smart boy.

A mother and three kids made their way down the aisle and sat in the booth across from ours. The two boys, about eight and six, shoved each other while a girl, fourish, screamed that she wanted a milkshake. The mother buried her head in her hands. I stared at her, wishing I were the one sitting with the energetic kids. Let her be the one listening to Kyle trying to talk her out of wanting a baby. The little girl stopped wailing. She reached for her mother's hands and tried to pry them apart. "I'm sorry, Mommy. Don't be sad," she said.

I sipped my drink, trying to swallow the lump in my throat, but I couldn't, and tears streamed down my face.

"Hey now." Kyle reached across the table for my hand. "It will work this time." His fingers were ice cold.

Chapter 2

The injections, the endless trips to the clinic, the egg retrieval—all of it was easy compared to waiting eleven days to take the blood test. A few minutes before six o'clock in the morning on the day following our trip to the city, I studied myself in the full-length mirror, hoping to see a sign the IVF had worked this time, even though I knew it was much too soon to tell. The image that stared back at me was a bloated version of my former self. The hormones caused me to pack on the pounds. I wondered if anyone else noticed my weight gain. Did Kyle? He would have to be blind not to. I hated looking like this, but it was a price I was willing to pay.

I leaned closer to the mirror. *Just give me a sign.* What I expected to see, I had no idea. People often said pregnant women glowed. Maybe I was glowing? Nope. My complexion appeared muted today, with yellow undertones dominating my olive-colored skin. The eyes of a mother-to-be sparkled. Mine were bloodshot, with sleep dust clumped in the corners. I wiped it away and blinked hard. *Please work this time.* Inside my head, I chanted it over and over again.

Outside, the wind howled, and a snowblower buzzed. I pushed open the curtains, expecting to see Kyle clearing our driveway, but it was already snow-free. He was across the street digging out the Abramses, who relied on him after every storm. I smiled, thinking of his kindness. It was one of the traits that had drawn me to him. He had spent a stressful day driving back and forth to the city yesterday and had a long day of work ahead of him today, and there he was, outside before the sun fully rose, lending a hand to our elderly neighbors. He also helped them in the fall, spring, and summer with raking, mowing, and any household repairs they needed. When my parents were alive, they had sung Kyle's praises, claiming he was the ideal son-in-law. He'd be the perfect father too. His crankiness yesterday was out of character. He was tired and frustrated. He wanted a baby as much as I did.

While I waited for him to finish at the Abramses', I made him scrambled eggs, brewed a pot of coffee, and poured him a cup, adding two sugars and two shots of half-and-half, just the way he liked it. The aroma made my mouth water, and I had to summon all my willpower not to pour a cup for myself. I had read a few studies that found a link between caffeine consumption and the ability to conceive, so I had stopped drinking coffee almost three years ago. Old me drank five to six cups a day, and new me always felt a bit sluggish without it.

Outside the snowblower stopped. A few minutes later Kyle stood next to me in the kitchen. His earlobes glowed bright red, and his hands were dry and cracked. I pointed to the plate and travel mug. "I made breakfast."

He leaned against the counter as he shoveled the eggs into his mouth. "Mr. Abrams has a nasty cold."

"I'll make him soup." I smiled, glad to have something on my agenda today. Determined to do things differently this time so that we'd have different results, I'd taken the rest of the week off to relax, but I was afraid that with nothing to do, I would spend my time obsessing about whether this cycle would work.

Kyle's eyes fell to my abdomen. "I'll bring it over tonight. Don't go near them."

~

By two that afternoon, I realized that not going to the office had been a terrible idea. With nothing to do after I'd made the soup, I obsessed about whether I would get pregnant this time. I even thought about driving to the drugstore to buy a home pregnancy test. Instead, I decided to think good thoughts and figure out how I would decorate the nursery. To get ideas, I logged into Pinterest. I was looking at a room that had one wall painted like the sky on a starry night and the words **DREAM BIG** stenciled on another when I heard my sister Dana's car rumbling up the street. The muffler had fallen off months ago.

A few minutes later, Dana let herself in the unlocked front door. Water dripped off her duck boots onto the flagstone in the entryway. She bent to remove them before walking across the hardwood toward me. "Are you sick?" she asked, looking down at me over the back of the sofa. I swiped my finger across the touch pad, desperate to click off the web page showing pictures of nurseries. Other than my best friend, Sharon, I hadn't told anyone that Kyle and I were doing IVF. I was embarrassed to be failing at something so basic.

Dana leaned closer. I slammed the laptop's cover down. It closed with a loud click. "Holy shit, you were watching porn." As usual, she had an enormous grin that made me wonder if she was stoned even though she swore she'd stopped smoking in high school.

"Homemade," I said. "Kyle and I set up a camera in our bedroom."

"Ewww." She crinkled her nose. Unlike mine, which had two moguls across the bridge, hers was straight like our mom's. Looking at it gave me hope for my baby-to-be. Maybe he or she would have a perfect Greek nose too. *How's that for positive thinking, Dr. Evans?*

Dana slipped out of her ski coat and tossed it toward Kyle's recliner. It landed on the floor. Leaving the jacket where it fell, she plopped down on the couch next to me. "So what are you doing home?"

I stared at the coat, telling myself not to lecture her about what a slob she was. When we were growing up, she left cups, plates, and pieces of her clothing scattered all over every room, where they remained until my mother or I picked them up. "How did you know I was here?"

"I stopped by the office. Page told me you weren't there." Dana worked in the equipment-rental shop at Mount Stapleton and often had a day or two off during the week because she worked all weekend. She pulled off her hat and ran a hand through her short, flattened black hair until it spiked at the top. She continued talking, but all I could think about was her balled-up jacket lying on the floor, taunting me. I jumped up, picked it up, and hung it in the closet while Dana watched me with an amused expression. "Ninety seconds," she said. "Surprised you left it there that long."

Eight years younger than me, my sister had been pushing my buttons since she uttered her first word. "Mine," she had said, ripping my favorite doll out of my hands.

She waited until I sat again. "I have big news." The gold specks in her olive-green eyes sparkled the way they always did when she was excited.

All my muscles tightened with certainty she was about to tell me she was pregnant. Wouldn't that be something, my commitment-phobic, eternally single sister who swore she didn't want kids unintentionally getting knocked up by a one-night stand while Kyle and I had been trying for years? I straightened my back, bracing for the blow. Dana grinned. "I'm getting a puppy. Remember that woman, Marie, I saved from choking? She breeds golden retrievers and is giving me one. Sometime in March."

I relaxed. "She's giving you a dog?"

"I told her I always wanted a golden, and she said she'd give me one as a way to thank me for saving her life."

Dana had been riding the gondola at Mount Stapleton when a tourist sitting next to her choked on a granola bar. My sister gave her the Heimlich, dislodging the grainy snack from the woman's windpipe. Dana's friend captured the entire incident on video and posted it on social media. The local news stations all ran with the story. For a few weeks, Dana had been a big hero in our tiny mountain town.

"Will your roommates be okay with you having a dog?" My thirty-one-year-old sister lived with a bunch of twentysomethings, who, like her, all worked at Mount Stapleton during the winter. In the summer,

Dana lifeguarded on the Cape. Honestly, they were jobs she should have outgrown years ago and that didn't put the four years she'd spent studying computer science at the University of New Hampshire to use.

"They don't care."

"Is it a good idea for you to have a puppy? They need a lot of attention when they're being trained. They can't be left by themselves, or they'll destroy your place." I glanced toward the gnawed bottom shelf of the bookcase, which Cole had feasted on the first year we had him.

Dana fiddled with the zipper on her sweatshirt. "I'll figure it out."

I knew she didn't have a plan. She never thought anything through. I imagined the poor dog whimpering, locked in Dana's room with no food or water, or worse, left outside in the bitter cold. I counted to ten before responding and said in what I hoped was a nonjudgmental tone, "Dogs are a lot of responsibility."

"Don't be a killjoy, Nikki. I'm excited about this." She jumped to her feet and bolted for the kitchen.

I remained on the couch until my desire to lecture her on how irresponsible it was for her to get a puppy passed. When I finally followed her to the kitchen, I found her standing in front of my refrigerator, rummaging through the contents. "I'm starving," she announced, pulling a large red bowl from the back corner of the bottom shelf. "What's this?"

I had no idea. Whatever was in the bowl was something Kyle had made when I was at paint night last week. "I'll make you something."

"What do you think about Deeogee as a name?" She ripped off the tinfoil covering the dish, revealing a brownish-greenish mush.

I gagged when I smelled it.

"Guacamole?" Dana dipped her finger into the goo.

Horrified, I watched her lick it clean. Maybe it wasn't rank. Maybe I was sensitive to smell because I was pregnant? Could it have happened that fast?

Dana's face contorted, and she rushed to the sink to spit out the gunk in her mouth. "Definitely not guac," she said.

As I dumped the guck in the bowl down the drain, Dana returned to the refrigerator. For several seconds, she stood in front of it without opening it. A card Dr. Evans had given us to remind us of our next appointment and a New Horizons IVF magnet hung on the stainless steel door, where Kyle had placed them yesterday. My heart raced. I didn't want my sister to see them because I wasn't ready to tell her that I was trying to get pregnant. It wasn't that she wouldn't be supportive. It was the opposite. She'd smother me with support. I imagined my inbox filled with articles about how acupuncture could cure infertility or drinking apple-cider vinegar while standing on your head was sure to get you pregnant, or worse, she would relay stories about sixty-year-old grandmothers in India giving birth to beautiful, healthy babies.

"Let me make you a grilled cheese." I wanted to get her away from the refrigerator.

"Kyle had a hat trick. Good for him."

"What?" I bumped her out of the way with my hip so I could pull out the cheese and butter. She reached over me and tapped an article hanging on the fridge. In our sleepy small town, real news was hard to come by, so the local paper covered the hockey league Kyle played in all winter. Last week his picture had accompanied the story because he'd scored three goals. He hung it up along with the league standings that showed his team in first place. I imagined years from now his hockey clippings would hang side by side with our child's drawings and report cards.

Relieved that it was not the magnet or the appointment reminder that captured her attention, I laughed. "Honestly, he thinks he's playing in the NHL."

"It's great that he still has something he's so passionate about," Dana said.

Her words stung as much as if she'd slapped my face, because what crossed my mind was that I wished he were still that passionate about me. We hadn't had sex in the past three months.

Dana turned her attention to a cabinet above the refrigerator, where Kyle kept his fattening snacks. I asked him to put them there so I couldn't reach them, but my sister had no trouble pulling down the potato chips. At five foot eight, she stood a good four inches taller than me. My parents had both towered over me too.

I busied myself collecting the ingredients for our dinner. Dana returned to the refrigerator. Again, she paused before opening it. I focused on buttering the bread like it was the hardest thing I'd ever done. Why had Kyle put Dr. Evans's card and the magnet on display in our kitchen? We were so careful about keeping all the other evidence, the medicine and needles, upstairs, where guests wouldn't be able to stumble across them. We even had a mini refrigerator in our bedroom.

Dana finally opened the refrigerator door and pulled out a jug of iced tea. She turned to look at me. I prepared myself for a question about the magnet and appointment reminder. She had to have seen them. I would tell her the truth.

"Deeogee, like d-o-g, get it?" Dana said.

"What?"

"The dog's name."

Sitting at the table, she ripped open the bag of chips and popped one in her mouth. She chomped down on it, crunching loudly. I hated chewing sounds, and I could tell by her smirk that she was trying to push my buttons again. I wasn't about to let her win this time. "Deeogee is weird."

"Weird as in interesting?" She shoved another chip in her mouth.

"It's such an old, awful joke."

She smacked her lips together as she chewed. I couldn't stand it another second. I snatched the bag from her.

"You're so easy." She laughed.

"And you're such a child." In the five years since our parents' death, she seemed to have reverted from age twenty-six to twelve.

I plated the sandwiches and carried them to the table. We ate in silence for a moment or two. Dana faced the refrigerator and kept stealing glances at it. There might as well have been a neon sign advertising that we were trying to have a baby. I waited for her to blurt out a question. She smiled. "Are you coming to dinner with me and Aunt Izzie tomorrow?"

"Where are you going?"

Dana bit down on her lower lip. "Pendleton 88."

At the mention of that restaurant, the grilled cheese, which a moment ago had tasted delicious, felt soggy in my mouth. "Not a chance."

"Nikki, it's absolutely crazy that you've held this vendetta for so long. You need to get over it. It's not healthy. Uncle Hank didn't do anything wrong."

"He lied."

"He took over a failing restaurant, saving us from a mountain of debt, and made it more successful than it ever was when Mom and Dad owned it."

"He said he would preserve their legacy."

My hand dropped to my abdomen, and I took a deep breath to calm down. I couldn't allow myself to get worked up about Hank. Stress could ruin my chance of getting pregnant. "You and Aunt Izzie go. Have a good time."

"I'm definitely going. Never turn down a free dinner: Dana DeMarco rule number one." She stuffed the last bite of her grilled cheese into her mouth. I wondered when the last time she'd had a good meal was. She had definitely lost weight since I'd seen her last. Her cheekbones were more pronounced, and her jeans were baggy.

"Do you want another sandwich?"

"Only if you don't mind making it."

I finished mine and rose to make her another. Neither of us said a word as I cooked, but I could feel her eyes on my back the entire time I stood at the stove.

"You reminded me so much of Mom right then," she said when I handed her the plate. "The way you were hunched over the pan with one hand resting on the counter."

My eyes got watery. I blinked to clear them before Dana noticed. All I wanted was to be as good of a mother as our mother had been. "I . . ." I intended to tell her about IVF. I tried to say the words, but my stomach clenched, and I thought better of telling her. "I'll swing by Aunt Izzie's later in the week and spend some time with her." Dana didn't need to know all Kyle and I had struggled through. In a few days, I would tell her the happy news that I was pregnant.

Chapter 3

Tears stung my eyes as I noticed the single set of snowshoe tracks leading from Aunt Izzie's driveway to the woods behind her house. There should have been another set, my mother's. When she was alive, the two sisters always went together. Even five years later, the little reminders sprinkled through everyday life still sneaked up on me, making me think about all I had lost.

For a moment, I stood on Aunt Izzie's front steps with my eyes closed, breathing in the homey smell of a fire and imagining my mother in her orange ski jacket emerging from the woods with her infectious grin, teasing her big sister, Aunt Izzie.

Inside, my aunt sat at a card table by the roaring woodstove, working on a puzzle I had given her for Christmas a few weeks before. Her head whipped around at the sound of my boots on the hardwood, and her hand went to her chest. "Lord have mercy, Nikki. Are you trying to give me a heart attack, sneaking up on me like that?"

"You shouldn't leave your door unlocked."

"Sit down and help me with this." The border of the one-thousand-piece puzzle was complete, but none of the interior had been filled in yet. The image on the box showed a hummingbird feeding on a flower. Aunt Izzie slid me a pile of pieces, all with traces of pink. Before I started trying to fit them together, I pulled off my sweater. The woodstove threw off a ridiculous amount of heat, and the low ceiling trapped it all in place, making the room feel like a sauna. Aunt Izzie didn't seem to notice. A Bruins ski hat covered her salt-and-pepper hair, and she wore a turtleneck covered by a thick zip-up black sweatshirt. I tried to imagine my mother in a similar outfit but couldn't. She'd worn trendy sweaters and stylish jeans, often borrowing them from my closet. Although my mom was three years younger than Aunt Izzie and eighteen years older than me, when the three of us had gone out together, people sometimes thought Mom and I were sisters and Aunt Izzie was our mother. Strangers could never believe my mom was old enough to have a daughter in her thirties. Not only did she look young, but she was young. She'd given birth to me less than a year after her high school graduation.

For a few minutes, Aunt Izzie and I sat without speaking, working on the puzzle and listening to country music on the radio. Every so often, Aunt Izzie hummed along. On the mantel behind her, black-and-white images of my great-grandparents and great-aunts and great-uncles watched us. The house used to be my grandparents'. Besides filling a glass hutch with a collection of frog figurines, my aunt had done little to make the place her own.

"Are you hungry?" she asked. "I have leftover chicken parm that's out of this world." She leaned over the table, closer to me. "It's from Pendleton 88."

Like Dana, Aunt Izzie wanted me to reconcile with Hank.

"Did you and Dana have a good time last night?"

"It was a wonderful evening. Nadine came, too, because I made the reservation for three." She playfully slapped my hand. "Hank charmed the pants off her."

I rolled my eyes, imagining Hank flirting with the recent widow, teasing her with his deep baritone voice. I couldn't deny the man was charming. After all, he'd charmed my parents' restaurant out from under me and my sister.

"Hank asked about you. He always does."

I fit two puzzle pieces together and searched my pile for another piece that might go with them. "I wish you wouldn't talk about me with him."

"He would like to see you. Nadine and I are going back this weekend, and he said he hopes you'll join us."

"I'd rather starve." I snapped another piece of the puzzle onto the flower I was building.

Aunt Izzie pulled it off. "It looks like it belongs there but doesn't." She eyed my pile and pulled out a piece. "Try this."

The tab slid into the slot. I smiled at her, wondering if I should worry about her ability to identify two pieces that fit together. How much time did she spend doing puzzles?

"It's not healthy to hold on to anger, Nikki. Your mother would be so upset to know that you and Hank were at odds. He was a true friend to her, and she wanted the two of you to have a good relationship."

My head snapped up. I met my aunt's eyes. "Well, then he should have kept his word." I would never understand why Dana and my aunt weren't bothered by the changes Hank made to DeMarco's. He'd said he would preserve the diner, and now there was nothing left of it.

My aunt bit down on her lip and averted her gaze. I had a feeling she was debating whether to continue this old argument. Her hands fluttered over the table, and she accidentally knocked a pile of puzzle pieces to the floor. "It's his restaurant now. You need to let it go."

I said nothing and ducked under the table to retrieve the fallen pieces.

When I popped back up, my aunt's expression hardened. "It's one dinner."

I shook my head. She sighed as she stood and stomped off toward the kitchen. The refrigerator opened and closed. Cabinets banged shut. The microwave beeped a few times. Several minutes later, Aunt Izzie returned with two plates of the leftover chicken parm. She handed one to me.

"I don't want any." The smell of tomato sauce filled the air. My stomach grumbled.

"Don't be ridiculous. Hank won't even know you ate it."

The aroma and the sight of the gooey mozzarella over the golden bread crumbs made my mouth water. I gave in and cut off a small bite. Damn, it was good, the chicken juicy and the tomato sauce sweet on my tongue.

Aunt Izzie grinned as I finished all the food on my plate. "The recipe is from Dominic DeMarco's family," she said.

Shortly after my parents' death, my aunt had started referring to my father by his full name when she spoke about him to me. I thought she blamed him for the accident and avoided saying *your dad* or *Dom* as a way to distance him, but I never asked about her reason. I didn't want to hear anything bad about my father, and he and Aunt Izzie hadn't gotten along since I was a child.

She cut off a piece of chicken from her plate and transferred it to mine. "So this chicken is proof that Hank did carry on some of the traditions of DeMarco's Diner," she said.

"A man of his word."

"Yes, he is," she said, ignoring the sarcasm in my tone.

While I washed our dishes, Aunt Izzie continued working on the puzzle. She had pieced together a leaf by the time I returned. A Blake Shelton song came on the radio. "How's Kyle?" she asked.

I laughed. She insisted my husband resembled the country music star. He did not. "He's fine."

Aunt Izzie's green eyes, so similar to my mother's and sister's, bored into me. "Everything good between you?"

My hand froze on the puzzle piece I was about to pick up. *Should I tell her about trying to get pregnant and the strain it's placing on our marriage?* An image of her at church lighting candles for me and Kyle popped into my head. She would ask Father Doherty to pray for us. I could see the old priest's tightly pressed lips and hear the judgment in his faint Irish brogue. *Reproductive technology is immoral. Babies are meant to be conceived through the marital act.* No, I definitely couldn't tell her.

"Yes, of course."

"I haven't seen him in a while."

I nodded. "Come for dinner next week."

"Why don't we all go to Hank's?"

"I'll cook so you know what good food tastes like. It's not that slop Hank serves."

Aunt Izzie stood to tend to the fire. "You just inhaled his chicken parm."

"You said it yourself. It was a DeMarco family recipe. What I tasted was my father's love."

Aunt Izzie poked at the glowing embers. "Yes," she agreed. "You did."

Chapter 4

I didn't want to get my hopes up, but when I woke up Saturday, day six, I was sure I was pregnant because I had cramps—not the God-was-so-unfair-to-women cramps I usually experienced every month but a tingling with—well, I hated to admit it—a positive energy. During the first cycle, Dr. Evans had told me some women could feel when the egg attached to the uterus wall, and they often compared the sensation to a friendlier version of menstrual cramping. I wanted to call her to confirm I remembered her words correctly, but it was so early that darkness still masked my bedroom. The only light came from the fluorescent-green background of Kyle's alarm clock and the bright-blue LED numbers on mine that read 6:04.

Next to me, Kyle fought an imaginary demon in his sleep, his hands balled in tight fists as he bounced from his stomach to his side to his back. I wondered what was running through his subconscious and hoped it didn't have to do with the baby.

"Kyle." I whispered his name, though I had no idea why. After all, I was trying to wake him. He didn't stir, so I propped myself up on an elbow and leaned over him, poking his chest.

He jerked awake, jolting upright. "What's wrong?"

"I think it worked."

He yawned. "What worked?"

"I'm pregnant." *Did I jinx myself by saying it out loud?*

Kyle opened his mouth. No words came out, just the stench of his morning breath.

"I can feel him." At that moment, I was certain the baby was a boy. "Will. Let's name him Will." *This baby* will *be born. I* will *be a mother. See, Dr. Evans, I'm thinking positively.*

Kyle flopped back to a horizontal position. "Go back to sleep, Nikki." Minutes later, his snores rattled the bed.

I had been pregnant one other time. Almost seven years ago. Shortly after we got married. We weren't even trying. One night, Kyle and I were drinking margaritas. I couldn't hold mine down, which was weird. I had never had a problem before. I thought maybe I had a stomach bug. The next day I realized I was late. It took me a few days to work up the nerve, but I eventually peed on the stick. Three minutes later two pink lines appeared, confirming the pregnancy. My initial reaction was, *SHIT!* I had wanted to be married for a year before starting a family.

Kyle, on the other hand, was thrilled. He ran out and bought that scary-ass book, *What to Expect When You're Expecting*, and sent me daily texts with suggestions for the baby's name. Trevor and Jasmine were his favorites. Thinking they sounded like names of Disney royalty, I pooh-poohed them in a hurry. At week twelve, we went for an ultrasound. By then, I was on board with the idea of being a mother. Really excited about it. I had decided if it was a girl, we would name her Gianna after my mother, and if it was a boy, we'd name him Dominic after my father but call him Nico.

I wished I didn't, but I remembered the day of the ultrasound perfectly, so humid that the backs of my legs had stuck to the leather seats on the drive over. When we arrived at the doctor's office, two white vans with logos for a local heating and air-conditioning company were parked out front. The doors to the building were propped open. In the hallway, repairmen perched high on ladders fiddled with the vents. I had forgotten my phone at home. When we checked in, the receptionist said she had tried to call us to reschedule because the office was closing for the afternoon due to the excessive heat. Dr. Kaplan, our doctor at the time, said since we were there, we might as well do the ultrasound. The nurse helping with the procedure flung a hospital gown at me and told me to change. Less than a minute later she knocked on the door. When I told her I wasn't ready, she sighed so loudly I could hear it on the other side of the wall.

She walked several inches in front of me as she led me to the exam room. Occasionally, she looked back over her shoulder. "Come on," she urged.

We approached a restroom. "I need a minute," I said, stepping into it.

"No!" she snapped. "Your bladder needs to be full."

"But I really need to go."

"You can wait a few minutes."

In the exam room, she continued barking orders, getting me positioned on the table while Kyle and Dr. Kaplan, huddled in the corner, laughed about something.

Finally, Dr. Kaplan approached the table. She smiled as she squirted gel on my abdomen, the chilly wetness of it providing temporary relief from the stifling heat. I felt the pressure of the wand sinking into my skin as she maneuvered it around my belly. Kyle held my hand, grinning like an idiot as he watched the monitor. I, too, looked at the screen, but all I could see were black and gray swirls, reminding me of the radar image of a hurricane I had seen on the news before we left the house.

The wand froze in Dr. Kaplan's hand. The smile on her face faded as she peered at the screen. She and the nurse exchanged a look.

"What's going on?" Kyle asked.

I knew something was wrong. I could tell by the kind expression on the mean nurse's face when she met my eye.

"Please get dressed and meet me in my office," Dr. Kaplan said.

As she stepped toward the door, Kyle grabbed her arm. "What's happening?"

"I'm sorry. I'm not detecting a heartbeat," the doctor said.

My own heart sped up, threatening to explode as I remembered my reaction to the positive pregnancy test, certain this was the reason the baby would not be born. Her soul—yes, it was a girl—was moving on to a mother who was welcoming from the get-go.

Kyle hung his head so his chin rested on his chest. When I looked at him, I couldn't see his face, just the bill of his baseball cap and the Boston Bruins' logo, a menacing bear. I threw that hat away when we got home.

Dr. Kaplan called it a "missed miscarriage," a miscarriage where there were no symptoms.

"You didn't know anything was wrong?" Kyle asked the day of the D&C. The tone of his voice, the way he wouldn't look at me, made it clear he blamed me.

"I didn't."

Five years ago, after my parents' accident and Hank's closing of DeMarco's Diner, I became desperate to have a baby, feeling it was a way to bring a piece of my parents back to life. I was only thirty-four and didn't think I'd have trouble conceiving. Once I turned thirty-six, though, I started to worry that nothing was happening. I had read that women's fertility began to decline quicker after age thirty-five. I started tracking my cycle, using a kit to predict ovulation and scheduling sex. The romance vanished from our marriage, but I never conceived. I went for an exam and convinced Kyle to as well. The doctors said there was no medical reason we couldn't have a baby. Because of my age, almost thirty-eight by then, they recommended IVF. With the help of modern medicine, I'd thought getting pregnant would be a breeze, but I was wrong. Until now, it had been more like a category-five hurricane.

It was true what they said about the third time being a charm, though. I could tell by the energy I felt in my stomach and the metallic taste in my mouth. A baby was growing inside of me, a little boy we would name Will.

~

When Kyle got out of bed, he found me in the room we used as an office, emptying a desk drawer into a cardboard box. "What are you doing?" he asked.

"This is going to be the nursery. After breakfast we can get paint. Light brown. I think Will's going to want a mocha-colored room."

Kyle rubbed his chin and studied me for several seconds without saying anything. "Slow down," he finally said. "You don't even know you're pregnant." The large bags on each side of the bridge of his nose looked like pillows for his tired eyes.

"Did you sleep okay?"

"You woke me up at six."

"I thought you'd be excited."

"I'll save my excitement until after the blood test." His bare feet slapped against the hardwood floor as he made his way down the hall to the kitchen. It was as if he were stomping out my enthusiasm with each step he took, because he was right. After all, we'd been through this two times before with disastrous results. I should wait for Dr. Evans to confirm the pregnancy, but she'd told us to be positive. She'd said it would help, and hadn't I already lost a baby because I didn't make her feel welcome? I wasn't about to make that mistake again.

Chapter 5

When I was back at work on Monday, the scent of hazelnut floated into my office seconds before my coworker Page burst through the door. She carried a ceramic mug with the words *World's Best Mom* circling around it. That thing hadn't left her hands since her fifteen-year-old daughter, Mia, gave it to her for Christmas. Page flung herself into the seat across from me. "Andrew interviewed a tall woman yesterday," she said.

In heels, Page barely reached five feet, so almost everyone seemed tall to her, even me.

"He walked her out to her car, a red Range Rover, and hugged her goodbye. Hugged her. Carol told me the woman's an old friend of his." Page paused for a sip of her coffee. "You need to make it clear to him that you want the job."

Andrew Pollard was the publisher of *Mountain Views Magazine*, where Page and I had worked together for the past fifteen years. The magazine needed a managing editor. The previous one, Leo Timmerman, had retired at the end of September.

"Talk to Andrew today," Page urged. "Before it's too late."

At any other point in my career, I would have killed for that job, but these days I had other priorities. All my energy was channeled into trying to get pregnant. I didn't have extra to give to the magazine. If Kyle and I could have afforded it, I would have quit before we'd begun the third cycle. Deep down I knew it would be the last. I was going to get pregnant this time. Regardless of our financial situation,

I didn't plan to work away from the house after the baby was born and needed to convince Andrew to let me work at home. If I were managing editor, he certainly wouldn't allow that, but I wasn't going through all this trouble to have a baby only to drop Will off at day care every morning.

"Why don't you apply for the job?" I asked Page. The position paid a lot more than ours, and Page desperately needed the extra money. She was a single mom. Her deadbeat ex-husband lived on the other side of the country and didn't bother to send child support for their only kid.

"Andrew doesn't trust me. Besides, you're the one Leo groomed."

Leo hadn't groomed me. He'd taken advantage of me. I was his go-to girl, the one he relied on to pull all-nighters or come in on weekends to meet deadlines. Once I asked him why he always chose me for the unpaid overtime gigs. He twirled the pencil perpetually tucked behind his ear. "Because you're the only one without kids." While that was blatant discrimination, no one was holding protests or marching for the childless.

"I don't want the additional responsibility."

Page raised one of her overly tweezed eyebrows and cocked her head. "You've been doing the job since Leo left. You just haven't been getting paid for it."

As she spoke, my email pinged, bringing the total number of unread messages in my inbox to 217. Most of them had come in last week while I was out. Before Leo left, I hadn't gotten that many in a month, never mind a few days.

"At the very least, you deserve a big fat bonus," Page said. Her cell phone rang with a ringtone she had set for Mia, a teenage girl repeating the word *Mom* in a whiny voice. "Everything okay?" she answered. As she listened, she headed toward the door. "Not again, Mia. All right, I'll be there as fast as I can." Before leaving, she looked back at me over her shoulder and rolled her eyes. "Do you want a kid? Because I have a teenage girl I'm willing to give away."

My jaw tightened. Parents made that type of offhand remark all the time, and I always wanted to shout at them, *You don't know how lucky you are.*

I tried to focus on reading my emails but kept thinking about what Page had said about the managing editor position. From a picture on a shelf next to my desk, Kyle stared down at me. The question he'd asked on the drive home from the city last week played on a loop in my mind. *Where's the money going to come from, Nikki?*

Page was right. I was doing the job. I should get paid for it. We could pay off some of our debt with the extra money or, if the worst happened, pay for another round. The higher-paying job was the perfect insurance policy. When the time came, I would convince Andrew to let me work at home. I called Carol, his assistant, and told her I wanted to speak to him about the job. "It's about time you expressed an interest," she said. My interview was scheduled for later in the week.

∼

Andrew's office was dark. There was no sign of him or Carol in the area. I knew he was at work because I had seen him in the parking lot on my way into the building that morning. He had looked at me as if he were trying to remember who I was when I said hello. Fewer than twenty of us worked on the magazine, but Andrew knew only one person's name, Carol's.

I made myself comfortable in the chair outside his office and scrolled through my personal email on my phone as I waited. The only interesting message was a reminder that tomorrow was day eleven and I had to go to the clinic for my blood test. As if I would forget. I knew exactly how Dr. Evans delivered bad news: the removal of her glasses, the watery buildup in the corners of her eyes, the way she rolled her chair away from her desk as if trying to create distance between herself and Kyle and me. Now I tried to imagine how she would announce tomorrow's good news. Her glasses would remain perched on her nose.

She'd walk around to the side of the desk where Kyle and I sat and lean against it. She'd grin and not have to say a word. I'd stand, and we'd hug.

Lost in my thoughts, I didn't notice Andrew until he looked down at me. He carried a pizza box, and his salt-and-pepper hair seemed shorter than when I'd seen him earlier. "Do you need something?" he asked.

I stood. "We have a meeting." I was waiting to eat lunch until after the interview, and the smell of oregano was making me hungry. My stomach growled.

"About?" He unzipped his coat.

"The managing editor position. I'm interviewing for it."

He looked at me blankly.

"Nikki Sebastian," I reminded him.

"I know who you are, Nicole." He gestured with his head for me to follow him into his office. "Carol's out sick today, and I'm a little lost without her. Give me a second."

He placed the pizza on the desk between us. "Help yourself."

It was margarita, my favorite, but I didn't want to eat while talking with him, so I declined. He slapped two slices on a paper plate and eyed them hungrily while he asked me his first question. "Why did it take you so long to express interest in the job?"

Not a good start. I didn't have an answer I felt comfortable telling him. He bit into his pizza, but his eyes never left mine. I picked at my nails, thinking of something to say. "I've been doing the job for several months, and I'm good at it."

Andrew nodded and waited to swallow before speaking. "You sound surprised by that."

My shoulders tensed. "I'm not."

He stared at me without blinking. I held eye contact for what felt like several minutes but was really only a few seconds.

"I really like the position. I wasn't sure I would." I smiled, pleased with my response.

"Leo recommended you before he left, but you never seemed interested." He bit into his slice again.

"I'm very interested." I hoped I didn't sound disingenuous.

Andrew spoke with his mouth full. "If you had come to me when Leo left." He reached for a glass on his desk and gulped down the dark liquid. "There are a handful of strong candidates who are interested now." He wiped his hands on a napkin. "I'm going to have to think about it." He stood and looked toward the door. "I'll let you know."

Chapter 6

Before she said a word, Dr. Evans pushed her glasses into her hair and rolled her chair backward. My hand fell toward my stomach, a protective barrier between the baby I knew I was carrying and the words she was about to hurl.

She cleared her throat. "The test was negative."

Next to me, a strange garbled sound came from Kyle. I couldn't tell if he was laughing, coughing, or crying. I tried to turn toward him, but my head felt too heavy to move. Dr. Evans said something else, but I couldn't make it out. Her voice sounded far away and muffled. Her blurry image moved in slow motion, leaning across the desk toward me.

Kyle's hand was on my shoulder, shaking me. "Are you okay?"

I took a deep breath and squeezed my eyes closed. When I opened them again, the room came back into focus. "There has to be a mistake." Will was growing inside of me. I could feel him, had even had morning sickness today and had to bolt from the kitchen table after a few swallows of my breakfast. Kyle said it was because I'd made it with old eggs. As soon as the words left his mouth, his ears turned bright red. I knew with certainty then that he blamed me for our undiagnosed fertility problems.

"I'm sorry," Dr. Evans said. The way her eyes leaked with sympathy reminded me of why I liked her so much and how I was sure we would have been the best of friends if we had met under different circumstances.

I reached for Kyle's hand. He wiped it on his pants before giving it to me, but it still felt clammy.

"It's not unheard of to need more than three rounds, but it is unusual." Dr. Evans slid her glasses off again. "I think it's time to start considering other options. An egg donor, a surrogate, adop—"

I shook my head. "We want to do another cycle."

Kyle's hand slipped out of mine. "No, we're done. I'm done."

I twisted in my chair so I faced him. "One more time."

He flexed his fingers but said nothing.

Dr. Evans fidgeted with a candy dispenser on her desk, a peanut M&M with a surgical mask covering its mouth. "You don't need to decide anything today. Nikki, I want you to go through a natural menstrual cycle before we start over."

"I want another blood test."

"I think it might be a good time for you both to talk to Dr. Keezer again." Dr. Evans rummaged through her top desk drawer and pulled out a card for the therapist who'd evaluated us at the start of this whole process. Kyle reached for it. If it were up to him, he would have had me carried out of there in a straitjacket. I could still see the way he'd bitten down on his lip when he saw me painting Will's room. It was a miracle he hadn't bitten right through it.

I tore the therapist's card from Kyle's hand, folded it in half, and flung it toward the trash can. It bounced off the side and landed next to the desk. Kyle and Dr. Evans stared at it like it was a grenade about to explode. They were being unreasonable. It wasn't crazy to think the blood test could be wrong. Doctors made mistakes all the time. A guy at work had gone in for a right-knee replacement, and they'd operated on his left. A friend from high school had been told she was having a girl and instead gave birth to a boy. A neighbor had had a sponge left inside of him after abdominal surgery. "There could have been a mix-up in the lab," I said.

The noises outside Dr. Evans's office became louder as I waited for her to respond. Phones rang. Voices murmured. Doors closed.

"Fine," she finally said. "We'll do another test."

~

The smell of fresh paint mocked me.

The IVF didn't work, the mocha walls screamed.

I cranked the windows open as wide as they would go, letting in the icy air, trying to get rid of the odor.

On the other side of the room, the empty crib bullied me. *You will never be a mother.* Standing in front of it, I closed my eyes and saw Will, the baby who never was, his mass of curly dark hair a tangled mess, his thumb stuffed into his mouth, his pudgy legs hanging out of his baggy diaper. I lulled him to sleep by singing a lullaby. *Stop, you'll give him nightmares,* Kyle said in that joking tone of his that I hadn't heard in months.

I didn't know how long I stood there staring into the empty crib, living my imaginary life. I only knew I was putting Will on the bus for kindergarten. He bent to give his three-year-old sister a kiss before bravely marching up the stairs. Reality came crashing back when a bright light came on in the room and the windows banged shut. Kyle hovered behind me, wrapping me in a blanket and guiding me to the living room, where he built a fire while I shivered on the couch, tears streaking down my already wet cheeks.

The following Tuesday when I arrived home from work, the entire house smelled like paint, the room was green again, the crib had been replaced with the desk, and the medicine, the needles, and all other traces of IVF were gone. Kyle slept soundly in his recliner, paint specks in his hair, an empty bottle of scotch and small glass on the table next to him.

~

A few days after Kyle had converted the nursery back into an office, I called Dr. Evans to discuss next steps. There was a long pause on the other end of the line before she spoke. "You and Kyle need to get on the same page."

"Why do you think we're not?"

She hesitated. "He called me."

"He called you?" I was the one who made all the appointments. I was the one with the clinic on speed dial. Kyle had never once contacted them. He always left that for me, acting as if the staff spoke a different language than he did. I pictured him in the driveway calling Dr. Evans from his Jeep and stealing glances at the living room window while they talked to make sure I wasn't watching. "When?"

"A few days ago. We had a long discussion. Look, Nikki, this is a highly emotional time. It's hard on you and Kyle as individuals and hard on your marriage. I strongly encourage you both to talk to Dr. Keezer."

Hard on our marriage? What exactly had Kyle said? Why was he talking to Dr. Evans and not me? My stomach fluttered. "She has a nice way about her," he had said after our first meeting. "How old do you think she is?" he'd asked another time. "She has a young face, but the gray hair throws me off."

When had he ever speculated about someone's age before? "You have a crush on her," I had teased.

His earlobes had reddened. "Don't be ridiculous."

Now I paced our bedroom. "I'm not sure what he told you, but we're doing another round. When can we get started?"

Dr. Evans sighed. "We need to retrieve more eggs, and we'll need more sperm from Kyle." She said the last part as if it were as likely as me experiencing an immaculate conception. "Instead of another round, you might want to think about other options." She paused. "Adoption?"

The word caused my chest to tighten. "Absolutely not." I was determined to carry on a piece of my parents. I wanted a baby with their blood. Someone I would look at and see my mother's smile, my father's bushy eyebrows, or the olive-green eyes my mom, sister, and aunt all had.

"Just think about it, Nikki, because many birth mothers prefer the adoptive parents to be on the . . ." She paused to clear her throat. I recognized her stalling technique and imagined her removing her glasses. "To be on the younger side."

I stopped pacing and sank to the bed. "You're saying I'm getting too old to adopt." Even though I had no interest in adoption, her words were more painful than any of the hormone injections or procedures I'd had over the past two years. If I was too old to adopt, surely I was too old to have my own baby.

"The longer you wait, the smaller your chance will become, especially if you want an infant."

"We need to start the next round as soon as possible."

"I'm ready when you and Kyle are." She said my husband's name as if it were written in bold font.

Chapter 7

Kyle's boots thumped on the wooden stairs as he made his way up from the basement. We'd been avoiding each other since I'd confronted him about his conversation with Dr. Evans. "Why would you tell her we're done?" I had asked after I spoke to her.

"Because I am." He kept his eyes glued to the home-improvement show he was watching.

"Well, I'm not."

He'd shrugged. "We're in a stalemate, then."

"We need to discuss this."

"We don't have the money to try again."

"I'll get the money. I talked to—"

"End of discussion." He'd reached for the remote as if he wanted to press the off switch on our conversation. Instead, the television screen faded to black, and he left for hockey practice.

That was two nights ago. Now his footsteps loomed closer. I thought about fleeing, but before I could move, the door swung open. Kyle and I stood face to face in the tiny hall, neither of us saying anything. Our worst fights were fought without words.

I wanted him to reach for me. Hold me. Tell me he'd overreacted, that everything would be okay. We would try again, and this time it would work. Instead, he slipped by me, skimming the wall with his shoulder so he wouldn't accidentally touch me.

He stopped at the end of the hallway. "Are you going to get dressed?" It sounded more like an accusation than a question. "We have to be there at one."

My best friend, Sharon, was hosting a birthday party for her son Cameron, who was turning seven. "I'm not up to a party." I didn't want to spend time with a bunch of mothers and their adorable kids. Also, Cameron's birthday was always a tough time for me because for a couple of months, I'd thought I would have a child close to his age and imagined the two children becoming great friends. The day, the mere sight of Sharon's oldest son, always reminded me of the baby I'd lost.

"We have to go," Kyle said.

"Sharon will understand."

"I don't want to disappoint Cameron or Noah."

The way Kyle loved my best friend's children was one of the reasons I knew he'd be a wonderful father.

"We don't have to stay long." He pleaded with his eyes.

Maybe going to the party together will get us back on track. Seeing all the kids will remind Kyle how much he wants to be a father and convince him we should try one more time. "I'll be ready in a half hour."

~

Cars filled the driveway and lined both sides of the street. Kyle reversed direction in the cul-de-sac and parked two houses away from Sharon's. "How many people did she invite?" he asked.

"Cameron's entire first-grade class." Twenty-four reminders.

"Seems excessive." He walked around to my side of the Jeep and waited for me to remove my seat belt. I took a deep breath and braced myself for the onslaught of mixed emotions. Kyle reached for my gloved hand with his bare one. I wished it were a gesture of support: *We're in this together.* But I knew him enough to understand that he was afraid I would slip on the mushy layer of snow and slush covering the street.

The driveway was clear down to the shiny black pavement. When we reached it, Kyle released my hand.

Sharon's husband, Rick, greeted us at the door and took our coats. "Thanks, Fr . . ." I stopped. I always wanted to call him Freddie. His full name was Fredrick, and all through elementary, middle, and high school, he'd gone by Freddie. He'd attended college in Georgia, where he apparently rebranded himself. When he returned to Stapleton, he insisted on being called Rick, wore crisp oxfords instead of flannel shirts, and spoke with a slight twang. Every time I saw him, I was shocked that little Freddie Grey had transformed into handsome Rick Grey and was the man Sharon vowed forever with. He'd had a crush on her when we were teenagers, but she hadn't given him the time of day. On a wintery Saturday night almost a decade after graduation, Rick was drinking at the same bar we were. He spotted Sharon and me across the room and made his way toward us. As he worked his way through the crowd to the corner where we stood, bumping shoulders with people he passed and spilling his beer, she scrunched her nose. "Would you look at this putz," she said. He told her he'd gone to school with us, but she didn't remember, insisting she had never seen him before, even though we'd known him since kindergarten.

My heart broke for him, but Rick was unfazed. He asked Sharon out a dozen times before she agreed to a first date. Once they started dating, she dumped him at least four times. She even turned him down when he proposed. Good ole Rick had persisted, though, and here he was, married to the woman of his dreams, the father of her two sons. I bet a few failed IVF attempts wouldn't have stopped him like they had stopped Kyle.

In the playroom, a group of boys and girls stood around an air hockey table while their parents engaged in friendly conversations off to the side. Kyle and I paused in front of a cluster of mothers sipping white wine who were dressed in black stretch pants and designer sweatshirts like they'd all come from a yoga class. I didn't know any of them. I scanned the area, looking for Sharon, but didn't see her.

Cameron lit up when he saw us. He dropped his paddle and raced across the room, screaming, "Aunt Nikki! Uncle Kyle!"

I sank to my knees to hug him. He kissed me with sticky lips that smelled like grape.

"Hey, little big man. Happy birthday," Kyle said, bumping Cameron's fist.

"Look what I got!" Cameron excitedly pointed to the air hockey table. "Play with me." He pulled on Kyle's arm and led him away.

I stood by myself, not making eye contact with anyone. Pieces of conversation floated toward me.

"Chelsea got the lead in the school play."

"Brandon's playing Little League this spring."

"Meghan's applying to University of New Hampshire."

These women were all talking about their children. I had nothing to contribute to the conversation. I folded my arms across my chest, trying to think of something to say. The three mothers standing closest to me broke into laughter, and one of them smiled at me. "The kids are having a great time," she said.

"Sharon knows how to throw a party."

She jutted her chin toward the kids. "Which one is yours?"

My face heated up the way it always did when I was asked questions like this. I forced a smile. "None." The corners of her mouth slanted downward. "I'm a friend of Sharon's." She blinked fast. "We've known each other our entire lives." No response. "We were next-door neighbors growing up." I could have kept going, pummeling her with useless information until she forgot her original question. It was a strategy I had used before.

"How nice," the woman finally said. She inched back toward the other mothers and turned her back to me again. I swallowed hard, feeling judged and, worse, invisible because of my childless status. My heart raced, and my shoulders rose until they were parallel with my earlobes. I fled the playroom to look for Sharon in the kitchen.

As soon as I walked through the threshold, my shoulders relaxed and my heartbeat slowed. Love and warmth oozed out of the gray walls. Sharon's kitchen always smelled like cookies, brownies, or muffins. I inhaled deeply to take in the aroma and wondered if when her boys were older, the scent of baked goods would remind them of their mother's love the way garlic and basil did for me.

The trays of cupcakes sitting on her counter looked like they'd been bought at the popular bakery in town, but I knew Sharon had been up all night baking. She crouched over the table, putting the finishing touches on a cake. Her blonde hair was pulled away from her face and tied in a short ponytail. She wore a sweatshirt I guessed was Rick's by how baggily it fit her. I stood less than a foot away, watching her do her magic, but she was so focused on her work she had no idea I was there. Her sixteen-month-old son, Noah, sat in a high chair next to her, sucking a pacifier. Seeing me, he bounced in his seat and banged his fist on the tray. The pacifier tumbled from his mouth. "Nik, Nik," he squealed, raising his arms toward me. My insides turned warm and gooey.

"You made it." Sharon paused to greet me. With the pastry bag still in her hand, she pulled me into an embrace. "So sorry," she whispered. The night of the blood test, I had called to tell her I wasn't pregnant. "Next time," she had said, but I could tell by how tight she hugged me now that she, like Kyle, had run out of hope.

Sharon returned to decorating the cake while I extracted Noah from his chair. His almond-shaped blue eyes stared into mine. I had been looking into them for my entire life because they were exactly like his mother's. He pulled on a strand of my hair until it straightened and released it, watching it curl again. He giggled and did it again. If I let him, he would spend hours doing that. I hugged him tighter, loving the feel of his soft, chubby arms wrapped around my neck. For just a second, I pretended he was mine. The warmth in my belly threatened to turn into a red-hot flame of yearning that burned me alive. I inhaled through my nose and exhaled through my mouth.

Sharon watched me with her eyebrows knit together. We had known each other so long that I had no doubt she could feel my yearning. I smiled at her so she wouldn't worry.

"The first cake I made burned to a charcoal-like consistency because somehow the little beast got hold of the bag of flour while Rick was watching him," Sharon said. "I didn't hear the timer go off over the sound of the vacuum cleaner."

I cringed at Sharon's nickname for her younger son and pulled him even closer. "You're not a little beast."

"Oh, he is." She reached for her phone. "What do you think?" The cake was decorated like a skating rink, with nets on each end and players with hockey sticks battling for the puck at center ice. Sharon planned to open her own bakery one day and had even put a deposit down on a storefront before she found out she was pregnant with Cameron. I suspected the reason she baked so much was to keep her skills fresh. Once Noah started school, she planned to pursue her dream.

"It's a masterpiece."

She snapped picture after picture of the cake and the cupcakes. Before anyone had a bite, her photos would be posted to social media. Scores of her friends would post comments about how talented she was. Their praise would keep her dream alive. She knew she just had to wait for time to pass to make it come true. Passing time, on the other hand, meant the death of my dream.

∼

"I'm glad we went to the party," I said. Kyle and I were stopped at a red light in the center of town on the way home from Sharon's. "Cameron had so much fun playing with you."

"He's a good kid."

"You're great with him. And Noah too."

The light turned green, and Kyle punched the gas. Without using a signal, he turned right onto Gorham Road, a cut-through to the other side of the mountain where we lived, but a street I didn't like to drive down. Usually when I was with him, Kyle didn't use the pass-through, either, because he knew being on it upset me. That he turned on it today told me he knew what I wanted to talk about and was trying to distract me. I had seen a vicious side of him when he played hockey, but I had never seen it off the ice, and certainly he had never directed it at me. Granted, driving down a road wasn't exactly vicious, but by taking the turn onto Gorham, my husband let me know he would no longer treat me with the consideration he always had.

Ahead on the right, Pendleton 88, the reason I avoided this road, came into view. The marquee was the same maroon color it had been when it read **DeMarco's Diner** and my parents owned the place. I felt queasy, the way I always did when I was reminded that I had given away my parents' legacy.

Directly in front of the restaurant, the driver in the car ahead of us flipped on his blinker and stopped, waiting for a parking spot. As Kyle braked again, I shifted uncomfortably in the passenger seat and felt him watching me. He placed a hand on my knee. I knew by that simple gesture he regretted his decision to drive by Pendleton. I didn't, though. If anything, seeing the place my parents had sacrificed so much to build with Hank's last name and stupid hockey number on the door made me more determined to carry on a piece of them.

I covered Kyle's hand with my own and turned toward him. "I interviewed for managing editor. The position pays a lot more than my current one. If I get it, we can use the money for another cycle."

Behind us, someone beeped. Kyle slid his hand out from under mine and continued down the road without saying anything. The Jeep's engine hummed, the road noises got louder, and the street in front of us became less congested as we drove away from downtown.

Less than a mile from home, Kyle finally spoke. "Remember how we used to go to Eastham every summer, with Sharon and Rick . . . what a blast it was?"

"Of course." I thought of the four of us slugging down mojitos, watching the sunset at Thumpertown Beach, and how Sharon and I wouldn't be able to stand, never mind climb the stairs, when it was time to leave. Kyle and Rick would carry us up piggyback-style, and we would collapse in the back of the Jeep in a fit of laughter.

"Once they had Cameron, they stopped coming," Kyle said. "But we still go, and we have fun. It's the highlight of our year, and they're always jealous, wishing they could come with us again."

"Don't."

"We can be happy without kids, Nikki. We've been happy without them."

"I've been happy because I've known children were in our future. Without that knowledge—" I stopped and shook my head.

"We can't take another twenty-thousand-dollar hit."

"Don't exaggerate."

He tapped his hand on the steering wheel, and his wedding ring clanked against it. "Think about all the jobs I've turned down."

He had passed up an opportunity to work on major renovations for a few of the houses on the mountain because with our frequent trips to the city, he couldn't commit to the timelines.

We were on our street, driving by the Abramses'. A shadowy figure stood in the window, watching us. "We aren't going to have kids, Nikki. It's not in the cards. Accept it."

"The increase I get with the managing editor position will be more than enough to pay for another round."

Kyle turned in to our driveway and killed the ignition. The sun was beginning to sink behind the mountain, and the sky was turning pink. I let myself believe the color was a sign from my parents. *You'll get pregnant next time, and you'll have a girl.*

Kyle unfastened his seat belt. "Talk to me about another round when the job's yours."

Chapter 8

On Wednesday, Page and I sat at my desk, reviewing the latest issue of the magazine, which had just arrived. My IM pinged with a message from Carol. Please come up to Andrew's office right away.

"He must have made a decision about the managing editor position," I said.

Page squeezed my arm. "Promise you'll take care of your good friend when you're the boss."

The elevator took forever to get to the fourth floor. When I finally arrived at Andrew's office, his door was shut. He sat with his feet up on the desk, talking on the phone while tossing a ball in the air. He saw me peeking in the window and motioned with his finger that he would be a minute.

Carol came up behind me. "Is he still on the phone?"

"He is." I smiled, hiding my frustration. I wanted to get back to my office and call Kyle to tell him I got the promotion and we could pay for another round.

Carol pointed to her guest chair. "Have a seat."

"I'd rather stand."

The latest edition of the magazine was spread open on her desk. "I'll definitely try this place," she said, tapping an article I had written about a new restaurant in town named Declan's.

"The steak tips are out of this world," I said.

She studied me with her head tilted to the side. "I didn't know DeMarco's was your family restaurant. It used to be my favorite place in town."

Her comment stirred a strange mix of pride and sadness in me. "How did you find out?"

Her lips curled downward. "Andrew told me."

"I didn't know he knew."

Her face flushed, and she busied herself straightening papers on her desk. "Hank told him." She pointed toward Andrew's office. He had finished his phone call and waved me in.

As I took my seat, he composed an email, pecking away at the keyboard with his two index fingers. Impatient for the good news, I picked up the stress ball and squeezed it. Andrew's monitor was set up kitty corner on his desk. I leaned to the left to see the screen. Squinting, I tried to make out his words, but the font was too small. I bent closer and thought I saw the words *Managing Editor* in the subject line. I scooted closer still. The font came into focus, and I read, I'm pleased to announce.

Before I could read another word, Andrew hit the send button, and the message disappeared into cyberspace. He swiveled in his chair to face me. I expected him to smile. His eyes narrowed, and the vein in his forehead pulsated.

Oh no. I squeezed the ball tighter. The last issue of the magazine sat on the corner of his desk. He pulled it toward him and opened to the center spread, the article on Declan's. "Want to tell me what this is?"

"It's the new it spot in town. Tourists and the locals love it."

"You know who doesn't love it? Hank, proprietor of one of our largest advertisers, Pendleton 88."

The ball slipped from my hand and rolled across the desk toward Andrew.

"He says you have some sort of vendetta against him for taking over the space where your parents' restaurant used to be."

My neck muscles tensed as I pictured Hank a month after my parents' death, hiking Mount Stapleton with Aunt Izzie, Dana, and me to spread their ashes. His salt-and-pepper curly hair blowing across his bearded face in the wind as he spoke. The sincerity in his deep-set, dark-brown eyes as he presented an argument on why Dana and I should sell the restaurant to him. *I know what their dreams were for the place. I'll carry on their traditions, make sure their vision becomes a reality.* My parents had been in deep debt when they'd died, and Hank's offer would cover their loans. Selling to him seemed like a no-brainer, especially because he promised to honor their memories.

I rolled my head, trying to loosen my neck muscles. "What does that have to do with the article on Declan's?"

"Hank thinks you ran it to hurt his business."

"That's not true." Page had suggested running an article on Declan's after having dinner there one night. "I ran it because it's a trendy new restaurant."

"You ran an article promoting the competitor of one of our biggest advertisers."

"He doesn't get to dictate the editorial content of the magazine just because he runs a few ads every now and then."

Andrew picked up the ball. He gripped it so tight it nearly flattened in his hand. "It's not just a few ads. He's our second-largest advertiser, and after he saw the article on his competitor, he called to pull all his ads."

"Well, I'm sorry, but—"

"I had to talk to him in person to smooth things over." He spoke through gritted teeth. "Had to comp him an ad on the back cover in next month's issue." He emphasized the word *comp*. "And promise we would do a similar feature on his place."

I glared at him, wishing he would have stood up to Hank instead of kowtowing. "I'll ask Page to schedule some time with him."

Andrew tossed the ball high into the air. When he caught it, he grinned. "Hank would like you to interview him and write the article."

My stomach churned. "I'd rather not."

"It will give you a chance to bury the hatchet." He threw the ball up again. It bounced off the ceiling and ricocheted to the right, landing on the floor near where I was sitting. "I do have good news."

I sat up straighter. This wasn't how I'd imagined my promotion would go down, mixed with an unjustified scolding, but I'd take it.

"You're going to have some help starting next month."

Heat coursed through my body. "What do you mean?"

"I hired a new managing editor. Elizabeth Sanders. She starts on March first."

I couldn't swallow. I couldn't breathe. I tried to open my mouth to say something, but no words came out.

"She used to work for Condé Nast. Recently relocated to the area from New York."

"But I've been doing the job since Leo left." I rubbed the back of my neck, trying to unknot the muscles.

"You filled in admirably, but you're not ready."

"I am."

Andrew shook his head. "The whole Hank mess proves you're not."

Rage constricted my throat. Hank had already stolen my parents' restaurant, and now he was going to cost me the opportunity to pass on their genes. "We can't ignore every other restaurant in the area because he advertises with us."

"I think you'll like Elizabeth," Andrew said. "She has fresh ideas."

"I want a raise and a bonus. For all the work I did filling in for Leo."

Andrew stood and slid into his jacket. "You got a raise in the fall." He made his way around his desk.

I jumped from my chair to block his path. A musky scent filled my nostrils. "That wasn't really a raise. It was a cost-of-living adjustment."

"If you're not happy with your compensation, I encourage you to seek other opportunities." He bumped my shoulder as he breezed by me.

"Wait!" I rushed toward him, stumbling over the ball and falling forward. He caught me, breaking my fall. The odor was almost unbearable. "How about a onetime bonus?"

"No." He was holding me up, and now he released me. "I have to go." As he strutted toward the elevator, he looked back at me over his shoulder. "Hank's waiting for your call."

Even as he disappeared around the corner, the scent lingered, and I realized it was coming from me: the smell of desperation.

~

I slammed my office door and fired up my computer. The message announcing the new managing editor was waiting in my inbox. I wanted to punch my fist through my monitor. Instead, I took out my aggression on the keyboard, pounding on the delete button until the email vanished.

Page burst into my office. "That asshole."

"He's pissed about the article on Declan's because they compete with Hank's."

Page's face turned white. "Oh no, it's my fault."

"No. It's Hank's. He called to complain. Now I have to interview him. Honestly, I'd rather quit than talk to that prick."

"You can't quit."

She was right. I couldn't. Office jobs were hard to come by in this mountain community, where the service industry fueled the economy.

"I would if I could afford to." I shook my head. "I already had my raise spent. We need the money." My eyes filled with tears. I blinked hard to clear them.

"Oh, honey, I know. Things are tough. I had to take an early withdrawal from my 401(k) because that deadbeat dick didn't send child support for months."

This took me aback. I knew things were rough for Page, but I hadn't realized how bad they were. "Did he finally send you the money?"

"Part of it. Says he's between jobs."

"I'm sorry."

"Yeah, I might have to dip into it again."

"Isn't there a huge penalty?"

Page pressed her lips together. "You do what you have to."

Chapter 9

Snow had been falling on and off all day, and the sidewalks downtown hadn't been shoveled yet. Concentrating on keeping my balance, I inched along over the thin path of footprints stomped into the deep snow. Minutes before, I had dropped off Aunt Izzie at the front door of Sip and Strokes because I didn't want her walking in the treacherous conditions. Tonight, the paint bar was hosting their third annual beach party, which meant they'd be serving rum punch, and we'd be painting the ocean, beach chairs and umbrellas, and palm trees. The last two years, the event had sold out, and judging by the full parking lot, tonight looked like a sellout as well.

After being passed over for the magazine's managing editor position, I didn't feel like painting or socializing, but Dana and Sharon had already canceled. Aunt Izzie didn't want to go by herself, so I'd forced myself to come. At the least, by not going home after work, I hadn't had to tell Kyle that I didn't get the raise or even a bonus. I could picture what he'd say when I told him. *That settles it, then. We're not doing another round.* I had to figure out another way to get the money.

In the distance, the marquee for Pendleton 88 came into view, the name lit up in red lights. I considered turning onto Main Street, but that would add an extra block to my walk, and the snow-covered sidewalks weren't safe, so I forged ahead. As I passed the restaurant, I glanced in the windows and noticed pictures of Hank hanging on the wall: one of him and Arianna, his famous model wife, standing on a red carpet, and a large portrait of him dressed in his New York Rangers hockey uniform with the number 88 on his sleeve.

Despite the weather, a crowd huddled around the hostess stand, waiting to be seated. The magazine's article on Declan's hadn't hurt Hank's business like he had claimed. The man was a first-rate liar, and his latest lie had cost me not only a promotion but the money I needed to fund another round of IVF. My jaw tightened as I thought about all I had lost because of him.

At Sip and Strokes, Aunt Izzie sat at a table with four other women, who were all dressed in hula skirts and Hawaiian shirts. One of them smelled like coconut, as if she had slathered herself with suntan lotion before she came out on this winter evening. Even Aunt Izzie, in a sun hat and Cape Cod sweatshirt that Dana had given her, had dressed as if she were spending a day by the shore. In a turtleneck and sweater, I was the only party pooper at our table.

Aunt Izzie had set up my paint tray, and there was even a glass of rum punch waiting by my easel. The image we were painting was more complicated than the ones we usually did. It was a beach, crowded with sunbathers splayed out on beach chairs and blankets, some under an umbrella. Several people played in the ocean, some riding the waves on boogie boards.

"Can't wait to see what you do with this." Aunt Izzie laughed as she said it.

I stank at this painting thing and knew mine would end up as a smeared mess of blue, tan, and yellow. Aunt Izzie, on the other hand, was an artist. Until recently, she'd taught art to elementary school students. She was an old pro who took paint night seriously. Usually, Dana, Sharon, and I laughed our way through it. Like Aunt Izzie, Dana had talent, but Sharon was just as bad as I was, if not worse. Our paintings always looked as if we had accidentally spilled our paint trays over them or as if her kids had done them.

The instructor took her seat at the front of the class and eyed the crowd. "Don't worry if you're not a good painter," she said. "I'll walk you through this picture step by step. Everyone will leave with a painting they're proud of." She spotted me and frowned. "Well, almost everyone."

Aunt Izzie laughed and tapped her glass against mine. "You can do this, Nikki."

Once we started painting, Aunt Izzie focused solely on the canvas in front of her, shushing me whenever I spoke. I tried to concentrate and listen to the instructor's directions but found myself eavesdropping on the beach ladies next to us. One of them owned an oceanfront bungalow in Maine. "The cottage next door is for sale," she said. "One of you should buy it." Her friends all laughed.

"I wish I could," said the woman who smelled like suntan lotion. "We just don't have the cash right now with Tyler's tuition."

"Christine was starting BU when we bought ours. I wanted it so bad nothing was going to stop me. I borrowed from my 401(k)."

My paintbrush froze in my hand. This was the second time today I'd heard someone mention withdrawing money from their retirement fund. *It's definitely a sign that I should do the same.*

Aunt Izzie tapped my shoulder. "You're making a mess." Yellow paint had dripped off my brush all over the bottom of my canvas, where the ocean was supposed to be. I painted over it with blue, but the yellow paint wasn't dry, and the colors combined to a stormy green.

~

My foot bounced off the floor under my desk as I navigated to the web page to download the 401(k) withdrawal form. My account had more than enough money to fund another round of IVF, and taking an early withdrawal rather than borrowing from it would save us from going further into debt. While I was confident that using the money now to start a family was the right thing to do, I knew I'd have a hard time convincing Kyle. He worked for himself and was still investing in his business rather than saving for retirement, so for now, we were counting on living off my account in our golden years.

The investment site loaded. I took a deep breath and scrolled to the appropriate part of the page. My grip on the mouse tightened as I read the bold red font above the link to the withdrawal form: Taking an early withdrawal on your 401(k) should only be done as a last resort. I scanned the rest of the text. The warnings jumped off the screen. Do not make the decision to withdraw money early from your 401(k) lightly.

As I read, the voice in my head morphed into Kyle's argumentative tone. *An early withdrawal carries serious financial penalties.* I could picture the vertical line between his eyebrows becoming more pronounced, the way it did whenever he was tense. *The withdrawal is taxed.* I saw him thrusting his chest forward. *You'll incur a ten percent penalty.* In my mind, he narrowed his eyes and rubbed his temple. *You will net only six thousand three hundred dollars on a ten-thousand-dollar withdrawal.* Now imaginary Kyle laughed as if to say, *This is so ridiculous; of course we're not doing it.*

I let go of the mouse and flexed my hand. For several seconds, I stared at the online form without moving. Was this the right thing to do? Early in the process, we had applied for a second mortgage but had been declined. This was the only remaining option that wouldn't increase our debt. If we wanted a baby, we had to do it. My fingers flew across the keyboard, pausing only on the question about how I wanted the disbursement paid, direct deposit or check. I clicked the box next to Check, not sure why, and submitted the form. The money would be available in five to seven business days. I had a week to convince Kyle this was a good idea.

Chapter 10

Our kitchen table sat six and had a built-in lazy Susan. Kyle had picked it out before we got married and added it to our wedding registry. At the time, we'd both imagined two or three kids sitting down to eat with us. Instead, the empty chairs had turned into a scab I couldn't stop picking at. Maybe that was part of the reason we had started eating in the living room, plates balanced on our thighs and the television on so we didn't have to talk.

Tonight, though, I had set the table for two and made one of Kyle's favorite Italian dinners: manicotti, meatballs, and garlic bread. More than a week had passed since I found out I wasn't being promoted to managing editor, and I still hadn't told him. I'd been putting it off because when I told him, I'd also have to tell him about withdrawing from my 401(k). But I had to tell him tonight. We had to get back to the clinic.

"We're eating in here?" he asked when I called him in from the living room. "Must be a special occasion?"

I winced. Had our marriage really deteriorated to the point where he thought sitting down to dinner together marked some type of celebration?

He looked at me with a hopeful expression. "So are we celebrating?" He smiled as he asked the question. *Is he happy because he thinks I got promoted and we'll have the money for another cycle?*

I didn't want to watch his face crumple, so I turned away from him toward the stove. "I didn't get the promotion. Andrew hired someone from the outside."

Sound from the television in the living room drifted into the kitchen, a commercial for some type of medication. The announcer recited a long list of potential side effects.

"I'm sorry," Kyle said. He placed a hand on my shoulder, and I jumped as if a bug had landed on me. I didn't know how to respond to his sympathy. In the script I had rehearsed, he said, *Well, that seals it, then. We're done with Dr. Evans.*

Kyle sighed as he shuffled to the other end of the counter to open a bottle of red wine. My chest tightened, and I wondered if we would ever go back to being us. Telling him about the withdrawal from our retirement account wasn't going to help.

After he filled our glasses, he sat at the table and studied me at the stove. My hands shook as I plated the food. A manicotti slipped off the spatula and landed on the floor, splattering red tomato sauce on the gray tile and white cabinets. As I cleaned up the mess, I tried to imagine Kyle agreeing that withdrawing the money was a good idea, but all I could picture was him storming away from the table.

Finally, I slid into the seat across from him. The commercial on TV ended, and the home-improvement show came back on. I fiddled with my silverware as I rehearsed my speech in my head. "Black mold," someone on the television said. "Dangerous."

I looked up, ready to tell Kyle, but lost my nerve. He took a bite of his pasta.

"Is it too dry? Do you want more sauce?" I spun the lazy Susan so the gravy boat was within his reach. He poured more sauce on his plate.

We sat without speaking, both of us staring at our dishes like parents mesmerized by their newborn. It was the most uncomfortable I had ever been with him, and that included our awkward chance meeting on a chairlift at Mount Stapleton. Halfway up the mountain, high above the trails, our chair had jerked to a stop, swaying from side to side when the wind blew. The air was so cold and dry that my nostrils stuck together every time I inhaled. I tapped my poles against the bar, waiting for the chair to move again. It didn't. Shivering, I pulled my hood over my hat and zipped my coat to the top so that it concealed my mouth and half my nose.

"This will help." Kyle extended a flask toward me.

I raised an eyebrow.

"Don't judge." He pulled it back and took a swig. "I only do it to keep warm."

"You're not really warm," I said. "You just don't know you're cold."

"Same difference." He licked his lips and thrust the flask at me again.

This time I accepted his offering. He laughed as I sipped. "First drink?" he asked. I tilted the flask back and took a large gulp. Whiskey gushed into my mouth. I squeezed my eyes closed and twisted my lips as I swallowed, my throat burning.

I handed the flask back to him, but he refused to accept it. "Try again. This time without the face," he insisted.

My throat was still on fire. "Nope." I dropped the container into his lap. At that exact moment, the lift lurched forward. The flask tumbled downward, bouncing off the seat and plummeting through the chilly air into the deep, ungroomed snow beneath the lift line.

Kyle's eyes widened in horror as he watched it fall. "That was my granddaddy's," he said. "Had it since I was seventeen."

"So it was probably time for a new one." I thought if I could make him laugh, I wouldn't feel as bad for losing his grandfather's flask.

By the time we reached the top of the mountain, I had agreed to buy him a new one. We exchanged numbers. For the next two weeks he sent me links that led to ridiculous flasks, one disguised as a bottle of suntan lotion, another as a folded tie, and others with funny sayings. I never did buy him a replacement, but he bought me dinner. Nineteen months later we were married.

Now Kyle took another bite of manicotti. The recipe I used was passed down from my maternal grandmother, who had moved from Palermo to the States. It had been on the menu at DeMarco's Diner only on Sundays and was the most popular meal on that day. "Delicious," he said.

He was trying to make things better between us, and I was about to ruin it all. I shredded the napkin in my lap into tiny pieces, ready to tell him. "I . . ." A clump of tomato sauce smeared his chin. It made him look so vulnerable that I couldn't go through with what I was about to say. "I got a bonus." I blurted out the words, not knowing where they had come from.

He put down his fork, and he waited for me to continue.

"A big one. To thank me for filling in for Leo." My face burned with shame. I had never lied to him before.

"How much?" He wiped his chin with his napkin.

I swallowed hard and forced myself to maintain eye contact. "Fifteen grand."

I could tell by his arched eyebrows that he was surprised. "Wow."

"I couldn't believe it."

His hand had frozen on his wineglass. "Unbelievable." He whistled.

Neither of us said anything else. The home-improvement guru's voice floated into the kitchen. "You can't fix it. You need to tear it down and rebuild."

"We can use it for another round." I tried to make the words sound nonchalant, but they came out as a desperate question.

Kyle reached for a piece of garlic bread and dunked it in his gravy. "Or we could pay off some of our debt."

"We have the rest of our lives to make payments, but time is running out to start a family." That line, I had rehearsed.

"Do you really want to go through all that again? Start from the beginning? We're still recovering from the last time."

"I promise, one last try. No matter what happens."

Kyle stood and carried his plate across the kitchen. When he opened the dishwasher, a foul odor escaped from inside it. With just the two of us, we rarely had to run it, and dirty dishes sat in it for long periods of time. He loaded his dish and turned to leave. At the doorway, he paused, chewing on his lower lip. "It's almost like a sign that we should try again."

My stomach knotted, and my dinner threatened to come back up. "I thought so too."

"Promise me that no matter what happens, this will be the last time."

"On my parents' grave."

Chapter 11

As soon as I woke up the next morning, I called Dr. Evans's office to make an appointment. The answering service told me I would have to call back during normal business hours and speak with someone in the office. I set the alarm on my phone for nine o'clock and showered and dressed for work. The buzzer went off while Page and I were brainstorming with the graphic designer about what photographs should accompany an article on the Mount Stapleton Ski Museum. I excused myself from the meeting to call the clinic. The soonest they could see us was in two weeks.

I texted Kyle the date and time of the appointment. He responded with a thumbs-up. Staring down at his response, I grinned, thinking he was as excited as I was to try IVF again. At some point, I would have to tell him where the money for the round really came from, but I would wait until after my pregnancy was confirmed or even until after I delivered. I imagined Kyle holding a baby boy when I finally told him. He would smile and stroke the baby's cheek. *I'm just glad we tried again.* In my head, his voice had a lilt as he spoke the words.

That night when I got home after work, Kyle had dinner waiting for me, homemade baked-potato soup with fresh-baked Pillsbury rolls. A vase with a bouquet of red sunflowers sat in the center of the table with a card that said *I'm sorry.*

"What are you apologizing for?" I asked.

"I've been so cranky about trying again. You need to know—it's not just the money I'm worried about. It's you too."

"Me? I'm fine."

He stirred his spoon around his bowl. "Each time we do this, you get your hopes up, and then when things go wrong, I can't console you. No one can. It hurts to see you that way."

My throat tightened as I saw myself standing over the never-used crib after our last try. I swallowed hard and pushed the image away. "If it doesn't work this time, I'll know we gave it all we had, and it just wasn't meant to be. I can live with that."

~

The next day, we rented snowmobiles, a bright-blue one for me and a lime-green one for Kyle. We rode them over a fifty-mile loop of connected trails that wound around enormous pine trees. I took my time navigating across the snow, enjoying the scenery, but Kyle let it rip, going full throttle when the path opened up. At one point, he got so far ahead that I lost sight of him. I caught up to him at an overlook where he had stopped to wait. It was the exact spot where he had proposed the first time we ever went snowmobiling together.

That day, he'd ridden beside me at a slow speed. About a mile from the spot, another snowmobile raced by us, going the other direction. "Pick up the pace," Kyle hollered.

As we approached the overlook, I noticed red spots dotted over the bright-white snow. We steered closer. I realized the red spots were painted rocks arranged in the shape of a large heart. I braked hard, coming to an abrupt stop. Kyle and I both climbed off our sleds.

He undid his helmet while I unfastened mine. "What do you think is going on here?" he asked.

"No idea." Weighed down in layers of clothes and numb from the cold, I felt as if I were dreaming. There was no one else around, and all I could see in front of me was a blanket of snow and tall trees, and all

I could hear was wind. "Maybe we stumbled across Stapleton's version of Stonehenge?"

Kyle reached for my arm and guided me away from our snowmobiles. Together, we trudged through the snow to the center of the heart. He inhaled deeply and dropped to one knee. I started to shiver.

"Nikki, the day we got stuck together on that chairlift, I wished it would never start again, because I knew even then I wanted to be with you forever." He pulled a box from his pocket. "Marry me." Later, when we started our snowmobiles again, I wore a sparkling diamond ring under the glove on my left hand.

Today, there was no heart, but Kyle did have a thermos of hot chocolate spiked with butterscotch schnapps stowed away in his backpack. He filled two paper cups, and we sipped, looking out at the mountain view. Before he put the thermos away, he rummaged through the knapsack's outer pocket and pulled out a red rock.

I took it from him. "I can't believe you kept that in here all this time."

"It's my good luck charm."

I smiled, thinking of him all those years ago collecting and painting each rock and waking up at sunrise on a cold January day to arrange them. He'd told me he had started preparing the rocks in August.

"Would you do it again?" I asked now.

He wrapped his arm around my shoulders. "Of course."

Chapter 12

Pots and pans banging together, cabinet doors slamming, boots stomping on the hardwood. These were the sounds that woke me the following Saturday. It was so unusual for Kyle to be noisy in the morning that I knew something was wrong before I got out of bed.

As I descended the stairs, he leaped up from his recliner and stalked toward me. "What the hell is this?" He waved a sheet of paper above his head.

I couldn't see it, but I knew exactly what it was by the tone of his voice: the check stub from my 401(k) withdrawal. I had hidden it in the glove box of my SUV so he wouldn't see it.

"How did you get that?"

"Doesn't matter."

"What were you doing in my car?"

"That's not the issue."

I tried to walk past him, but he grabbed my arm, pressing his fingers so hard into my skin that I was sure they would leave marks. "You're hurting me."

He winced as he released me and stepped back. I knew he wasn't trying to harm me. That wasn't who he was. The only time I had ever seen him violent was when he checked someone while playing hockey. Before we'd started trying to have a baby, Kyle never got angry with me. Even the time I'd backed the car through the garage door, he had been perplexed, not mad. "I just don't understand how you . . . how that could have happened," he'd said, scratching his head but careful not to judge me, though clearly it was an idiotic thing to do.

Now, he took a deep breath in and slowly released it. "I can't believe you lied to me. This whole thing has changed you into someone I don't even recognize anymore. Someone I don't like." His face glistened with perspiration, or maybe it was disappointment oozing from his pores.

"I knew it was the only way you'd agree to try again."

"It's going to take us years to get out of the debt we're already in. I won't have you sacrificing our retirement."

"We could just as easily lose that money if the market crashes. Let's put it to good use for one last time."

"There's not going to be another time." The veins in his neck bulged as he inched closer to me. "It's over!" He shredded the stub into tiny pieces, cocked his arm like he was going to fling them at me, but thought better of it and dropped them to the ground. "Even if we win millions in Powerball, I wouldn't do another cycle. I can't have a baby with someone I can't trust."

~

Later that day, when I left to have lunch with Sharon, I noticed the salt and sludge had been washed off my car, the water bottles that littered the passenger seat were gone, the interior had been vacuumed and polished, and my gas tank was full. Damn, Kyle had been doing something nice for me when he came across the check stub. I always ruined whatever momentum we built.

I wanted to run back in the house to thank him for his kindness, but he had left while I was in the shower. I glanced toward the corner of the garage where he kept his hockey gear, but the equipment wasn't there. Even though his game wasn't until this evening, he'd taken it with him, so clearly he planned to stay out and avoid me for the rest of the day. This realization made my heart ache, as I remembered the days Kyle had hated being away from me even for an hour on weekends, insisting I come to the rink and watch his games. I enjoyed seeing him play, too, witnessing an aggressive side to my mild-mannered husband. Now if I wanted to see that aggressive side, all I had to do was open my mouth.

Chapter 13

Sharon waited for me in a booth at the back of the restaurant. Unlike how she usually was when I saw her, she wasn't in mom mode. Instead of her trademark messy ponytail, her hair hung past her shoulders and curled. Concealer hid the dark circles and bags that often punctuated her eyes, and she wore an argyle sweater instead of a baggy sweatshirt. I expected Noah and Cameron to be sitting next to her, pushing toy cars across the table, but to my surprise, she sat alone. "Where are my favorite boys?" I asked, removing my jacket and hanging it on the hook.

"I left them with Rick so we could talk. You sounded upset when you called."

"Yeah, Kyle and I had a huge fight. He found the check stub in my car."

Sharon tilted her head. "What check stub?"

A waitress walked by with a plate of chicken wings. I could practically taste how spicy they were by their strong scent. My eyes even watered. "The check from my 401(k) withdrawal. I told you. I took it so we can do a fourth round."

"You didn't tell me that. If you had, I would have told you it's a terrible idea."

I forced a smile. "Do you have a better one?"

She pulled her chin toward her chest and bit down on her lower lip. I had seen her do the same thing countless times through the years, always right before she said something I didn't want to hear and she usually regretted saying. "Let's look at the menu."

We were at the Stapleton Tavern, where we had been coming for years. Sharon always ordered the barbecue-pulled-pork sandwich, and I got the grilled-chicken-salad wrap. Every single time. Still, she studied the menu like she had never been here before, so I knew that whatever she was about to say, she was thinking of the least offensive way to word it.

A group of teenagers done with a morning ski run sat down at the table next to ours. One of the kids removed his hat, revealing a mop of chocolate-brown hair that reminded me of Kyle's. I studied the boy's face. Like Kyle, he had a cleft chin and large puffy lips, but his eyes were dark like mine. *Our son will look like him,* I thought.

"Nikki!" By how loud Sharon said my name, I realized she'd been trying to get my attention for a while. "Do you know him?"

"When Kyle and I have a son, that's what he'll look like."

Sharon squeezed her eyes shut and pinched the bridge of her nose. "You have to stop this. Really."

The light in the restaurant seemed too bright and the conversations around us too loud. "Stop what?"

"This obsession with having a baby. It's making you insane."

I looked at the kid again. "He looks like a young version of Kyle, but his eyes are sort of like mine. A similar color anyway."

The kid turned his head and caught me staring. He nodded as if saying hello. "That lady's totally checking me out," he said to his friends. They all turned to look at Sharon and me. Her cheeks reddened, and she muttered under her breath.

"You look like a younger version of my husband," I shouted over, causing the table of teens to break out in a fit of laughter.

"I'm really worried about you," Sharon said.

"Why?" We hadn't been greeted by a server yet. I searched the room for one. I needed a drink. Fast. A few tables away a waiter leaning against a wall gabbed with customers. I waved him over. "Two blueberry beers."

Sharon fiddled with her silverware. "Bring a water for me. With a lime."

"Two waters," I said.

Sharon started to say something else, but the waiter was already walking away.

"What did Kyle say about the withdrawal?" she asked.

I wasn't about to confess to her that I had lied to him about where the money came from. Even thinking about that fib now made my stomach cramp. "He refuses to try again."

"And you used the last of the embryos?"

I nodded. There had been seven in all. We used two in the first round, three in the second, and the remaining two the third time. "How am I going to convince him? Any ideas?"

Sharon reached across the table and squeezed my hand. "Maybe just give the baby thing a rest for a few months. Until things are better with him."

The waiter dropped off our drinks and took our food order. Despite studying the menu earlier, Sharon ordered the pulled pork. She waited until the waiter left and continued. "Have some fun trying to conceive the old-fashioned way." She winked, and I was reminded of sophomore year in college, when I'd planned to lose my virginity with my then boyfriend, Anthony. Sharon had given me advice. "The first time is awkward and kind of painful, so don't expect fireworks or anything, but it gets better. Much better." She'd grinned. "Make sure you don't just lie there like a statue. Be an active participant, and speak up. Let him know what feels good and what doesn't."

God, I was so worried about getting pregnant when I was with Anthony, despite being on the pill. I would stress so much about it that I threw off my cycle and would be in panic mode when my period was late. I actually cried in relief every month when it finally arrived.

"I can't wait. I'm running out of time."

"Women our age get pregnant all the time," Sharon said.

"They don't."

"Believe me, they do." Something about the way she said it caused me to study her. Her cheeks reddened, and she looked away. I continued to watch her as she picked up a glass—the water glass. She hadn't touched her beer. Every muscle in my body tensed. This couldn't be happening. It wasn't fair. "You're pregnant." It came out as an accusation.

She flinched. "Fourteen weeks."

When she was pregnant with Cameron and Noah, she told me the day she took the home pregnancy test.

"Why didn't you tell me?"

She pressed her lips together.

"You don't think I can be happy for you?"

"Are you?"

My throat burned the way it sometimes did before I started to cry. I hated myself. She was right. I wasn't happy for her. I was pissed. I should have been the one who was pregnant. "You don't even want another kid. You call Noah the little beast."

"It's a funny nickname. I love that kid to death. You know that."

"No, all you do is complain about how much work the boys are. Noah's impossible to potty train. Cameron won't eat anything and has to be entertained all the time."

"I don't think you want to hear about the good stuff."

"Why wouldn't I?"

"I feel guilty telling you about it." She picked up her beer glass and took a sip.

I slumped against the back of the booth. We had always told each other everything. "You shouldn't be drinking that."

She pushed the mug across the table to me.

"What's the best thing about being Noah and Cameron's mom?"

She shook her head. "Nikki."

"Really, I want to know."

Her face softened. "Their unconditional love. The way Noah's entire face lights up when he sees me in the morning. How he giggles as he reaches for me."

I turned to look at teenage Kyle and imagined him as a two-year-old, the smile on his face as he wrapped his soft arms around my neck. *I love you, Mama,* he said. My lip quivered.

"Are you okay?" Sharon asked.

No, I'm not. You were right. I can't handle hearing about the good stuff. What kind of person does that make me? "That's beautiful."

"Yeah." Sharon's eyes welled up. I knew she was sad for me.

I forced myself to smile. "Are the boys having a sister or another brother?"

"Sister."

"Were you trying?"

She looked down at the table. "We weren't not trying."

Noah was also unplanned. Life was not fair.

Sharon fiddled with her silverware again. "I want so much for this to happen for you too."

"It will." I didn't sound convincing even to myself. Tears threatened to spill from my eyes. I picked up my beer and chugged it down to stop them from coming. The waiter arrived with our food. We were silent as he slid the plates in front of us.

"Have you thought of names?" The french fries were limp, and my sandwich was soggy.

"Sharon," she said.

I stared at her while chewing, waiting for her to say she was kidding.

"Don't look at me that way," she said. "Why can't a mother name a baby after herself? If I were having another boy and we named him after Rick, you wouldn't think twice."

She had a point, but still.

We stayed at the restaurant for another half hour. Sharon ate her entire meal. I boxed up most of mine to take home. When we stood to leave, I noticed her sweater stretched across a small bump in her belly. I wondered how I had missed it the last time I saw her, but more than that, I wondered when Sharon had decided I was someone she could no longer confide in.

Chapter 14

The queen-size bed felt as big as Mount Stapleton without Kyle's large body next to mine. Usually his snoring kept me awake, but without it tonight, I couldn't fall asleep. I hadn't heard from him since he stormed out of the house after confronting me about the 401(k) withdrawal. The numbers on the clock next to me glowed: 1:11. I knew Kyle had hockey earlier in the evening, but his games always ended by nine.

I had stopped myself from texting him before I went to bed because he needed space, but enough was enough. I pounded out a message: Where are you?

I stared at the screen, waiting for a response. After a minute or so, I gave up and tossed the phone on his pillow. Closing my eyes to try to fall asleep, I pictured Kyle in his red-and-gold uniform with number seven on the back, sprinting across the rink toward the puck. Out of nowhere, an opposing player slammed him into the boards, knocking him off his feet. Kyle's head smacked the ice, and he lay unconscious— or worse, lifeless.

I jerked upright and inhaled, trying to slow my racing heart. *He's fine. Just angry. And he has every right to be.* Even I didn't like the person I had become, a liar, a sneak, willing to do anything to get my way. I should have told him the truth. At the same time, the money was deducted from my paycheck every week. Didn't I have a right to spend it however I wanted?

I tried to fall asleep again and almost succeeded. In my groggy state, I imagined Kyle drinking with his friends at a bar. Tipsy, he climbed into his car and headed home. He sped around a sharp, slippery curve and lost control. The Jeep tumbled over the edge of a deserted narrow mountain road.

The images made me think of my parents. I often wondered if they'd seen the other car racing toward them. If my father had tried to swerve out of the way. Sharon's dad, who was chief of police at the time, had broken the news. Sharon was with him. I thought they'd come over for a friendly visit, even offered them pizzelles that I had just made, the taste of anise still in my mouth. When they both declined, I knew something was wrong. My hands started to shake. "I don't know how to tell you this, Nicole." I knew right then he was about to say something devastating. People always called me Nikki, except when they were breaking my heart. "Your parents were in an accident. A wrong-way driver on the interstate."

They were coming back from visiting Dana on the Cape. "It's my fault," she'd said at the funeral, as if she had been the one driving the car that hit them.

I shook my head to clear the horrible images. *Where the hell are you, Kyle?* I tried to reach him again. This time I called instead of texting, but his phone went straight to voice mail. It was after two. Should I call the police? Check hospitals? I texted his teammate Luke. Fifteen minutes later, Luke responded.

As I read his message, my grip on the phone tightened. He's sleeping one off. Spending the night at my place.

~

I didn't fall asleep until hours later, and I slept fitfully before waking with a sore jaw from clenching my teeth all night. I heard the first-floor shower running and marched downstairs. My back felt stiff, and my legs wobbled. Just as I reached the last step, the water shut off. A minute or so later, Kyle, a towel wrapped around his waist, a cloud of steam behind him, opened the bathroom door.

I wasn't sure whether to punch him in the throat or hug him. "Where were you all night?"

His bloodshot eyes avoided mine. "I was with Chris, had too much to drink after the game and didn't want to drive." His shoulders slumped as he spoke.

"Chris?"

He stared at the floor while nodding.

"Luke told me you were with him."

He ran a hand through his wet hair. After a long silence, he said, "Chris and I stayed at Luke's."

"You could have let me know. I was out of my mind with worry."

"My phone died."

"You couldn't have borrowed one of theirs?"

He wouldn't meet my eye. "I didn't think of it."

"You didn't think of it?"

He pulled himself back to his full height and pointed at me. "You lied to me."

I stepped closer to him. "So you were punishing me by making me worry?"

"No, I didn't want to talk to you." The fan in the bathroom clicked off, making his voice sound even louder than it was. "I still don't want to talk to you."

He stormed past me, leaving his woodsy scent behind. I thought about chasing after him but decided to give him space. This was my fault. I should have been honest about where the money came from.

My phone whistled with a text from Dana. **Just spoke with Marie. This dog thing is happening.**

I sighed and jammed the phone into my pocket. I had too much to think about with Kyle to engage with my sister about this ridiculous idea of her getting a dog.

I made myself a mug of tea. Heavy footsteps stomped across the living room ceiling, and drawers banged closed. A few minutes later Kyle trudged down the stairs, a baseball cap on his head, a large duffel bag with that menacing Boston Bruins bear logo thrown over one shoulder, and his toiletry bag on the other. The green tea I was drinking felt like sludge in my stomach. "What's all that?" I asked.

He fiddled with the zipper on the bag. "I'm gonna stay with Luke for a while."

The cup in my hand shook so hard that tea spilled out over the side. I set it down on the coffee table. "What are you talking about?"

"I can't live like this anymore, Nikki."

The recliner that was usually so comfortable hurt my back. I shifted in the chair. "Like what?"

"Fighting all the time."

"We don't fight all the time." Of course, it came out confrontational. I waited for Kyle to smile at the irony. His lips remained flat.

"We should be supporting each other through all this, but we can't because we're on different pages, so we end up doing and saying hurtful things. Things we regret." His chin quivered, and his next words came out shaky. "I've accepted that we're never going to have kids. If you can't come to terms with that, I don't see how we can make this marriage work. It may already be too late."

His words brought me to my feet. "What exactly are you saying?"

"You need to figure out what you want more: me or a baby."

I swallowed hard, wondering what he'd say if I told him I wanted the baby more. Would he ask for a divorce? We stared at each other without speaking. A picture of my parents on the shelf behind him caught my attention. They sat at the counter in their diner. My mother's smile radiated happiness. My father slumped in his stool with his head hung low and his lips pressed tightly together. I had always thought he was trying to stifle a laugh, but today I wondered if he was trying to hide his disappointment.

"I'm going to leave, figure out what I want, and give you time to figure out what you want," Kyle said.

"We'll figure it out together." I inched closer to him, but he dropped the duffel bag off his shoulder so it acted as a buffer between us.

"This is something we each need to figure out on our own."

With four long strides, he crossed the room, then opened the front door and closed it gently behind him. The soft way it clicked masked the fact that he was slamming the door on my dream of becoming a mother.

Chapter 15

Exhaustion overtook me after Kyle left, and I lay down on the sofa to nap. I told myself he was bluffing and he'd be back. Several hours later, the front door banged off the wall guard, waking me from a deep sleep. I sighed with relief, happy Kyle was home but too tired to sit up. "Please don't make me choose between you and a baby."

Footsteps on the hardwood too light to be Kyle's approached the couch. "A baby? What are you talking about?" Dana stared down at me.

A blast of cold air had sneaked in with her. I pulled the blanket up to my chin. "What are you doing here?" Outside the living room window, the sky over the mountains glowed a brilliant shade of red. I had slept the day away.

"You look like hell."

I couldn't argue with that. I hadn't changed out of my pajamas.

"Where's Kyle?"

"He left." Saying the words out loud took my breath away. He wasn't bluffing. He was gone.

Dana's phone rang. She pulled it from her coat pocket to see who was calling but didn't answer. "What do you mean?"

"He left me."

Dana slipped out of her jacket. Instead of tossing it on a piece of furniture, she hung it on the closet doorknob, which was her way of showing support. "You had a fight. He'll be back. It happens." She tapped on my legs with the palm of her hand until I moved them and she could sit.

"It was more than a fight."

"What happened?"

I gripped the blanket tighter. "It's a long story."

Dana bent to remove her boots. When she finished, she curled her feet under her. "I'm not going anywhere."

"I don't want to talk about it."

"Was it about IVF?" she asked.

I sat upright. "How do you know about that?"

"Dana. Can. Read," she said. "I saw the card and magnet on your refrigerator."

Of course she'd seen them. "Why didn't you say anything sooner?"

She poked her tongue against the inside of her cheek. "Why didn't you tell me about it? Did you tell Sharon?"

I didn't answer but could feel my face heating up.

"You told her. You tell her everything. You do realize I'm your sister, not her." For once, Dana wasn't smiling.

"I don't like to talk about it because it's embarrassing."

"Embarrassing?"

"Women get pregnant all the time. Without even trying. Why can't I?"

Dana frowned, an expression I'd rarely seen on her. With the frown, she looked like me. I wondered when I had become so unhappy. Was it after I'd had the miscarriage, when my parents had died, or after the first failed IVF attempt?

"Lots of couples have trouble conceiving, Nikki. That's why fertility clinics exist," Dana said.

"I never expected it to happen to us."

"'Cause bad shit never happens to the DeMarcos." Dana's tone was as sharp as the blade on Kyle's skates. "Anyway, that doesn't explain why you told Sharon and not me. Was it less embarrassing telling her?"

I opened my mouth but didn't have a good response, so I shut it again.

"You're the only family I have. You and Aunt Izzie," Dana said. "I always tell you what's going on in my life, but you never tell me anything."

The sadness in her voice made my heart ache. She was right, though. I never confided in her. In my mind, she was still the little sister who followed me around the house, the one I had to babysit when my parents were working at the diner, the little girl who rode the pink bike with the white banana seat through the neighborhood while I was driving around town in my parents' Accord.

"It's because of our age difference," I said.

Dana rolled her eyes.

"I know it doesn't matter now, but when I was thirteen and had my first crush, you were five. I couldn't tell you about it. When I was sixteen, going through my first breakup, you were eight and wouldn't understand. I just never got in the habit of telling you things, so I don't think of you that way."

Dana pointed to herself. "In case you haven't noticed, I'm all grown up now."

Of course I knew she was a full-grown woman now, but she would always be my little sister, someone I was supposed to look out for. I hated that I had unintentionally hurt her. I leaned toward her and pulled her into a hug. "I'm sorry."

Dana shook her head. "I don't want you to be sorry. I want you to understand that no matter what, I'm here for you. I want you to know you can trust me."

"I do."

"Then tell me what's going on."

I stood. "I will, but we need alcohol for this conversation." Dana followed me into the kitchen. I pulled out a bottle of Montepulciano from the built-in rack and tried to open the wide drawer under it for the corkscrew. The drawer stuck. I tugged hard, managing to open it just far enough to see a pad of bright-yellow sticky notes caught in the tracks. I used to write messages on them and leave them in Kyle's lunch cooler, telling him what time he had to be home to give me my shots. "You don't have to remind me," he had snapped during the most recent cycle. "It's the same damn time every day."

I wrenched at the notepad until it came free. The drawer slid open. Matchbooks and a screwdriver tumbled out. I rummaged through the contents, pulling out pens, menus, old postcards, elastics, and twist ties. Finally, I ripped the drawer from its brackets and flipped it over on the counter. The remaining junk spilled out, some of it crashing to the floor.

"Nikki." Dana nudged me to the side. "What are you doing?"

"Looking for the corkscrew."

She took the bottle from me. "It's twist off." While she opened the bottle and filled our glasses, I flung the sticky notes into the trash. We settled back on the living room sofa. Dana's drink sloshed over the side of her glass and left a small red wet spot on the couch's tan fabric. "Whoops," she said, soaking up the spill with the sleeve of her sweatshirt. I returned to the kitchen to grab paper towels and soda water.

"When did Kyle leave?" Dana asked as I tried to blot out the stain.

"Can you still see it?"

"It's fine."

"It's not." I dabbed more soda water on a clean paper towel and continued to blot. "He left this morning." Thinking about his ultimatum, I pressed hard on the stain, applying so much pressure that I thought my fist would break through the cushion of the sofa.

The living room floor lamp, set on a timer, clicked on. Five thirty. I wondered what Kyle was eating for dinner.

Dana stretched her leg, accidentally kicking me and pulling me from my thoughts. "Do you really want kids?" She had never liked children and had always claimed she'd never have them. As a teenager, she'd even refused to babysit.

"Yes, I want a family."

"You have a husband. Get a dog and call it a day. I'll ask Marie when she drops off mine."

I glared at her.

"The world is so screwed up. School shootings, terrorists, global warming. Wrong-way drivers on the interstate. Why do you want to bring a baby into it?"

I put down my wineglass and stared at her. "Do you really think that?"

"Do you ever watch the news?"

"Yeah, the world needs more good people."

Dana laughed.

"I don't want Mom's and Dad's genes to die with us."

Dana's lips quivered. "They would have loved being grandparents."

"You'd be a fun aunt." I pictured her on the slopes or at the beach with my and Kyle's son or daughter. Of course, I'd have to keep her in my sight at all times. She might be all grown up, but she was still Dana.

She disappeared into the kitchen with both empty glasses and returned with them full.

"I still don't understand why Kyle left."

"I want to try another round. He doesn't."

"You've already tried?"

"Three times."

"Three times." She sank against the back of the sofa. "I would have been there for you, Nikki. If you had told me."

I felt a pang in my heart. I had handled this whole baby thing wrong. It had already alienated me from Kyle and Sharon. I didn't want to lose Dana too. "I know. I'm sorry."

Dana sipped her wine. "Do you think Kyle will change his mind?"

I thought about how hurt he was when he found out I'd lied about the money. How he had said he didn't want to have a baby with someone he couldn't trust. The wine tasted sour. I put my almost full glass down on the coffee table. "No." I didn't want it to be true, but I knew it was.

"Well then," Dana said.

"Well then what?"

"What's more important, having a baby or staying married to Kyle?"

"That's what he asked me to think about when he left, but it's about more than having a baby. It's carrying on Mom and Dad's legacy. I already screwed up the restaurant."

"We sold the restaurant to Hank. They'd be happy about that, and they'd be ashamed that you threw away your marriage trying to carry on their legacy."

I sneaked a peek at my parents' picture on the shelf. My mother's smile didn't look as big tonight, and my father had that same disappointed expression that I'd noticed earlier. How had I missed it all these years?

I buried my face in my hands. "I don't want to lose Kyle."

"The one thing I know about Kyle is that he loves you. Tell him you're ready to move on, and he'll be back."

Chapter 16

The buzzing alarm clock woke me from a fitful sleep on Monday morning. My temples throbbed, and I felt nauseous, the beginning of a migraine. I'd never experienced one until I started taking fertility drugs. As I thought about this, my anger toward Kyle for refusing to do another round intensified. He hadn't sacrificed as much as I had, so it was easier for him to give up our dream of having a baby. I glanced toward my phone on the nightstand, expecting to see a message from him, but there was none. We hadn't communicated since he walked out on Sunday.

I'd been waiting for him to cool off, but he'd had enough time. I pounded out a text and waited for the dots that indicated he was replying to appear. They didn't. I flung my phone back on the bureau and pulled the covers over my head. If only I could stay in my cozy, warm bed all day, but I couldn't. Today was the new managing editor's first day at the magazine, and I didn't want to make a bad impression by calling in sick. I swallowed two ibuprofen and forced myself to make the drive across town.

As I circled the parking lot, my headache worsened. A candy-apple-red Range Rover with a New York license plate occupied the spot I had been using since my first day more than a decade ago. While there wasn't a sign designating the space as mine, everyone else knew not to park there. How could I tactfully bring this up with my new boss?

There were no empty spaces in the lot because the maintenance crew had plowed the snow into mountainous piles that swallowed up the last four rows. I drove a quarter of a mile down the street to the overflow lot, a property of an abandoned warehouse, and huffed back over the slushy sidewalks. My phone, tucked away in my coat pocket, vibrated. I sighed in relief, expecting a response from Kyle. The message was a group text to Dana, Kyle, and me from Aunt Izzie, reminding us she was cooking us dinner tomorrow night. Artichoke gratinata because Kyle requested it, she wrote. A gust of icy wind blew as I stared down at my screen, waiting for my husband's response. Surely he wouldn't ignore my aunt. He'd come up with an excuse: working late or hockey.

My phone vibrated in my hand, and Page's name flashed across the screen. Where are you???????

The series of question marks at the end of her message made me quicken my pace. Inside the building, my coworkers sat at attention behind their desks, focused on their monitors. Usually, at this time of morning, they milled through the hallways, cups of coffee in their hands, chitchatting with one another. In the corner office that used to be Leo's, a pale, dark-haired woman sat behind the enormous mahogany desk, talking to Andrew. She stared toward the door as I passed. Our eyes locked. I smiled. The corners of her mouth curled downward. She glanced at her watch and pointed at me. Andrew turned and looked in my direction. As he spun around to face her again, he nodded. I wasn't sure if his nod was to acknowledge me or a response to whatever Elizabeth had said. *Are they talking about me?*

As I made my way down the hall, Page called out to me. "Andrew was looking for you to introduce Elizabeth. They stopped by three times."

"Did you meet her?"

Page wrinkled her nose. "Yup." I waited for her to elaborate. "I stopped by Eli's, bought her a blueberry muffin and coffee to welcome her."

"Kiss-ass."

"It didn't work out so well. She's allergic to blueberries and doesn't do caffeine."

I laughed. "So I get to have them?"

"Andrew scoffed them down while she droned on and on about the importance of native advertising." I tilted my head, and Page clarified. "Advertorial content."

~

Elizabeth wiped her mouth with a napkin when I entered. A greasy paper plate rested on the desk in front of her, and the room smelled like bacon. She certainly hadn't wasted any time making the corner office her own. Framed posters of inspirational quotes hung from the walls.

PLEASURE IN THE JOB PUTS PERFECTION IN THE WORK.

THE FRUIT OF YOUR OWN HARD WORK IS THE SWEETEST.

THE DIFFERENCE BETWEEN TRY AND TRIUMPH IS JUST A LIT-
TLE UMPH!

If Kyle and I weren't fighting, I'd sneak a picture with my phone and send it to him. I smiled as I imagined his snarky response. *You didn't tell me Tony Robbins was your new boss.*

Covers of past issues of the magazine that had decorated the walls when the space belonged to Leo spilled out of an overflowing garbage can. A chill ran down my spine. Elizabeth wouldn't think twice about making all kinds of changes. Would I survive her regime? Would Page? Or would Elizabeth discard us as easily as she did those old issues?

"I wasn't particularly impressed with any of those covers," she said.

She had spoken fewer than ten words, and I already thought I might not enjoy working for her. I pulled my eyes away from the trash. "I look forward to seeing your ideas."

She rolled her chair back and stood, extending her hand. "Elizabeth Sanders. I've heard a lot about you, Nicole. It's nice to formally meet."

"Nikki," I corrected, wondering exactly what she had heard.

"Andrew tells me you wanted the managing editor position."

Andrew had told me she had moved to Mount Stapleton from Manhattan, so I had expected her to be a fast-talking New Yorker. Instead, she spoke excruciatingly slow, pausing after each word as if there were a period there.

We were still standing. I wondered if she was trying to intimidate me with her height. She was at least six feet tall. I drew up my shoulders and stood as straight as I could. "I've been doing it for the past six months."

"Will you have trouble working for me, then?"

I admired her directness. "I'm going to be a sponge, learning everything I can from you so if the opportunity arises again, I'll be ready."

"Good plan." She pointed toward the window. Outside, it had started to snow again. "I'm not sure I'm built for this snow. We didn't get as much in the city." She dropped to her chair, and I felt like I had passed a test. "Andrew tells me you grew up here."

I sat on the edge of her guest chair, still on alert. "What else did he say?"

"You're not a fan of Pendleton 88."

I felt like I was having a conversation with Dana or my aunt, like Elizabeth was purposefully trying to push my buttons. "I hear the macaroni and cheese is good."

"That's all my daughter will eat. We'll have to try it."

My mouth went dry the way it always did when I met someone new and the conversation veered to children. *How old is she? What's her name? Do you have others?* They were all questions I knew I should ask but didn't because then I would be expected to answer them myself.

"I have two. How many kids do you have?" she said.

Her assumption made me feel vulnerable. After all, what married woman my age didn't have children? "None." It was barely a whisper. I rubbed my hands on my thighs as a way to comfort myself. I was too embarrassed to look at her, so I stared out the window. A dusting of snow covered the pine trees. Seeing the beauty of the white on green reminded me why I loved living here despite the frigid winters. "That would make a beautiful picture for the cover." I pointed at the window.

"We're putting Hank on the cover of the next issue. I'm introducing a new service. We'll write an article for anyone who commits to four full-page ads a year. Hank's the pilot, since we owe him a piece." She stared at me as if she expected me to react. I kept the temper tantrum going on inside my head silent and focused on being still. "Today's my kids' first day with the new nanny. Hallie's four, and Danvers is six months."

Her eyes glazed over. If I knew her better, I would have reached across the desk to squeeze her hand. It couldn't be easy moving to a new state and leaving your children with a stranger. Elizabeth reached into a messenger bag resting on the corner of her desk. I expected her to pull out photographs of her kids. Instead, she took out a small notebook. She looked at me again, all traces of the vulnerability she had shown a second before gone. "How's the article on his restaurant coming along?"

I rocked back and forth. "I haven't been able to pin him down for an interview yet." I was getting good at lying. I hadn't even bothered to call him.

"I'll set it up. We'll talk to him together," she said. "I should meet him, considering that he's one of our biggest advertisers and isn't happy."

Chapter 17

The overpowering scent of garlic assaulted me as soon as I walked into Aunt Izzie's house. Kyle hadn't responded to the group text or my messages, but I hoped he had let my aunt know he wouldn't be here tonight.

As I slipped out of my coat, she stood at the top of the staircase with her arms folded across her chest, watching me. "Where have you been?" Her annoyed tone made it seem as if I were hours late instead of a mere ten minutes.

I held up a bakery box. "I stopped to get dessert."

Dana's head popped out of the kitchen doorway. She mouthed words behind Aunt Izzie's back, trying to convey a silent message. Whatever my sister was trying to tell me, I couldn't figure it out. She became desperate, making exaggerated movements with her lips and pointing at my aunt, but still I had no idea what she wanted me to know.

Aunt Izzie looked over her shoulder at Dana. Dana reshaped her wide-open mouth into a broad smile. "There better be cannoli in that box," she said.

Aunt Izzie's eyes flickered from Dana toward me and back. She knew something was going on.

"You'll have to wait until after dinner to find out," I said as I reached the top of the staircase. Aunt Izzie blocked my path, her expression still stern.

"I'm sorry I was late."

"Why isn't Kyle with you?" she asked.

"Hockey practice." The words fell from my mouth without my even thinking about them, and they were a perfect excuse. Still, my face burned with shame. I didn't want to be good at lying.

Behind Aunt Izzie, Dana slid her index finger across her throat.

"Nicole, I saw him at the grocery store this afternoon."

I swallowed hard, picturing Kyle in the frozen-food aisle, his shopping cart filled with TV dinners, Cape Cod Café pizzas, and Oreos. Right away, Aunt Izzie would have known something wasn't right. Had he told her that he'd left me? Had he told her why?

"What did he say?" I stared down at the hardwood. *Please don't have told her that I stole from our retirement fund.*

Aunt Izzie placed a hand on her hip. I braced myself for a lecture about lying. *My sister raised you better than that.*

"That he wouldn't be here for dinner. The two of you were separated and you could explain why."

Separated? Is that what we are? My legs wobbled, and I reached for the banister to steady myself.

"I'm starving," Dana announced. "Can we eat?"

Aunt Izzie turned toward the kitchen. I scooted by her, rushing into the bathroom and banging the door shut behind me. I eyed the window, wishing I could climb out. How could I go back out there and face my aunt again? How could I explain what I'd done? There was no excuse. I turned on the faucet and washed my hands, imagining how she would reprimand me. *If you have to resort to lies to get what you want, you're clearly not ready to be a mother.* I turned away from my reflection in the medicine cabinet mirror, unable to stand the sight of myself. Aunt Izzie spoke the truth in her imaginary scolding. What kind of role model would I be for a child?

In the kitchen, a timer buzzed. "Dinner's ready," Aunt Izzie called.

There was a soft knock on the door and then Dana's voice. "You can't hide in there forever."

I reached toward the toilet and pulled the chain. "I'll be right out."

When I returned to the kitchen, Aunt Izzie stood in front of the stove, banging a wooden spoon against a pot as if she were trying to beat it to death. Dana leaned against the counter next to her, eating bruschetta off a cookie sheet. Aunt Izzie whacked my sister's knuckles with the spoon. I winced, sure the smack was meant for me.

Dana flinched and shook out her hand. "Ouch, that hurt."

"Transfer those to a platter," Aunt Izzie barked.

I sank into a chair, and Dana slid into the one next to me. Aunt Izzie placed the baking dish with the artichokes in the center of the table. The bread crumbs topping them were golden-brown perfection, making my mouth water. Aunt Izzie had done a lot of work preparing this meal for Kyle. I should have told her he wasn't coming. "Those look delicious," I said.

Aunt Izzie didn't respond. She hadn't looked at me since I came out of the bathroom. As much as I wanted to avoid a conversation about Kyle, I knew I couldn't. "Look, Kyle and I, we're—"

"Nicole," Aunt Izzie interrupted, holding up a hand. "What's going on between you and Kyle is none of my business. What I don't understand is why you let me believe he'd be here tonight."

"I'm sorry."

"I know I can never replace your mother, but I hope you know that if you ever need to talk, I'm here for you. I'll always be here for you." She turned toward Dana. "For both of you."

Her reference to my mother did me in. If my mom were here, Kyle and I wouldn't be in this mess. That I was sure of. "Thank you." My voice cracked. I took a giant sip of wine, trying to swallow the lump in my throat. "Kyle and I will work things out."

"Of course you will. You love each other," Aunt Izzie said.

I heard Kyle's angry words on the day he'd left. *This whole thing has changed you into someone I don't even recognize anymore. Someone I don't like. I can't have a baby with someone I can't trust.* I sliced into my artichoke as if I were trying to carve the memory from my mind.

"You know, your mother and Dominic went through some rough patches too," Aunt Izzie said. "Talking to Father Doherty helped."

"When did this happen?" Other than a few arguments around the time Hank moved back to town, I didn't remember my parents fighting. "Talking to a priest about marital problems is beyond ridiculous," Dana said.

Aunt Izzie shot her a warning look. Kyle had argued something similar when my aunt had suggested pre-Cana after our engagement. "How is a priest going to prepare us for marriage?" he'd asked. I wondered now if we could have better worked through our fertility issues if we'd taken the course.

"Their arguments had to do with Hank," I said.

Aunt Izzie dropped her piece of bruschetta to her plate and broke out into a coughing fit. I watched, paralyzed with fear, as her face turned red. "Can you speak?" Dana asked. She jumped up from her chair.

Aunt Izzie reached for her water. "I'm fine," she croaked. "Chunk of tomato went down the wrong pipe." She waited until she composed herself. "What do you remember about their arguments?"

I shrugged. I'd been ten when Hank came back. "Not much. Dad told me Hank was a hockey player, and he was sad because he hurt his knee and couldn't play anymore. Mom was mad that Dad was talking to me about Hank. I don't think she wanted Hank around me," I said.

Aunt Izzie raised an eyebrow. "You're misremembering something."

"I'm not."

"Then you didn't understand something you heard." She sighed. "Nikki, Hank isn't the villain you've cast him to be."

"Let's not ruin dinner by getting her going on Uncle Hank," Dana said to my aunt. "Instead, let's talk about my big day this weekend." She grinned. "Marie's dropping off my puppy on Friday."

"Are you sure you want a dog?" I asked.

"Lord help that poor animal," Aunt Izzie said.

"Why do you both think I can't take care of a dog?" Dana asked.

Aunt Izzie passed Dana the dish with the bread. "I give you one to two months before you're trying to hand him off to someone else."

Dana jabbed her food with her fork. "Thank you for the vote of confidence."

"Prove me wrong," Aunt Izzie chided.

There's a better chance of Dana keeping the dog than there is of Kyle coming home. The thought popped into my head with no warning. I feared it was the truth.

Chapter 18

Friday night, I passed row after row of empty cubes in the silent building on my way out. Before I boarded the elevator, I flipped the hall lights off. My SUV, parked in the far back corner, sat alone in the dark lot. I shivered as I made my way toward it, walking cautiously so I wouldn't slip on ice. Somehow I had made it through a week's worth of endless meetings with Elizabeth. They had helped keep my mind off Kyle during the workday, but now, a long, lonely weekend stretched in front of me.

Kyle and I still hadn't spoken. All week, I had come home from work, expecting to find him sitting in his recliner, waiting for me. I fantasized he'd stand when I came through the door and rush across the room to embrace me. *I'm sorry I left,* he would say. I'd hug him tightly and tell him I was sorry. Then we'd make love, and of course, I would get pregnant. After five nights without him, I missed him and wanted him to come home.

Last night, I'd texted him, asking if we could talk. As with all the other texts I'd sent, he'd ignored it. As I waited for my car to heat up, I took a deep breath and called him. After six or seven rings, his voice mail picked up. Even as tears stung my eyes at the sound of his voice, I smiled, remembering sitting across the table from him as he recorded his outgoing message. "It's Kyle Sebastian." He had started in a serious, businesslike tone, but I'd made faces at him while he spoke until he cracked up. In the message now, I heard him trying not to laugh. "Sorry

I missed your call." He hadn't been able to stifle his laughter, though, so at that moment in the dark, cold parking lot, he laughed in my ear. He rushed through the end of the message without taking a breath. "Leave your number. I'll call you back." When he'd disconnected, he'd lost it, giggling so hard that he'd had to bend over until he composed himself. I had expected him to rerecord, but he said he liked how I always made him sound happy.

I pressed disconnect without leaving a message and drove out of the parking lot.

Traffic snarled through town, as cars with skis loaded on their roof racks clogged the roads. During weekends and school vacations, the population in Stapleton doubled from less than two thousand to almost four. I hated dealing with the crowds, even if the tourists kept our economy running. At the light in the center of town, I turned right to break free of the gridlock. This route brought me by Luke's street. I turned onto it.

The lamppost at the end of his driveway emitted a welcoming glow, Kyle's Jeep was parked by the garage, and a table lamp lit up the living room. I imagined Kyle inside, watching a home-improvement show. I sat in the driveway for a long time, thinking about what I would say. I'd tell him I was sorry, because I was, and I'd ask him to come home. We could figure out the rest together.

Someone had sprinkled sand over the ice on Luke's walkway, but it was still slippery. I trod carefully across it. At the front landing, I squared my shoulders and rang the doorbell. No one answered, so I pressed the button again. Still, no one came to the door. I looked up at the windows, wondering if Kyle was hiding behind a curtain, watching me shiver on the front landing.

"You just missed them," a high, shrill voice hollered: the neighbor across the street. She stood on her walkway in a long red bubble jacket, staring me down. Luke had a million and one stories about her, how she was in everyone's business. I'd met her once, a few summers ago, when Kyle helped Luke build a sunroom. She had stomped across the road to complain about the pounding of hammers and buzzing of saws, saying it was too early in the morning for all that commotion, even though it was after ten.

She must have been wondering why Kyle was staying with Luke. Was that why she'd come outside—to get the story? I put my head down, hoping she wouldn't recognize me, wouldn't realize my connection to Kyle. I didn't want him to know I had been here. "I can tell him you stopped by," she said, walking farther down her flagstone.

"I'll text him." I rushed back to my car, almost losing my balance on the slick walkway.

By the time I started the engine, she had made it to the end of her driveway. She watched me pull away, probably memorizing the make and model of my vehicle or license plate. Kyle would definitely know I'd been there.

I would have no trouble finding him if I wanted to. He and Luke were probably having a beer, and in this small community, there were only so many places they could be. I also knew if I showed up at a bar looking for my husband, we'd become the talk of the town. Heck, with Luke's busybody neighbor, we already might be.

A few miles down the road, I passed the ice rink. Kyle would be playing hockey there tomorrow night. No one would think twice if I showed up to watch his game.

~

Sharon and I hadn't spoken since Saturday at the restaurant, when she'd told me she was pregnant. Still, instead of driving home, I stopped at her house because I didn't want to be by myself. I knocked on her door. When after a minute, no one answered, I rang the bell. Inside, the pitter-patter of small feet sprinted toward the door. It flew open, and Cameron stood there, a milk mustache above his lip and a dark stain on his green sweatshirt. Without saying a word, he leaned to his left to see around me. "Where's Uncle Kyle?"

"It's just me, bud."

He frowned. "I wish it were Uncle Kyle instead."

I winced.

"Cameron," Sharon scolded. "That was mean and hurt Auntie Nikki's feelings." She stood in the living room just outside the kitchen door, watching us. Seeing her dressed in maternity clothes, a pink-and-black shirt and black yoga pants, hurt more than her son's honesty. "Tell her you're sorry, give her a hug, and go finish your dinner."

He reached up to hug me and ran off.

"You're just in time for dinner," Sharon said. She led me into the kitchen, where Rick and the boys were eating. She quickly made up another plate, steak tips, salad, mashed potatoes, and carrots.

"Where's Kyle tonight?" Rick asked.

My face flushed. Several seconds passed before I answered, and when I did, I stared down at the floor. "He's with Luke." I felt Sharon watching me and took another bite of my steak. The sweet taste of teriyaki filled my mouth.

"Probably watching the game," Rick said. "The Bruins are playing the Canadians."

After dinner, I helped Sharon clean while Rick bathed the boys. "So where's Kyle, really?" she asked. I hesitated, not wanting to tell her because I was afraid she'd take his side. "Is he still mad about the 401(k) withdrawal?"

"You could say that." I wiped crumbs off the counter as I answered. "He moved out."

She stopped drying the pan in her hand and turned toward me. "What?"

"He's staying with Luke."

"When did this happen? Why didn't you call me?"

With the dishes still needing to be loaded into the dishwasher, we sat down at the kitchen table. I told her what had happened the day Kyle left. "He won't take my calls or answer my texts. He told Aunt Izzie we're separated."

She scratched the back of her hand. It was the same thing she used to do when we were kids and her mother asked her if her homework was finished or her father wanted to know if she knew where the bottle of rum was. "He needs time to cool off."

"I'm going to his hockey game tomorrow night."

She shook her head. "Not a good idea. Give him space right now."

"I gave him a week. We need to talk about it to move on."

I expected her to argue with me more, but she stood without saying anything. As she loaded the remaining dishes into the dishwasher, I said good night to the boys.

She hugged me goodbye at the door and watched as I walked to my car. Just before I slid behind the steering wheel, she called down to me. "I'm coming with you tomorrow, with Cam and Noah. He won't ignore them."

Chapter 19

While Sharon unbuckled Noah from his seat, Cameron burst from the car and ran through the parking lot toward the entrance. Shouting his name, I chased after him. He ignored me as he pulled the door open and rushed inside. A group of teenagers crowded the concession stand, but the lobby was otherwise empty. I glimpsed a flash of Cameron's green coat heading for the rink. When I caught up with him, he was standing by Kyle's team's bench, calling my husband's name. Kyle took shots on the ice with several players, warming up. He didn't acknowledge Cameron, probably because he couldn't hear him over the sound of the music and sticks slapping pucks into the boards. For a few minutes, Cameron and I watched Kyle shoot. He bent his knees, shifted his weight to his back leg, and pushed off it, directing all his energy toward the net as he shot. The first three shots missed wide to the left. The next two banged off the right goal post. I'd never seen him miss an empty net so many times.

Luke sat on the bench, lacing up his skates. He looked up at me with such sympathy that I wondered if he knew Kyle was never coming home. "Nikki." The way he said it made my name sound sad. "Good to see you."

"Cameron wanted to watch Kyle play."

Luke's right cheek twitched as if he was trying to stop a laugh. He knew I was the one who wanted to see Kyle play and the kid was a cover.

"It's going to be okay," he said, standing and placing a hand on my shoulder. He turned his attention to Cameron. "Long time no see, little man. Did you come to see your Uncle Kyle play?"

Cameron nodded, edging closer to me. I reached for his hand.

Luke grabbed his stick and tousled Cameron's hair. "I'll tell Uncle Kyle to score a goal for you." Stepping onto the rink, he winked and sprinted toward his teammates. He skidded to a sudden stop in front of Kyle, spraying tiny particles of ice into the air.

Kyle paused his shooting as Luke leaned toward him, pointing in my direction. My husband turned toward the bench. The edges of his lips curled upward when he saw me, the way they did when we were arguing about something stupid and he was trying not to smile. Their curl boosted my confidence. Cameron waved wildly, and Kyle saluted him with his stick. He nodded at me before resuming his practice shots. The next three landed in the center of the net.

Cameron headed up the bleachers to a spot about four rows down from the top. I climbed the stairs behind him, happy about my decision to come here tonight. We had just settled in our seats when Sharon appeared, carrying a kicking and screaming Noah.

"I should have left him with Rick," she said. "He's overtired." With circles under her eyes as dark as the puck, she looked exhausted too. She should have been home cuddled under a blanket with her feet up on the ottoman, not traipsing through a cold, loud ice rink babysitting me. I was lucky to have her as a friend.

A family of four sat a few rows in front of us. The teenage boy carried a large tub of popcorn. Its scent floated back to our row, making my mouth water.

"I want some," Cameron whined. He grabbed Sharon's hand. "Let's get some."

"I'll take him," I said.

"I want Mommy to take me."

Noah's cries became louder. Sharon shifted him to her other shoulder. "Let's go, Mommy," Cameron said.

"Stop it," she snapped.

"Take Cameron to the concessions, and I'll stay with Noah."

Sharon handed the baby off to me like we were playing a game of hot potato. Pulling Cameron by his arm, she raced out of our row. Noah's cries became bloodcurdling screams. Sharon froze on the concrete steps next to our bench. "We'll be fine," I said, shooing her away.

Below us, all the players had cleared the ice. I searched the bench for Kyle. He sat at the end, taping the top of his stick.

I held Noah tighter and whispered to him. "It's okay, little guy." I bounced up and down on my tiptoes and made a song of it. "It's okay. We're gonna watch Uncle Kyle play." I repeated the words so many times that the girls next to us started to sing along and make faces at Noah. His crying wound down. With his head resting on my shoulder, I sank down to the bench and swayed back and forth. By the time Sharon and Cameron returned, Noah slept soundly in my arms, covered by his small blanket.

"You're a miracle worker," Sharon said. She bit into a hot dog loaded with mustard and relish. "I had a craving."

My chest tightened as I connected her words to her pregnancy. *Just be happy for her.*

The players skated onto the ice. As the national anthem played, Cameron extended a huge tub of popcorn toward me, and I took a handful. The salt stung my tongue. The game started with Kyle winning the face-off. Three minutes later, he scored on an assist from Luke. The crowd erupted. Noah stirred but didn't wake. Cameron poked me in the side. "Uncle Kyle scored that for me!"

In the row behind Kyle's team's bench, two women wearing cute hats with pom-poms screamed his name. I squinted down at them, trying to figure out who they were, but couldn't place them.

Three minutes before the first period ended, the other team scored a goal. A horn blasted, waking Noah, who started to cry. "I'll take him," Sharon said.

I shook my head and slid him down to my knees. Bouncing my legs up and down, I sang a song my dad used to sing to me: "Noah climbs up the mountain." I lifted my knees higher. "Noah gets to the top of the mountain. Noah slides down the mountain." I opened my legs and lowered him to the ground.

Noah giggled. "'Gain," he said.

We played the game until the period ended. All the players skated toward their benches. When Kyle and Luke stepped off the ice, the women with the hats approached them. The men laughed at something the woman in the red hat said. She placed her hand on Kyle's forearm, and he quickly moved it away, looking up into the stands in my direction. My stomach flipped. "Do you know who the woman in the red hat is?" I asked Sharon.

She peered down. The woman's head tilted toward Luke as she listened to something he said. "Probably Luke's latest fling."

I let out a deep breath.

When play resumed, I kept my eyes on the two women. They spent more time looking at their phones than watching what happened on the ice. At the end of the second period, with the game tied two to two, they got up to leave. Red Hat waved toward the ice. Luke pointed his stick at her in acknowledgment, and Kyle raised his hand as if he was about to wave but looked in my direction and lowered it. I reached for more popcorn. It was time for him to come home.

Kyle's team won four to two. At the end of the game, while they celebrated on the ice, Sharon, the boys, and I made our way down the concrete steps to the team's bench. By the time we descended to the ground floor, some of the players had left for the locker room, but Kyle waited by the bench, clutching his helmet. He had been overdue for a haircut when he left, and he still hadn't had one. Because his hair wasn't cropped close to his head, the gray strands that were just starting to mix with his dark hair were more pronounced than usual.

He kept his focus trained on Cameron, then glanced at Noah, who was in Sharon's arms. Kyle's eyes widened, and his head jerked backward. I knew exactly why. He had noticed the small bump in Sharon's stomach. It was hard to miss under her tight-fitting, zipped-up ski jacket.

By the time we reached him, he had a white-knuckle grip on the helmet and kept rolling his shoulder as if he were trying to work out a kink. Cameron flung himself at Kyle, who placed his helmet on the bench and scooped up the boy. "Your goal was nasty," Cameron said.

"That was for you, champ." Kyle had turned so that his back was to me, Sharon, and Noah.

"Ky, Ky," Noah babbled, extending his arms in Kyle's direction.

Kyle rotated back toward us and deposited Cameron back on the ground. His eyes met Sharon's as he took Noah from her. "So you're . . ." He glanced in my direction and stopped. His Adam's apple danced as he took a few hard swallows.

"She's having a girl." I hoped my voice was steadier than it sounded to me.

"Congratulations," Kyle said, his tone more appropriate for saying something like *sorry for your loss.*

"We're excited." Sharon folded her arms across her belly as if she were trying to conceal evidence.

"They're naming her Sharon." I knew this would get a reaction from him because he thought Sharon was vain.

"Seriously?"

"Yes," Sharon snapped. "What's the big deal."

Kyle raised one eyebrow. Nostalgia overpowered me as I remembered him trying to teach me how to do that when we were first dating. We'd been sitting on his black leather couch. The eye under the eyebrow I wasn't trying to raise kept closing. "You look like you're having a seizure," he'd said. I bet him dinner I could learn.

After a month of trying, I made him manicotti to pay off the bet. It was the first time I had used a recipe from my parents' diner to cook him something.

Most of the crowd had left, and the rink was quiet, except for a few bangs coming from the locker room.

"Cameron wanted to see you play," I said.

Kyle nodded. I felt like a teenage girl pretending not to have a crush on a boy instead of a wife talking to her husband of seven years.

A small popping sound came from Noah. Kyle's face contorted, and he extended the baby away from him. "Someone needs a diaper change."

Sharon reached for Noah. "I'll take him to the ladies' room. Cam, come with me."

We watched them walk away before facing each other. I had so much I wanted to say to Kyle but didn't know where to begin.

He glanced at the clock on the scoreboard.

"Please come home." I shouldn't have started with that, but I couldn't help it.

Kyle picked up his helmet from the bench. "I'm giving you time to figure out what you want."

"I figured it out." My voice cracked.

"This isn't the time or place to talk about this."

"When, then?"

He squeezed his eyes shut and brought a hand up to his temple.

"Why did you tell Aunt Izzie we're separated? That word makes it sound so official."

He tilted his head. "I told her we're taking a break. She put me on the spot about dinner."

Across the rink, a door banged. Luke's voice called out. "Hey, buddy, we're waiting on you. Put a move on it."

"I gotta run." He headed toward the locker room, his stride unsteady, as if he were adjusting to being off the ice.

A wave of exhaustion rolled over me. I could barely support my own weight and sank to the bench. The chill of the ice rink had settled into my bones. I shivered in the cold, watching Kyle disappear into the locker room.

Chapter 20

As I tried to fall asleep, I kept hearing those women in the hats at the hockey game calling out Kyle's name. The image of him raising his hand to wave goodbye to them and glancing at me replayed on an endless loop, and then I saw him walking away from me, without looking back, leaving my questions unanswered. Trying to sleep was useless. I popped out of bed hours before the sun came up and made my way downstairs.

The bright light glowing from the floor lamp hurt my eyes. When they adjusted, a trail of sand leading from the mat in the entryway to the living room caught my attention. Sweeping up sand and salt tracked in from the outside was a daily activity in the winter, but I had always accused Kyle of making the mess because he traipsed all over the house in his work boots.

As I swept up the mess now, I realized I was responsible for it. My sweeping became frantic. When I was done, the hardwood still didn't look clean, so I mopped. Then I cranked up a country station on the radio and washed down the walls. I pushed so hard against the sponge that I was afraid the paint would come off.

I attacked the kitchen next, scrubbing the counters and cleaning out the cabinets. Singing along with the radio to drown out my thoughts, I zipped right along until I pulled out a box of Cheerios. I couldn't stomach the little round oats, but Kyle loved them. They were his go-to meal when we didn't feel like cooking. Was he living on them at Luke's? The music changed from an upbeat Zac Brown melody with happy lyrics to a song by Cole Swindell about surviving a breakup. I reached into the box, grabbed a handful of cereal, and stuffed it into my mouth.

I snapped the radio off before starting on the downstairs bathroom, which we referred to as Kyle's. Because he got up for work earlier than I did, he showered down here during the week so he wouldn't wake me. The memory made my throat burn. He was such a considerate husband, and I had paid him back by lying. *I'm sorry. I'm sorry. I'm sorry.*

I reached toward the shower shelf for his bodywash. The bottle belched as I squeezed soap into my hand. The masculine cedar scent made me imagine Kyle, a towel wrapped around his waist, pulling me into his arms, planting little kisses on my neck and leading me back upstairs. The image seemed like a crazy fantasy, but there was a time it had been real. How had we let trying to have a baby cause this rift between us?

By the time I finished cleaning, it was almost four in the afternoon. I collapsed on the couch. My shoulders and back ached, but my house sparkled. If only it were that easy to clean up the mess I had made of my marriage.

~

Several hours later, I awoke to the sound of the doorknob jiggling. I jerked upright as the door slammed against the rubber stop. Dana burst into the house, cradling a small four-legged bundle that yelped in her arms. She really had a puppy. She lowered him to the floor, and he scampered across the room, leaving tiny grimy paw prints on the just-cleaned hardwood. I balled my hands into tight fists, but when the dog trotted over to the couch and looked up at me with his adoring dark-brown eyes, I released them. With fuzzy golden fur, he made it hard not to immediately fall in love with him. I scooped him up, and he licked my cheek as I patted his silky-soft hair. His kiss made my face wet and sticky, but I laughed and hugged him tighter, thinking of my and Kyle's old black Lab, Cole. We were so happy when he was alive.

"Meet Deeogee," Dana said. "I think he likes you."

"She really gave you a dog."

"Told you she was going to."

Deeogee leaped off the sofa and wandered toward Dana, who had just sat in Kyle's recliner.

"How's it going? Training the puppy and working. Are your roommates helping?"

Dana picked at her thumbnail. "What do you have to eat?"

She left for the kitchen and returned with Oreos. She extended the package toward me, and I pulled out two. The only thing I had eaten all day was a handful of cereal.

Deeogee looked longingly at the cookies. Dana pulled a stuffed penguin from her bag and tossed it to him. He settled in front of the recliner, chewing on it, sending a chorus of squeaks through the room.

"Kyle's still not back?" She twisted an Oreo open and scraped the white crème filling off with her bottom teeth.

"I'm not sure he's coming back."

"Give him time," Dana said.

The squeaking was incessant. I glared at the noisy penguin. "It's been a week."

Dana cracked open another cookie. "That's nothing."

It was something. Seven days, a quarter of a month, 168 hours. I strode to the recliner and ripped the penguin out of the dog's mouth. Deeogee whimpered.

"Nikki," Dana scolded. "Give that back to him."

I stomped back to the couch and hid the stuffed animal behind my back. The puppy followed and stared up at me, still whimpering. For such a small animal, he made a lot of noise. I imagined him whining in the middle of the night when he had to go to the bathroom and Dana sleeping right through it, one of her roommates stumbling out of bed to take him outside, or worse, the dog leaving puddles of pee all around the town house that Dana didn't bother to clean up. "Are your roommates okay with you having a dog?"

"Come here, Deeogee," Dana called, clucking at the puppy. He didn't budge.

His name grated on my nerves almost as much as the squeaking. "You have to call him something better than Deeogee."

I picked him up and placed him in my lap. His wagging tail brushed against my arm, tickling it. "You need a new name." I spoke with the same type of voice people often used with babies. The puppy stared at me with his big chocolate-drop eyes. My heart melted. I pulled the penguin out from behind me. The puppy's head bobbed up and down as he took it with his mouth, almost as if he were nodding. "Oliver. You look like an Oliver." The penguin squeaked. "See, he agrees," I said, patting the puppy's head. "What do you think?" I asked Dana.

She shrugged. "You can call him that if you want." She was back to picking her thumbnail. "At least for the next few months."

"Why for the next few months?"

She reclined in Kyle's chair with her hands laced behind her head and grinned at me.

"You want me to take him."

"He'll be a good distraction for you and Kyle."

I thought about when we were kids, how one spring Dana had badgered our parents to let her sign up for softball. It wasn't easy for them to take time away from the restaurant to drive her to practice and games, but they relented and let her join the team. She lost interest and quit before the season ended. Same with guitar lessons. She took two before declaring instruments were not for her. Working at Mount Stapleton and lifeguarding on the Cape were the only things she had ever committed to.

"You're sick of him already?" I asked.

She flinched. "Don't say that."

"I'm not taking your dog." I looked down at the adorable puppy cuddling in my lap. "No offense, buddy."

Dana sighed. "The landlord was in town and stopped by. No pets allowed."

"Dana, how could you not know that?"

"I did know, but he lives on the other side of the country. I didn't think he'd find out."

"What are you going to do?"

"He's going to stay with you until I leave for the summer."

"Until June?" I set the dog on the floor and stood. "I'm not taking your dog."

"It's three months away. In the grand scheme of life, that's nothing."

"I have too much going on."

Dana looked pointedly at the pillow and blanket I'd been using while napping on the couch. "What exactly do you have going on?"

"I can't take care of a puppy right now. I can barely take care of myself."

"You're wallowing in self-pity because Kyle left. A puppy will cheer you up. Studies prove that people with dogs are hap—"

"No." Even as I said it, I pictured Cole, his shiny black hair, wagging tail, and unconditional love. I saw him waiting by the window for me to get home from work and racing to the door as I made my way up the walkway. I could hear his excited bark and feel his paws on my thighs as he jumped up to greet me.

"Just for a few days? Until I figure out something else," Dana pleaded.

I was so lonely here without Kyle. The dog would be company.

"Kyle loves dogs," Dana said. "If you tell him Deeogee's staying with you, he'll come over to meet him."

My lip curled, and I stopped petting the puppy. "Really. You're suggesting I use your dog to trick Kyle into coming home."

"No worse than lying about getting a bonus."

I flinched, regretting that I had confided in her. She had a point, though. Kyle loved dogs, and dogs loved him. When possible, he used to take Cole on jobs with him. Throughout the day, he'd send funny texts with pictures of the two of them. Dana's dog nudged my arm with his nose, almost as if he were telling me that he could help me turn things around with Kyle. I studied the puppy's face, noticing patches of fur on each side of his mouth were lighter than the rest of his face. The lighter fur made him look like an older dog, and I wondered if he was wise beyond his years.

"He can stay, but there's no way I'm calling him Deeogee." I studied the little guy. "You like Oliver better, don't ya?"

Apparently Dana had come over knowing the puppy could stay, because her car was packed with all his belongings. She dumped it all in a pile in my living room: dog bowls, puppy chow, squeaky toys, biscuits, two leashes, a crate, a dog bed, and a blanket. Oliver came with more stuff than Kyle had left with.

∼

After my sister drove away, I took Oliver outside. My heavy winter coat and hat didn't protect me from the early-March frigid air. I shivered as we walked, but Oliver seemed unbothered by the cold. He chased after the beam of light coming from my flashlight, yapping and pulling on the leash with a strength I didn't expect. A few yards down the road, he paused, sniffing at something in the enormous snowbank. The snow had been piled there since late November. Anything could be buried under it.

The wind howled, blowing icy air through me. I pulled my hood over my head and tugged lightly on the leash to get Oliver moving again. Behind us, tires crunched over snow, and seconds later the Abramses drove past us. When Oliver and I neared their house, Mr. and Mrs. Abrams were climbing out of their car. Mrs. Abrams called out to me, so Oliver and I turned in to her driveway.

"Who is this little guy?" Mrs. Abrams asked, bending to pick up Oliver.

"My sister's dog. He's staying with me for a few days."

"Oh, you're not going to want to give him back." Mrs. Abrams snuggled with the puppy. Oliver bathed the old woman's cheek with his tongue. Mrs. Abrams's hearty laugh echoed through the quiet neighborhood.

"Oh, Miriam, don't let him lick you like that," Mr. Abrams said, his face flushed from the cold, his teeth chattering.

Mrs. Abrams extended the puppy toward her husband, but he took a step backward. She laughed and pulled Oliver back to her chest.

"Where's Kyle been?" Mr. Abrams asked. "I haven't seen him lately."

I started to sweat under my heavy coat. "Oh, you know," I said. "It's hockey season."

The way he looked at me made me think he suspected my husband was buried under the enormous pile of snow at the end of the road.

I snatched Oliver back from Mrs. Abrams and turned to leave before he could ask any more questions. "Good night," I yelled with my back to them both as I crossed the street.

Chapter 21

Sunday night, I set up Oliver's crate on the floor next to my bed. That sweet puppy didn't even whine when I placed him in it. For a few moments, he stood on his hind legs with his front paws resting on the crate's wall. Exhaustion overtook him, and he collapsed on his blanket and fell into a deep sleep. He woke up whimpering just after midnight. I took him outside and led him down the path I had shoveled earlier in the day from the back door to the side of the house. The frigid air hurt my lungs every time I took a breath. When we reached the bush at the end of the cleared snow, Oliver sniffed around before crouching to do his business. I jumped up and down on the balls of my feet, trying to keep warm. It didn't work. My face stung every time the icy wind hit it. After Oliver finished, he gnawed on a branch sticking up through the snow. I pulled on his leash to bring him back inside, but he resisted, so I picked him up and carried him like a baby back to his crate. Behind the metal bars, he stood on his back two legs, watching me as I tried to fall asleep. Every now and then, the crate rattled as he shifted positions, but again he didn't cry.

I took him out two other times during the night, each time cursing my sister. In the morning, my mind felt foggy from being sleep deprived. I tried to figure out something I could do with Oliver for the eight hours I was at the magazine. I definitely didn't want to leave him locked up in his crate all day as if he were in prison. In the end, I couldn't think of anything, so I called in sick and stayed home with him.

Oliver was a good companion. He helped me keep my mind off Kyle. We played tug-of-war and fetch. Every few hours, we braved the cold so he could relieve himself. He made a few messes in the house, but they were confined to the mat by the back door. Clearly Marie had spent time training him before handing him over to Dana.

While Oliver napped at my feet, I called doggy day care places, but no one was willing to take on a puppy who hadn't been potty trained. Late in the day as I walked Oliver down the street, Mrs. Abrams joined us. When she found out that I had skipped work to take care of him, she volunteered to watch him during the day. "That's too much to ask of you," I said.

"You didn't ask. I offered. He'll be better company than Cranky Pants." I stared at her blankly, and she clarified, "Joel."

~

Tuesday morning, I walked Oliver across the street with his squeaky toys, puppy chow, and dog bowls. It had snowed overnight, just an inch or so, but it was enough to make the walkways and roads slippery. Mr. Abrams was outside, hunched over as he spread ice melt on the driveway, which was something Kyle would have done for him if he had been home. The old man straightened and watched me approach. I braced myself for a question about my husband's whereabouts. He pointed to Oliver. "This isn't a good idea."

"You want me to take him home?" As I waited for him to answer, I tried to think of something else I could do with Oliver. I knew Dana was working all day, and Aunt Izzie had made it clear she wanted no part of the dog. My only option was to leave him in a crate, and I really didn't want to do that.

"We're too old to chase a puppy around all day," Mr. Abrams said.

"Speak for yourself, Joel," Mrs. Abrams shouted down from the front door. "Bring him up here, Nikki."

Mr. Abrams muttered under his breath as I led Oliver past him to the landing, where Mrs. Abrams scooped him up. "He's precious," she said.

"Are you sure this is okay?"

"Ignore Cranky Pants." She jutted her chin toward her husband. "Go on, now." Still, I hesitated, not sure I should leave Oliver with them. "Don't worry. I'll take good care of him," Mrs. Abrams promised.

~

An email from Elizabeth marked urgent sat at the top of my inbox. Pressure built behind my eyes as I read it. I've scheduled an interview with Hank at one thirty on Wednesday afternoon at Pendleton 88. The pressure intensified. He said to come with an appetite.

I hadn't seen Hank or stepped inside the restaurant since it reopened with its new name four and a half years ago, and now Elizabeth had arranged for me to see him tomorrow with no time to prepare for the meeting. I couldn't imagine how I would sit at a table across from him and eat a meal. No matter how much I dreaded it, though, I knew I didn't have a choice. I would have to suck it up. Ringing from the other side of my office pulled me from my thoughts. I scrambled around my desk to the back of my door, where my coat hung on a hook, and reached into a pocket for my cell phone.

"How's Deeogee? Why haven't you sent any pictures?" My sister's jovial tone grated on my nerves. No doubt she'd slept like a rock last night while I stood outside, freezing my butt off and waiting for her puppy to do his business.

"Oliver is fine. If you want to see him, stop by. Take him for a walk."

"Someone got up on the wrong side of the bed."

"Three different times when I took your puppy outside to pee."

"Three times? You only have to take him out every five or six hours."

"You're an expert on training dogs now?" Back in my chair, I scrolled through my email as she spoke.

"Obviously I did research before I got him."

"Maybe you should have researched if you could have a dog in your town house."

"Still no word from Kyle?" Dana asked.

I sighed. She was right. I wasn't mad at her. Oliver was a godsend. I stopped scrolling and turned toward the window. In the parking lot below me, Elizabeth maneuvered her SUV into the space next to my Acura. "I have to interview Hank this week. At the restaurant."

"You're talking to Hank? In person?"

"Yes."

"Ugh. Listen to me. Hank . . . he isn't . . . he's not a bad guy. Give him a chance."

"I'm afraid I'll have a meltdown when I walk in and see all the changes he made."

"Want me to come with you?"

A warmth spread across my chest. As much of a pain in the butt as Dana could be, she was always there for me. Once again, I regretted not having confided in her when Kyle and I were trying to have a baby. She might have been able to help me through the darkest days.

"Thank you, but my new boss is coming." I watched Elizabeth step out of her ridiculous status symbol of a car, shaking my head as she wobbled across the icy parking lot on three-inch heels. Did she have any sense at all? No one wore shoes like that this time of year here. Just before she made it to the clear sidewalk, she slipped and fell to the ground. I jumped to my feet, but before I could move, Jerry from IT was by her side, helping her up. Elizabeth appeared to laugh as she brushed herself off, and in that brief moment, I liked her more than I had at any other time since I'd met her.

"It will be fine," Dana said. "Just fake smile your way through it."

"I'm not sure I can."

Dana sighed. "You have to get over your anger, Nikki. Hank didn't do anything wrong."

"He lied."

"Well, let's hope Kyle's more forgiving of your lie than you are of Hank's."

Chapter 22

On the day of my interview with Hank, I woke up groggy from lack of sleep. I'd only been taking care of Oliver for a few days, but waking up to take him outside in the middle of the night was taking its toll on me. I briefly wondered if this meant I wasn't cut out to be a mother, but I realized the issue wasn't getting up; it was going outside in the freezing-cold, pitch-black night. With Cole, Kyle and I had taken turns. Sometimes, we even got out of bed and went outside together. If the stars shone brightly, we'd spend time staring at the sky until Cole barked, reminding us we should be sleeping. Remembering it now, I felt the tug of the leash in my hand and the weight of Kyle's arm around my shoulders and smiled. I should have listened to him. We were happy without a baby. We could be happy again. I had to find a way to convince him that being with him meant more to me than having children.

Before I got ready for work, I plucked Oliver from his crate, snapped his leash on, and carried him outside. Even this early in the morning, the March sun shone brightly in a brilliant blue sky, reminding us better things were on their way. We'd almost made it through winter. I lowered the puppy to the ground and hoped he would be quick. Instead of crouching, though, he walked in circles, sniffing the snow. "Come on, buddy. Go to the bathroom," I pleaded.

He tugged on the leash, leading me to the bush.

"Good boy."

He dipped his head, picking up a stick with his mouth. I sighed in frustration and checked the time. It was already after seven. I had to be at work by eight thirty because Elizabeth had scheduled a morning meeting to discuss redesigning the magazine's website.

"Oliver, if you have to pee, now is the time," I said. It occurred to me then that training this puppy would be the closest I ever came to potty training a baby, and I felt a hollowness in my chest.

After a few minutes of standing in the cold and watching Oliver play, my fingers and toes tingled. "It's now or never," I threatened. The dog ignored me and continued chewing on his stick, so I scooped him up and brought him back inside. Upstairs, he struggled in my arms, kicking his back legs as I returned him to his crate. Even in the bathroom over the sound of the running water, I could hear his heartbreaking whimpering. I couldn't bear to listen to him crying, so before I climbed into the shower, I opened his crate and shut my bedroom door, giving him the freedom to wander around.

When I returned to my room, Oliver was asleep in his crate, but the room stank like a dirty diaper. A heap of dog poop soiled the rug on Kyle's side of the bed. I cursed under my breath as I cleaned the mess, but I knew it was my fault. I shouldn't have been so impatient. I should have considered what the puppy wanted and spent more time with him outside.

∼

On the way to work, I realized I didn't have my phone. The realization made me as uncomfortable as if I had forgotten to put on pants. Still, I couldn't turn around to get it. Between cleaning up the mess in my bedroom and talking to Mrs. Abrams when I dropped off Oliver, I was already running late.

As I entered Elizabeth's office for our meeting, she looked pointedly at her watch. "Sorry, I was dealing with puppy chaos this morning," I said.

"I had to deal with a fussy infant and a misbehaving toddler, and I still managed to be on time. Early even."

I swallowed hard, forcing down the nasty words I wanted to say. "Well, let's get started, then."

For the next forty-five minutes we brainstormed ideas for driving traffic to the magazine's website. We came up with more than twenty ideas and then narrowed the list down to ten that she would present to Andrew.

"Good work," she said as I got up to leave. Just before I stepped through her doorframe back into the hallway, she called my name. I looked at her over my shoulder. "I want to remind you that Hank's business is extremely important to this magazine."

I nodded.

"I trust you'll be professional enough to put your personal differences aside."

I glanced at one of the posters on the wall before answering. IT'S ALWAYS IMPOSSIBLE UNTIL IT'S DONE. "Of course," I said.

～

Elizabeth and I stood in front of my parents' old restaurant, ready to interview Hank. She pulled the door open and motioned for me to step inside, but I couldn't move. The good memories I'd made in this building all came rushing back: watching my father pound and fry chicken while he sang "Piano Man" or another Billy Joel song; standing at the stove next to my mother, learning how to make Sunday gravy; sitting in a booth in the back corner, eating tiramisu and playing Connect Four with my sister while we waited for my parents to close.

"Go on," Elizabeth said.

I lifted my foot to step inside, but it was as if the slushy sidewalks had turned to ice and encased my feet. Almost five years had passed since I had last been here. "I'm going to do some renovations," Hank had said. "Make the place more modern." He'd stopped to take a swig of his scotch and soda. "I'd also like to change the name. To Pendleton 88, my old hockey number. Fans will eat that up."

"No." Dana and I both said it together. She laughed and slugged my shoulder. "Jinx. You owe me a Coke." We thought Hank was asking for permission.

"It's my restaurant now, girls. I don't need your blessing. I was just letting you know so you're not surprised when the new sign goes up."

I'd been eating Italian wedding soup. That day was the last day I ever had that kind of soup. Ever since, the smell of it has caused me to gag.

Now Elizabeth took my arm and guided me past the threshold. Nothing looked familiar. When my parents owned the restaurant, it had been decorated like an old-fashioned diner with a black-and-white checkered floor, red vinyl booths, and a counter with swiveling stools. Hank remodeled to give the place an urban-chic look because he wanted to attract the wealthy tourists instead of the hardworking locals. Dark hardwood replaced the tiled floor. White linen covered tables set with bone china, and the mahogany-colored leather chairs appeared as if they were standing at attention with their high backs. The portrait of Hank in his hockey uniform hung behind the hostess stand. There was another picture of him dressed in a tux and standing on a red carpet with his arm wrapped around the waist of his gorgeous model wife, Arianna. Nothing in the place reminded me of my parents.

The hostess, an older woman who resembled a plumper version of Dr. Evans with her long silver hair, greeted us. Elizabeth told her we were there to see Hank, and the woman strode across the empty dining room to the back office to fetch him. My stomach fluttered, and my body felt like it was on fire. I slipped off my long wool coat and backtracked toward the stand by the entrance to hang it. Outside the sky was a calming shade of blue. I thought about bolting through the door so I didn't have to face Hank. I forced myself to turn back toward the hostess stand, and that was when I noticed the framed menu from DeMarco's Diner hanging on the wall. It looked so out of place among the watercolor paintings on the other walls that the old Sesame Street song "One of These Things (Is Not like the Others)" popped into my head. I would have bet anything that Hank had placed the menu there today because he knew I was coming.

On the other side of the restaurant, the hostess emerged from the office followed by a clean-shaven Hank. I couldn't remember ever seeing him without a beard. He wore a walking boot on his right foot and grimaced with each step he took. As he came closer, I could see the crow's-feet etched around his dark-brown eyes, and my heart cracked. After all these years, he was still so familiar, even without his trademark thick black beard. I stared over his shoulder, hoping to see my mother and father trailing behind, because those last years of my parents' lives, they had always been together here, the three of them.

He smiled, and I could feel something in my chest start to soften. "Nikki."

"Uncle Hank." My voice cracked as I said his name. He pulled me into an embrace. I rested my head on his shoulder, dampening his crisp blue shirt with my tears. For a brief few seconds, he was the fun uncle who took Dana and me tubing and taught us how to ski. He was the confidant I called who got me out of trouble when I was seventeen and got caught with a bottle of Captain Morgan in the high school parking lot. He smelled like smoked hickory, and that scent, so different from the fried foods and marinara sauce he used to smell like, pulled me out of my trancelike state. Similar to Cinderella's midnight transformation, he changed from the adored, fun-loving uncle back to the coldhearted family friend who had betrayed us. I stumbled backward to get away from him.

"What happened to your foot?" I asked.

"I gave snowboarding a go. Didn't turn out so well." He extended his hand toward Elizabeth. "Hank Pendleton."

"I grew up in New York. My brothers were such fans. They had your poster hanging on the wall of their bedroom."

Hank grinned, and two dimples appeared, one on each cheek. I had never seen them before because his heavy beard had covered them. Seeing them now unsettled me in a way I couldn't make sense of.

"How are you two related?" Elizabeth asked.

Hank's face blanched. "Friend of the family."

Elizabeth turned her attention to me. "Oh, you called him Uncle. I just assumed."

Hank tugged at the collar of his shirt. "You know what they say about assuming. It makes an ass out of you . . ." He pointed to a four-top by the window facing the street. "Let's sit."

Once we were seated, he wasted no time with small talk, launching into his story of the restaurant's origins. I shifted uncomfortably in my seat. I didn't need him to tell me how it had started. It was my family's folklore. I tuned out and stared out the window.

"I signed with the Rangers, a lucrative contract. I used some of the money to fund the opening of the restaurant."

My attention snapped back to the table. "I never knew that."

Hank cleared his throat. "Well, there were some things your parents didn't think you needed to know."

A waitress appeared at our table with a platter of sliced oven-roasted tomatoes sprinkled with cheese. "A new appetizer I want you to write about," Hank said. "You'll love them."

Elizabeth plated one and handed me the dish. She and Hank both watched me eat. The sweet flavor of the tomato filled my mouth, offset by parmesan and mozzarella cheese. There were also hints of garlic, onion, and basil. Damn, I didn't want to admit it, but it was delicious.

"You like it," Hank said, grinning.

"It reminds me of pizza."

"Without the calories!" His dimples seemed to get deeper as his smile grew bigger. I couldn't take my eyes off them. The tomato left an acidic aftertaste in my mouth. I gulped down my water, staring out the window with a hollow feeling in my chest.

"A knee injury ended my hockey career. I came back to the area for a visit and decided to buy a vacation home here. Gianna and Dom were having trouble with the diner, and they agreed my being here would be good for their business, attract some of the tourists from out of state, so I picked up a few shifts at the restaurant. I ended up spending more time here than in New York."

His words triggered a partial memory, my father and mother arguing about him working at the restaurant.

"My mother didn't want you anywhere near the restaurant," I said.

"You were ten, Nikki," Hank said. "Too young to understand what your mother wanted."

I wanted to argue with him. Tell him I knew my mother better than he ever had, but the warning look Elizabeth shot me kept me silent.

The waitress returned with another appetizer, grilled eggplant slices topped with tomato, a creamy sauce, and a fresh basil garnish. I bit into one. Damn, when it came to appetizers, the man knew what he was doing. The sauce tasted like a combination of garlic, parmesan, and mayonnaise. It offered a spicy contrast to the eggplant and tomato.

"Don't pretend you don't like it." Hank's dimples appeared again. They softened his appearance, made him look like a nice man, a trustworthy man, a man who would have kept his promise to preserve my parents' legacy.

Chapter 23

As soon as I pulled into the Abramses' driveway, their front door flew open. Mrs. Abrams rushed onto the landing in her slippers. The spotlight on the front of the house struck her face, making it appear ghostly white. "I've been trying to call you all afternoon." The emotion filling her voice conveyed that something awful had happened.

With one leg still in my car, I froze, not wanting to hear whatever bad news she was about to break but knowing I had to. "Is Mr. Abrams okay?"

Her body went rigid. "The dog is quite ill," she sputtered.

"Oliver?" I raced across the pavement, not bothering to close my car door. At the bottom of the walkway, I jerked to a stop. A trail of watery dog feces and vomit led from the front stairs to the snow-covered lawn. "What did he eat?"

She folded her arms across her chest. "The food you left for him."

Zigzagging across the flagstone to avoid the foul mess, I hurried toward the house. "Where is he?"

"Kyle took him to the vet."

"Kyle?"

"You didn't answer your phone, so I called him." The defensive way Mrs. Abrams spoke left no doubt that she knew Kyle and I were going through a rough patch.

"I forgot it at home," I mumbled. "How long ago?"

"Just after two." Her tone softened. "I took him for a walk. He was fine. Panting a little more than usual, but fine. I was standing in the driveway, talking to the mailman, and he threw up. He's so small." She shook her head as if trying to vanquish the memory. "I didn't know what to do."

I placed my hand on her shoulder. "You did the right thing calling Kyle."

Mr. Abrams stepped outside. Patches of Oliver's red hair clung to his black track pants. "I warned you leaving that dog here wasn't a good idea," he said.

"Joel," Mrs. Abrams said, the one word a warning.

"I would have never thought a little dog like that could make such a big mess," he continued.

"Have some compassion, Joel." Mrs. Abrams's eyes clouded with tears. "Such a sweet thing. I hope he's all right."

"I need to get my phone. See if Kyle left any messages." I took off down the stairs.

"Let me know as soon as you hear anything," Mrs. Abrams called out after me.

Please, let him be okay. I chanted it to myself as I moved my car across the street and ran into my house. In my bedroom, my phone sat on the charger on the nightstand, where I had placed it last night. The indication light blinked green, signaling I had missed calls, seven of them—five from Mrs. Abrams, starting at a few minutes past one, and two from Kyle, the last one fifteen minutes ago. There were no voice mails.

I scrolled to Kyle's name and hit the call button. He answered with a gruff hello. "Is Oliver okay?"

He didn't speak for several seconds. "I'm around the corner. I'll be right there." A feeling of foreboding seized me. Why couldn't he tell me what happened over the phone? Why did he say *I'm around the corner,* not *we're around the corner*? The sound of his truck crunching over snow in the driveway pulled me from my thoughts. I sprinted through the hallway and down the staircase toward the front door but slipped on the last step and fell on my butt.

Kyle found me in a heap at the bottom of the stairs and rushed to my side. My heart pounded. Oliver wasn't with him.

"Are you okay?" He reached for my hand to help me to my feet.

"Where's Oliver?"

"He's at the vet. Hooked up to an IV. He's in rough shape, dehydrated."

"Dehydrated?" I glanced toward the kitchen, where Oliver's silver water bowl, half-full, rested on a black mat. "I don't understand. I always make sure he has water."

"Dr. Drago thinks he ingested ice melt or something like it."

An image of Mr. Abrams dumping shovelfuls of the small blue pellets on his walkway popped into my head. Tears spilled from my eyes. When I went to wipe them away, I realized I was still holding Kyle's hand. I let go, and Kyle took a small step backward.

"He needs to get fluids in him. He'll be fine."

"I won't forgive myself if something happens to him. I should have taken him to the office with me."

"You can't think that way, Nikki. Some things are out of our control."

He had said similar things after the first two rounds of in vitro had failed. Like then, his words didn't make me feel better. If anything, they made me feel worse because they highlighted the fact that we had so little control over our lives and there was nothing we could do to prevent bad things from happening. We were all doomed.

Kyle walked to his recliner and picked at the dog hair stuck to it. "How long have you had him?"

"Since a little after you left."

"Where did you get him? You told me you didn't want another dog." It might have been my imagination, but he sounded hurt that I had made this decision and picked out a puppy without him.

"He's Dana's dog. Only she can't have pets in her condo, so she asked me to take care of him."

"Typical Dana."

"Yeah, well, at least this screwup benefits us. We get a dog." I used *us* and *we* without thinking, but once the words were out, they hung in the air like a storm cloud about to burst.

Kyle brushed more dog hair off the chair and sat. "I told you months ago we should get another dog."

I remembered how I had dismissed his suggestion out of hand, thinking a puppy was no substitute for a baby. While that might be true, having Oliver these past days was having someone else to love and be loved by. He taught me that life went on.

"I should have listened. We were happy when we had Cole."

Kyle closed his eyes and nodded. I imagined scenes from the earlier years of our marriage, before we'd started trying to have a baby, played through his mind.

"I'm sorry I lied about the money."

Kyle's eyes opened and met mine.

"I wanted a baby so bad that I wasn't thinking clearly. I mean, with all those hormones getting pumped into me, it's no wonder." I smiled, trying to lighten the mood.

He remained stone faced.

I inhaled deeply and blew out my breath. "You were right. We can be happy without kids." I couldn't even take care of a dog. Why had I thought I could handle the responsibility of being a parent?

"This change of heart seems sudden."

"More like long overdue. These past weeks without you." I shook my head. "I miss you. Being with you is more important than being a mother."

"Even if I believe you've changed your mind, I'm afraid that down the road you'll resent me."

"No. Having a baby isn't as important to me anymore." I swallowed hard, trying to convince myself of that. "All I want is for Oliver to be okay and for you to come home."

Kyle stood. I was afraid I had pushed him too far, that he was leaving. Instead, he slipped out of his jacket and hung it over the railing. He sat down next to me on the couch. "I miss you too," he said. "Who you used to be. Before all the . . ." He stopped and looked at the ground.

I finished his sentence in my head. *Before all the craziness.* I couldn't defend my past actions, so we sat in a heavy silence until his phone rang.

"Dr. Drago." Kyle jumped to his feet and paced as he spoke to the vet.

I stood too. After a few minutes, he smiled and gave me a thumbs-up. "The IV worked wonders. Oliver is fine. They want to keep him overnight to be sure, but we can pick him up in the morning."

I threw my arms around him, not sure which made me happier: that Oliver was going to be okay or that Kyle planned to go to Dr. Drago's with me to bring the little red fur ball home.

Chapter 24

The next morning, Kyle picked me up, and we drove to the vet together. Oliver was as happy to see me as I was to see him. He ran across the room with his tail slashing back and forth like a windshield wiper on the highest speed. I scooped him up, and he drenched my cheeks with doggy kisses. On the drive home, he curled up in my lap and fell asleep as I petted him. Every now and then, Kyle glanced over at us and smiled.

"What will you do with him today?" he asked.

"I can work from home, but I need to figure something out for the rest of the week. I don't want to ask Mrs. Abrams again. Maybe Aunt Izzie will help out."

Kyle reached over and petted Oliver's head. "I'm doing a kitchen remodel at the Gunthers'. They won't mind if I bring him. I can pick him up on my way."

The next morning, Kyle stopped by at seven thirty. I had homemade cranberry-and-orange muffins and a thermos of coffee ready to go for him. Over the next week, we slipped into a pattern. Kyle would stop by in the morning to pick up Oliver. I always packed a lunch for Kyle. Throughout the day, he'd send pictures of the puppy. My favorites of the week included Oliver curled up in a ball and sleeping on top of Kyle's toolbox with the caption, Someone's sleeping on the job. In another picture, Oliver held one end of a tape measure in his mouth while Kyle held the other end across the room. The caption read, Oliver's reminding me to measure twice and cut once.

In the evenings, when Kyle dropped Oliver off, he'd linger, telling me how the project was going and asking about my day. Each night, he stayed longer. When I got home from work on Friday, I made chicken parm. By the time Kyle arrived with Oliver, the entire house smelled like tomato and basil, and I easily convinced Kyle to stay for dinner. Unlike the last few weeks that he'd been living in the house, we sat at the table with no television on and talked to each other, even making each other laugh.

That night when Kyle left, I walked him to the door. We stood there awkwardly for a moment, and I felt as if I were on a first date, waiting for him to kiss me good night. He didn't, though. He thanked me for a delicious meal and pushed the door open. I stood on the landing, watching him back out of the driveway. He honked and waved before he drove off.

The next week, Kyle stayed for dinner most nights. On Monday when he left, he hugged me quickly. On Tuesday, he pulled me into a tight embrace. On Wednesday, he kissed me goodbye, and on Friday he paused by the door. "If this is going to work . . ." He pointed to himself, me, and then Oliver, who was curled into a ball at my feet. "If we're going to work, we have to be on the same page about having a baby."

I closed my eyes and pictured myself saying the words I knew Kyle needed to hear, the words I needed to be true. *I can be happy without a baby.* All I had to do was make myself say them out loud, and he'd move back home. I thought about a time, years ago, when Sharon, Rick, Kyle, and I had been vacationing on the Cape. Sharon and I went for a walk on the beach while the guys grilled dinner back at the cottage. Sharon looped her arm through mine. "We're so lucky we married men who love us more than we love them," she said.

Her words brought me to a dead stop. "That's not true."

"Of course it is."

I freed my arm from hers. "That's a horrible thing to say."

We walked in silence for a few moments, listening to the waves break on the shore.

"In every relationship, there's one partner who loves more and one who is loved more. It's just a fact," she said.

Above us, a seagull cawed.

"Why do you think Kyle loves me more than I love him?"

We'd reached the part of the beach that was roped off to protect the nesting piping plover and reversed direction. In the distance, a group of surfers carrying their boards over their heads descended the stairs to the beach.

"The man dotes on you," she said. "He moved to Stapleton to be with you because you didn't want to live in the city."

"I've made sacrifices for him too."

"Name one," Sharon said.

As hard as I tried, I couldn't think of anything. A rogue wave crashed ashore, drenching my shorts with salt water.

Sharon laughed and wrapped her arm around me. "Consider yourself lucky that you're the one who's loved more. I sure do."

I didn't feel lucky. I was embarrassed and ashamed and promised to do better by Kyle. I hadn't, though. Throughout our entire marriage, he was the one who sacrificed. It was my turn, and I was making the ultimate sacrifice. I would never be a mother.

Oliver jumped up on my leg, pulling me from my thoughts. His front two paws rested on my shin. I scooped him up and cradled him as if he were a newborn. "All I need are the two of you."

Oliver bit my finger, his sharklike teeth breaking the skin, but the only pain I felt was in the center of my chest.

Chapter 25

The walls in my office closed in on me as I struggled to write the article on Hank. I reread my notes from the interview, but my mind drifted. I couldn't stop wondering why my parents had never told me that Hank had invested in the diner. I decided they must have mentioned it at some point, but I had forgotten, so I called Dana to find out what she knew. It was after eleven, but I could tell by her groggy voice that my call had woken her. "Did you know that Hank gave Dad money to start the diner?"

Dana yawned. "What are you talking about?"

"When I interviewed Hank, he said he gave Dad money."

"Okay," Dana said. "So what?"

"Don't you think it's weird Mom and Dad never told us?"

Dana yawned again. "Your fascination with Hank is what's weird. Who cares if he gave them money? It should make you feel better about selling the place to him."

"Why wouldn't they tell us?"

"Probably because it doesn't matter," she snapped. "Look, Nikki, the last thing Mom and Dad would have wanted was for us to run the restaurant if we didn't want to. We did the right thing selling to Hank."

"It's never felt like the right thing."

"It was a sinkhole that sucked money into it. There was no other option." She paused and then continued in a gentler voice. "You should be focusing on Kyle, not Hank."

The temperature in the room spiked. Beads of sweat collected above my lip. Dana was right. I was obsessed with Hank. Why had I started our conversation with my encounter with him and not the more critical news about Kyle moving back home? Somehow the sacrifice I was making for Kyle to come back home and losing the restaurant to Hank were knotted up in my mind. I had to find a way to untangle them. "Great news. Kyle moved back home." I spoke softly because I felt ridiculous telling her now.

"What the hell, Nikki. Why didn't you tell me?"

I forgot. I couldn't say it out loud, so I remained silent.

"Never mind. Just listen to me," Dana said. "Focus on Kyle and your marriage and forget about Hank."

That my little sister was dishing out advice to me indicated how much I had screwed up my life. Still, I hung up determined to heed her warning. First, though, I needed to finish the article on Hank so I could get him out of my life. I flexed my fingers, thinking about how to start the piece, but the words wouldn't flow. I knew the only way to cure my writer's block was to visit the restaurant again, this time with an open mind.

~

Kyle parked his Jeep in a spot a few blocks from Pendleton 88 on the other side of the road. "You sure you want to do this?" he asked.

I didn't want to do it at all, but I knew the only way I would be able to write the article about Pendleton was to have a normal meal there without Hank sitting across from me, watching my every move.

As Kyle and I meandered toward the restaurant, a group of twentysomethings turned the corner and advanced in our direction. Kyle glanced at them, muttered under his breath, and lowered his head toward the ground. One of the women wore a red hat with a pom-pom like the woman who had been cheering for him at the hockey rink.

"Do you know them?" I asked.

Instead of answering, he took my hand and all but pulled me toward the restaurant, jogging across the street before we even reached the crosswalk.

By the time we arrived at Pendleton's entrance, I was out of breath. "What was that all about?"

"It's freezing." He made a big act of shivering. "Just want to get inside where it's warm." On the drive over, a local DJ had said the temperature was thirty-eight degrees, which was downright balmy compared to the single-digit readings on the thermometer over the past few days.

Alarm bells went off in my head. "You're acting weird."

He spun his wedding ring around his finger but didn't say anything.

As we waited to be seated, the door to the restaurant opened, blasting us with frigid air. Kyle's entire body tensed. I glanced over my shoulder. A man in his fifties helped a woman out of her coat and hung it on the rack. As they stepped forward and came into Kyle's line of vision, he relaxed.

The busboy finished clearing a table, and the hostess led us through the dining room to a small booth in the back corner. Because I was so focused on Kyle, I had forgotten to look for Hank, but I saw him now. He stood a few tables away with his back to me, talking to a young couple. Thick salt-and-pepper curls twisted over the nape of his neck. He glanced over his shoulder. His eyes met mine, and he nodded in acknowledgment. He excused himself to the couple and limped toward us. The thud of his walking boot striking the floor sounded ominous as he got closer.

"Twice in the same month, Nikki. I'm honored." He smiled at me, but his expression hardened when he looked at Kyle. "Kyle Sebastian, number seven," he said. "Your hockey team has had a lot of reason to celebrate this season." He made it sound as if that were a bad thing.

Kyle knocked on the table. "Let's hope our winning ways continue." He stood to shake Hank's hand.

Even though my husband towered over him, Hank appeared more commanding. He wore a quizzical expression as he spoke to Kyle. "You've been spending a lot of time at the Penalty Box after games," he said, hesitating before pumping Kyle's hand. "I've seen you there once or twice."

Kyle's ears reddened. "You should have come over to say hello."

"Didn't want to intrude."

Kyle sank back to his seat. I could tell by the way he ran his hand over his five-o'clock shadow that he was nervous.

"They have some good live entertainment," Hank said. "That girl, she can really sing. What's her name?"

Kyle pulled at the collar of his shirt. "No idea."

Hank shifted his attention back to me. "The food was so good you couldn't stay away." He flashed his dimples, and I got that same queasy feeling I'd had last time I was here.

"I wanted to eat here again before I finish my article."

"I'm looking forward to reading it." He placed a hand on my shoulder. "Order anything you want and enjoy. It's on me."

He took a step away from the table and turned to face us again, addressing Kyle. "I'll keep an eye out for you at the Penalty Box." Hank's words sounded threatening rather than friendly.

"What was that all about?" I asked.

Kyle shrugged. "No idea."

"Why do you think he shaved his beard off?" I twisted the napkin in my lap as I waited for Kyle to answer. Seeing Hank's clean-shaven face threw me in a way that made no sense. "Maybe the better question is, Why did he ever grow that nasty black beard in the first place?"

Kyle turned in his seat and looked at Hank, who was thumbing through the reservations book.

"Don't make it so obvious you're looking at him."

"He's not paying attention to us. He's helping a customer."

Kyle studied Hank for a few minutes. "He probably grew it to appear more intimidating. He doesn't even look like a hockey player without it. The beard made him seem meaner, unpredictable. Without it, he looks like a big ole teddy bear."

Thinking of Hank as a cuddly teddy bear made my stomach turn. "Doesn't the hostess look like Dr. Evans?" I blurted it out without thinking to change the topic.

Kyle shifted in his chair and fiddled with his silverware. "She's not as good looking."

Finally, he'd admitted he found our fertility doctor attractive. "I knew it. You have a crush on Dr. Evans." I laughed.

Kyle leaned back so he was as far from the table as possible without moving his chair. He folded his arms across his chest.

Damn, I should have never brought up Dr. Evans.

He took a loud breath and untangled his arms. "Good looking and smart. I bet she makes some decent coin too. What red-blooded male wouldn't have a crush." He winked.

A teenage waiter stopped by the table to tell us about the specials. He named one and stared off into space, seemingly trying to remember the others. After a few seconds of an uncomfortable silence, he yanked a piece of paper from his pocket and speed-read his way through it, quick to cram it back in his pocket when Hank came into view. He waited until Hank disappeared into the back office and pulled it out again. "He doesn't like it when we use cheat sheets."

He gave us time to peruse the menu. When he returned to take our order, he didn't have a pen or a notepad. "Don't you want to write it down?" Kyle asked after I gave pinpoint instructions on how I wanted my meal cooked and made mass substitutions on the sides that came with it.

"Filet, medium well, don't butterfly it, mashed cauliflower instead of a potato, and grilled brussels sprouts instead of carrots."

After we ate our meals and the waiter cleared our plates, Hank brought us dessert, even though we hadn't ordered any. "I remember how much you loved chocolate when you were a kid." He placed a lava cake with a scoop of salted-caramel ice cream and two spoons in the middle of the table. "You used to always ask for a piece of cake when you came into the diner." He had a faraway look in his eyes that made me wonder exactly what he was remembering. His dimples appeared. The back of my neck prickled. "Sometimes I'd sneak you dessert before your dinner."

Something about the look in Hank's eyes and the tone of his voice ruined my appetite. I let Kyle eat all the cake. Hank watched us from across the room. I couldn't shake the feeling that there was so much more he wanted to say to me.

Chapter 26

Admittedly, the article on Pendleton 88 wasn't my best work. If the piece had been on any other topic, I would have spent more time revising. I needed to be done with Hank and his memories, though, so I fired off the story to Elizabeth for her review. She must have attended Evelyn Wood's speed-reading course at some point, because minutes later, she summoned me to her office and handed me a printout dripping in red ink. "A good first draft," she said. "But I want to promote the angle about a local boy returning to conquer his hometown."

"I'm not sure what you mean."

"I want to get a sense of who Hank is. What kind of man is he?"

Her cell phone rang, and she glanced down at the name. She sighed before answering. "Is everything okay?" She held a finger in the air, telling me she needed a minute.

I studied the pictures on the credenza behind her desk. Most were of her kids, some with her, but none with the father. I wondered what her story was, why she would move from New York City to this Podunk mountain community.

"The nanny isn't feeling well," she said when she was through with her call. "She's vomiting, and apparently Hallie is having sympathy stomach pain." She stood and slipped into her jacket. "Hank said he left for hockey and came back after his injury for a visit and decided to stay. Find out more about what life was like for him when he came back."

"I don't think that's important. He just wants publicity for his restaurant."

"It's interesting. Humanizes the story." She grabbed her purse and headed for the door. "Sit down with the man. Get to know him. Tell his story as well as the restaurant's."

She left me alone in her office, thinking that Hank and my aunt had conspired to set up this entire article.

~

After leaving Elizabeth's office, I called Hank. The phone rang ten times before voice mail picked up. I hung up without leaving a message. I planned to tell Elizabeth that I couldn't get in touch with him and we should run the story as I had written it, but he called me back that evening while I walked Oliver. "I saw you called."

"I have more questions. For the article."

"Bring them on. You know my favorite subject is me." He laughed.

I stood under a streetlight in front of the Abramses' house, holding the dog's leash. Oliver tugged at a branch that was partially frozen in the remnants of a snowbank, trying to free it.

"Elizabeth would like the story to be more about you." I said my boss's name louder than any other word. He needed to know that it was her, not me, who wanted our readers to know more about him. "For example, what was it like when you returned to Mount Stapleton?"

Hank stayed quiet for so long that I thought the call had dropped, but then I heard him take a deep breath. "Really difficult."

"Why? Weren't you treated like a hero? Wasn't the town glad you were back?"

The curtains in the Abramses' living room shifted, and Mr. Abrams's face appeared in the window.

"I don't want to talk about that." Hank's tone had shifted to that of a hostile witness, surprising me. I remembered customers in DeMarco's Diner stopping to shake his hand, asking for his autograph and taking their picture with him. I'd thought he would want to boast about his celebrity status, which as far as I knew he still had today.

"Why does that matter?" he asked.

It doesn't, I thought as I repeated Elizabeth's words. "It humanizes the story."

Oliver gave up gnawing on the stick and climbed up on the snowbank, squatting when he reached the top. Mr. Abrams banged on the window, pointed at my puppy, and raised a fist. I pulled a plastic bag from my coat to let him know I would clean up after Oliver, but Mr. Abrams kept banging. I tugged on Oliver's leash and led him across the street to our yard.

"I was in a bad way, Nikki," Hank said. "I'd sacrificed a lot for hockey, and I couldn't play anymore."

"What did you sacrifice?"

The sound of Hank's heavy breathing filled the phone line. I pictured him younger, sprinting across the ice. "It's not a story for the magazine, but if you want to hear it, I'll tell you sometime."

The melancholy from his voice practically dripped out of my phone. I definitely didn't want to hear what he had to say.

He cleared his throat. "Send me a draft of the article." He barked the words out like a command. "I'll review it and let you know what I think."

"I'll email it tomorrow morning."

"Arianna and I are going to be traveling for the next few months, spending time in Rome, Paris, and London. Maybe Madrid too. We won't be back to Stapleton until the summer. If you still want to know what happened when my career ended, I'll have you over for a cookout or something."

I bent and scooped up Oliver, wanting to run into the house and away from this conversation. "That's okay. Elizabeth just wanted to know for the article. You don't have to tell me about it."

"I'd like to tell you. You might find out I'm not the asshole you think I am."

A car turned onto my road. Headlights flooded the street, momentarily blinding me.

"Think about it while I'm gone."

"I will." I had no intention of ever hearing his story, but I didn't want to get him mad before he signed off on the article.

"See you in a few months."

Chapter 27

The monstrous snowbanks that had outlined the streets of Stapleton since late November had melted. The ski lifts on the mountain had stopped running, and downtown, tourists wearing hiking boots had replaced those with skis on their roof racks. In our neighborhood, the dogwoods were blooming, and daffodils sprouted up in flower beds.

On this Saturday morning in late May, the sun shone with a ferocity usually reserved for sweltering days in late July or the dog days of August. I longed to sit by the ocean, look out at the endless blue water, breathe in the salt air, and listen to the waves crash against the shoreline. By dangling the reward of a lobster roll in front of Kyle, I easily convinced him to accompany me on the two-hour drive to the nearest beach. Almost two months had passed since he'd moved back in, and we were finally starting to feel comfortable with each other again. With each day that passed, I was coming to terms with the fact that I'd never be a mother. Sometimes after spending time with Sharon, Cameron, and Noah and hearing her talk to the boys about their little sister, Baby Sharon, who would arrive in August, I would cry on the way home. Mostly, though, I focused on the good in my life, the things I had—Oliver; Kyle; my aunt, sister, and friends; my health—and not on the baby I would never have.

Today as Kyle steered his Jeep down the winding roads, Oliver sat in the back seat with his head out the window and not a care in the world. I thought about the early years of our marriage, when Cole had sat behind us and the idea of a baby seat by his side had seemed like a certainty. *Don't go there, Nikki. Don't go there.*

I turned up the volume of the stereo to drown out my thoughts. A song by Blake Shelton came on the radio. Kyle grinned and sang along.

"I don't think you look like him," I said.

His earlobes reddened, and he stopped singing. "Why would you say that?" His voice had a defensive edge.

"Because of Aunt Izzie."

"What about Aunt Izzie?" He had a white-knuckle grip on the steering wheel. I didn't understand why he was getting so worked up about this. He was acting like I was accusing him of something.

"She always says you look like him."

His muscles relaxed. "I'd forgotten about that."

"What did you think I was talking about?"

He rubbed his palm over his stubbled chin but didn't answer.

We rode in silence until Blake sang a line about bringing fresh fajitas home. "I don't think fajitas work as takeout," Kyle said.

"Right, there would be no sizzle."

"And what are fajitas without the sizzle. That's the fun part." He reached across the console and poked me in the thigh.

We drove on, singing with the radio, sometimes making up our own words. The miles passed in a blur. The single-lane mountain road became a busy interstate. Office parks and chain stores replaced grassy marshes and empty fields. In the back seat, Oliver became restless, standing and spinning, changing his seat from behind Kyle to behind me.

Finally, we turned off the highway and onto the back roads of Gloucester. With my window open, I could smell the salt air. Soon the dark-blue, almost black waters of the Atlantic Ocean came into view.

Down on the beach, a smattering of people relaxed in lounge chairs and engaged in lively discussions, read books, or stared out at the waves, mesmerized. I held Oliver's leash in one hand and Kyle's hand with my other. Together, the three of us walked the long rocky shoreline. The bright-blue sky above me gave me a feeling of serenity, and the sound of the waves breaking against the shore soothed me. *This is perfect. This is all I need,* I thought.

We spread a blanket and napped with the hot sun warming our skin. I woke to Kyle playing fetch with Oliver, the little guy leaping and bounding through the waves to retrieve a rope with a large knot at the end, his red fur dripping wet. Each time he brought the rope back, he shook himself off, sending droplets of water flying through the air in all directions.

After a few hours at the beach, we headed to a seafood restaurant, the kind where you ordered at a counter and sat at picnic tables waiting for them to call your number. I ordered blackened-fish tacos, and Kyle asked for the twelve-ounce lobster roll with onion rings. When he went to retrieve our food, I fed Oliver a dog biscuit. Kyle's phone, sitting on the other side of the table where he'd left it, vibrated, catching my attention. A text flashed across the top of the screen. No name was assigned to the number it came from. I read the words before the message disappeared: We need to talk. It's important.

When Kyle returned, he picked up his phone and swiped at the screen. His facial muscles tensed, and his eyelid twitched as he stared down at it. He clenched and unclenched the fist of his free hand over and over again.

"What's wrong?" I asked.

He rubbed the hollow of his neck and slid the phone into his back pocket. "Pain-in-the-ass client."

"I thought you were working on the Gunthers' house."

"Different client. I forgot napkins." He took off for the counter. As I watched him walk away, a cool breeze blew, and I shivered.

～

"Give your aunt my apologies," Kyle said, zippering his coat. "Tell her I'll stop by sometime during the week to put her patio furniture out."

"You're really not coming?" For over a week, we'd had plans to have breakfast with Dana and Aunt Izzie this morning.

"I have to meet with this client." He held up his cell phone and shook it. I narrowed my eyes in confusion. "The one who texted me yesterday."

"But it's Sunday."

He shrugged. "He's threatening to use someone else. I don't want to lose the business."

"Can't you meet with him after breakfast? You haven't seen Aunt Izzie in ages."

"It's the only time he's available. Sorry." He kissed me goodbye, patted Oliver on the head, and slipped out the front door.

From the window, I watched him climb into the Jeep's driver's seat. With his chin resting on his chest, he held his phone to his ear. He sat that way for several seconds without moving, and then he slammed his phone down in the passenger seat. His tires squealed as he peeled out of his parking spot by the garage. On the road, a jogger approached our driveway. I pounded on the glass, trying to get Kyle's attention. His vehicle raced toward the street as if Dale Earnhardt Jr. were driving it. The jogger had her head down, staring at her phone. She reached the outer edge of our driveway. The Jeep kept rolling. I pounded harder, yelling, "Watch out." The brake lights lit up, and Kyle's car skidded to a stop. The jogger lifted her head and swerved to her right, the nylon from her jacket grazing the Jeep's bumper.

Kyle waved at her as if to say sorry. She glared at him and continued on her run. Whoever this client was, they had gotten under my husband's skin. His entire demeanor had changed since receiving that text yesterday. I'd never seen him so distracted.

~

When Oliver and I arrived at Aunt Izzie's, the dog charged up the stairs and into the kitchen, his tail wagging and his tongue hanging out of his mouth. Aunt Izzie and Dana sat at the table in front of plates with rivers of maple syrup running over them. Dana plucked a strip of bacon off a platter in the center of the table. Oliver barked and jumped up on her legs. "Not for dogs," she said, pushing the puppy off her. Oliver jumped up on her again. "Down, Deeogee." She pushed him again. "I see the training's going well."

"He responds better to his name," I said.

"Where's Kyle?" Aunt Izzie asked.

"He's working."

"Are you fighting again?" Dana asked.

"Things are great." I transferred a stack of blueberry pancakes from the griddle to a plate. "We drove down to the shore yesterday. Had a fun day."

As I took my seat, I noticed the June issue of *Mountain Views Magazine* in the center of the table. Hank smiled up at me from the cover, both of his dimples engaged. I flipped the magazine over. I didn't like looking at him without his facial hair. Kyle was right. The beard had made Hank look mean. The dimples made him seem good natured, like someone who would go out of his way not to hurt someone.

"I never realized he was so good looking," Dana said.

"It's easier to see now that he doesn't have that unkempt beard," Aunt Izzie said.

"Those dimples." Dana paused to take a bite of bacon. "Yummy." I wasn't sure if she was talking about her breakfast or Hank, and I wasn't about to ask.

"It was a lovely article on Pendleton," Aunt Izzie said. "I'm glad you were able to put your differences aside to write it."

"How come you never told me Hank invested in DeMarco's Diner?"

Aunt Izzie stilled. "Hank told you that?"

"He was lying, wasn't he?"

My aunt shook her head. It was the loudest headshake I'd ever heard. "What else did he tell you about that time?"

The way she leaned toward me as she waited for me to answer reinforced my gut feeling not to take Hank up on his offer of telling me about his life when he returned to Stapleton. Whatever he had to say, I didn't want to hear. "Nothing." I stood and busied myself at the sink, filling Oliver's portable water bowl. I didn't want to field more questions about Hank, so I made my way toward the basement door. "I'll put the patio furniture out."

"It's too heavy. I can wait for Kyle," Aunt Izzie said.

"Dana and I can do it."

I made my way down the steep, narrow staircase. With each step I took, the musty scent became stronger. At the bottom, I snapped on a light, revealing a chaotic mess that was the exact opposite of the neat and orderly upstairs. Wobbly stacks of cardboard boxes leaned against walls, threatening to tumble over if someone exhaled. Old wooden chairs formed a line in the center of the room, with a few others piled on top of each other off to the side as if a game of musical chairs had been interrupted. Clothes spilled out of plastic bins with cracked covers. Paperback books with yellow pages filled lopsided bookcases. Box and window fans coated with layers of dust lay on their sides.

I broke into a sneezing fit.

There were footsteps on the staircase. Dana reached the bottom. "What a dump."

"The patio furniture is in the back right corner," Aunt Izzie hollered. "Be careful down there."

As we made our way across the cellar, I noticed a familiar-looking long black-and-red aluminum rectangle sticking out from behind a pile of boxes, the sign from my parents' restaurant. I rushed across the room and pulled it out, tracing the dusty letters that spelled out DeMarco's Diner with my index finger. Touching the sign made me feel connected to my parents in a way I hadn't since they died. I looked around the room, expecting to see them, but of course they weren't there.

"I thought Hank threw this away when he renovated the restaurant," Dana said. She glanced at it, but something in one of the cardboard boxes seemed to catch her attention. She wandered off in its direction and knelt in front of it, rummaging through the contents. "Look at this." She held up a 1976 yearbook from Mount Stapleton Community High School. "This must be Aunt Izzie's. I wonder if Mom's is in here too." She dug through the box, pulling out old photo albums and another yearbook, this one from 1979, the year our mother had graduated.

As she went through the yearbook, I flipped open one of the photo albums. Baby pictures of my aunt and mother stared back at me. There were footsteps on the stairway. Aunt Izzie made her way down with Oliver trotting along behind her. "What are you gi—are those my old photo albums? Don't touch those." She rushed down the remaining stairs, tripped on the bottom one, and fell to the cement floor in a heap. Oliver whimpered as if he had been injured and stood guard over her.

Dana raced across the room while I froze, shocked by what I'd witnessed.

"Are you okay?" my sister asked.

Aunt Izzie grimaced as she pushed herself up to a sitting position. I shook myself from my trance, and Dana and I helped Aunt Izzie to her feet. "You were supposed to be down here getting the patio furniture, not snooping," she said.

"I saw the DeMarco's Diner sign. I didn't know you had that."

"I'd forgotten all about it. Hank gave it to me years ago."

"Can I have it?"

"Be my guest." Aunt Izzie limped toward the other side of the basement and returned the yearbooks and photo albums to the box. "The patio furniture is over there." She pointed to the back corner. Dana and I hoisted the table and chairs out of the bulkhead while Aunt Izzie stood by the box with her arms folded across her chest as if she were protecting the queen's jewels.

Chapter 28

Wednesday night, Kyle pushed his dinner around his plate but barely ate any of his food. "I'm just not hungry." He scraped the steak off his plate into the dog's bowl. He hadn't had an appetite all week, which was most unlike him.

Oliver charged into the room, almost knocking Kyle off his feet. "Damn it, Oliver."

"Hey, don't talk to him in that tone," I said.

"Sorry, buddy." Kyle stroked Oliver's back. The dog didn't notice. He had his face buried in his dish, gobbling down Kyle's meat.

"What's going on with you?" I asked. "You've been on edge for days." Twice this week, I had woken up alone in bed in the predawn hours and found him sitting in his recliner in the dark living room, staring out into the black night.

"Work stuff." He dropped a few ice cubes in a highball glass and reached for the bottle of scotch.

"That client?"

He stared at me blankly.

"The one you had to meet on Sunday."

"Oh yeah, right." He tossed back his drink, poured himself another, and left to watch television without answering.

After I finished cleaning the kitchen, I joined Kyle in the living room. As soon as I settled on the couch, he popped up from his recliner. "I'm taking Oliver for a walk."

"Are you sure?" Usually I took Oliver for his evening walk while Kyle watched his home-improvement show.

"Positive." With his head, he gestured toward the television. "I've already seen this."

An hour later, the side door clicked open. I heard Oliver lapping up his water. Kyle stood in the entrance to the living room, staring at me with an expression I didn't like, a mixture of sadness and worry.

"What's wrong?" I asked.

He clenched both hands into tight fists and released them. "I don't know how to tell you this." He bit down on his lip.

I assumed he had received a phone call on his walk, bad news. "Did something happen to Dana, Aunt Izzie?"

"Nothing like that."

I released a deep breath, resting my arm on a throw pillow.

"I did something stupid."

This got my attention because other than marrying me, a woman who hadn't been able to give him kids, Kyle had never done anything stupid. My eyes went to his, but he quickly looked away. "I was with someone else." His Adam's apple bobbed up and down as he swallowed.

"What?" I heard what he said, but I couldn't make sense of the words. He couldn't be saying what I thought he was. He wouldn't do that. Not Kyle. My eyes pleaded with him.

"I slept with someone else." He said those words that cracked open my heart with no emotion, as if he were telling me we were out of milk.

I hugged the throw pillow to my chest without saying anything. Who was she? How had he met her? At work? One of Luke's friends? The women calling his name at the hockey game popped into my head. I'd never gotten a good look at them. All I could remember was their hats with the pom-poms. One of them had touched him before she left the game.

Oliver scampered into the room. The clinking of his dog tags was the only sound. Maybe he sensed the tension, because instead of parking himself at my feet or jumping up on the couch next to me, he returned to the kitchen.

"Who is she?"

Kyle stood in front of the picture window, his head bowed so that his chin rested on his chest. "No one you know. I met her at the Penalty Box."

"The woman with the red hat. At your hockey game."

He pulled at the collar of his shirt. "It only happened once."

"What's her name?" I didn't know why I wanted to know this, maybe to get a better picture of who she was.

He blinked hard. "Why does that matter?"

"What's. Her. Name?"

He sighed. "Casey," he whispered, as if saying her name softly made her less real.

Casey, I repeated to myself, knowing I had heard that name recently but not remembering where. Had Kyle mentioned her? Had one of his hockey buddies said something about her? I imagined him sitting at the bar in his red-and-gold number-seven shirt, drinking a beer or sipping scotch, flirting with a tourist, one of the rich divorced women from Connecticut with a ski house on the mountain, getting her thrills with a local blue-collar guy. Or maybe she was one of the townies, a lonely waitress who had never been over the state line looking for Kyle to save her from her boring life. "Does she know you're married?" I spun my rings around my finger.

He nodded. I bet he'd told her I was crazy, the psycho wife obsessed with having a baby. *She bought a crib, turned our home office into a nursery,* I imagined him saying. She'd probably listened with that same sympathetic look Dr. Evans used to give him. They'd probably had a good laugh at my expense.

"Are you in love? Do you want to be with her?" I was afraid of how he would answer. My eyes darted toward the door. I wanted to leave, but my muscles had gone limp. I didn't think my legs could carry me across the hardwood floor.

"No. Nothing like that. It was just . . . I don't know. A bad decision."

Oh, okay then. A bad decision. You can use your Get Out of Jail Free card or maybe take a mulligan. Asshole!

"It didn't mean anything." Kyle's gravelly voice, which I used to find so sexy, hurt me now, scraping my heart with every word he said.

"Actually, it does mean something," I spat. "It means you're a cheater. Not at all who I thought you were."

His chest collapsed. "Nikki, listen to me. Things weren't good with us."

"Don't you dare." I balled my fists so tightly that my fingernails dug into the palms of my hands.

"It was the night I found out you lied about the bonus."

"So you decided to get even by having sex with someone else?"

"I didn't think we'd ever recover from that. I had too much to drink. I—"

I flung the pillow at him because I didn't want to hear any more. "Why are you telling me this? To clear your conscience? Get forgiveness? Because you're not going to get it."

He bit his lip and stared down at his feet. "She's." It was barely a whisper. "She's pregnant."

The room felt like it was spinning. The crickets outside became deafening, or maybe the sound was a buzzing in my head. I couldn't tell. "She's pregnant? It's yours?"

He collapsed on the couch beside me, leaving a foot of space between us. Still, I scooted away from him. "She says it is."

"She's lying. You can't . . ." Everything we'd done to get pregnant over the past few years flashed through my mind: the miscarriage, the ovulation-prediction kit, the injections, the needles, the implantations, talking to the therapist, Dr. Evans's grim face telling us the blood test was negative. "You slept with her one time, and you got her pregnant." My voice cracked. "It can't be. It's not yours."

He leaned forward with his elbows resting on his thighs. "I know. It's . . ." He buried his face in his hands without finishing.

It was a big *fuck you* from God to me was what it was.

"She doesn't want to keep it," he said.

There was a burning sensation in my chest. The heat crawled up my neck to my face. My entire body shook in anger. Kyle had gotten a woman pregnant, and she wanted to abort the baby. The whole damn universe was mocking me. "So why did she even tell you? Why didn't she just get an abortion?"

"She's going to have the baby. Give it up for adoption." He picked a clump of Oliver's red hair off the couch. "She's Catholic."

I laughed, a hysterical laugh, not because I thought what he said was funny but because the woman's reason was so ridiculous. "Someone should explain to her about adultery, or the church's view on premarital sex. Though apparently, she has that part about no birth control right."

"I don't want strangers raising my child."

His child. Kyle was going to be a father.

He scooched down the sofa in my direction and reached toward me, dropping his hand on my thigh. "I know this is crazy, but you've wanted a baby for so long, said we couldn't be a family without one. Now there's this baby coming that needs parents to raise her or him, my baby."

I jumped to my feet, unable to believe what he was suggesting. "Absolutely not!"

"I know it's unorthodox, but just think about it, Nikki, please."

I tried to swallow the lump in my throat, but my mouth was too dry. "I want you to leave."

"Nikki, please."

"Get your stuff and get out," I said louder.

Kyle sat there for several minutes with his head buried in his hands. Finally, he sighed and stood. The stairway creaked with each step he took as if it were moaning in sympathy. A few minutes later he slouched back down the stairs, slumping at the bottom. "Nikki, I'm sorry." His voice broke. He closed the door softly behind him on his way out.

Oliver loped into the room and nudged his head under my arm so that I would pat him. I sat on the couch for hours, comforted by the puppy who had saved my marriage once, only to watch it fall apart again.

∼

I couldn't sleep because I couldn't stop thinking about the grenade Kyle had detonated in our living room. For the past few months, I'd felt so guilty for lying to him about receiving a bonus when he'd done much worse. Yes, things had been bad between us. Working so hard to have a baby had ruined every good thing about our relationship, but if he loved me, he would have tried to fix it instead of running to someone else because he was angry with me. The worst part wasn't even that he'd knocked up some bar-going ho. No, the most devastating thing in all this was that I now had to admit that Kyle's and my fertility problems were my fault. I was the reason we couldn't have a baby together. Deep down, I had suspected this, but still, a part of me had blamed Kyle because blaming him hurt less than blaming myself. I thought about all the times people had said what a great father Kyle would be, but I couldn't remember anyone ever saying I'd be a good mom. Maybe they all knew I wouldn't be, and that was why I had been unable to get pregnant.

Then it occurred to me that a woman who hung out in bars and had no issues sleeping with someone else's husband probably had several partners and really had no idea if the baby was Kyle's. She'd probably picked him because he was the most likely to help her out. Yes, that was it. Kyle had not gotten her pregnant.

These thoughts circled round and round in my head until I finally fell asleep. Oliver's whining woke me. He stood on his hind legs with his two front paws on the mattress, looking down at me. I squinted toward the clock. It wasn't even five o'clock yet. "Go back to sleep," I said, gently pushing him off the bed and rolling over so that my back faced him. He barked as he jumped back up. Kyle usually took him out in the mornings while I slept. I petted his head.

"Okay." I reached toward the nightstand with my other hand for my phone. I expected to see a message from Kyle, letting me know where he'd spent the night, but the screen was blank. *Is he staying at a hotel? With Luke? He's staying with her.* The thought popped into my mind with a certainty, followed by an image of a dark-haired, dowdy woman having an ultrasound. Kyle stood by her side, holding her hand, watching the monitor like he had that one time I had been pregnant. *This woman is going to live the life I was supposed to live.*

Outside the sun crawled out from behind the mountains and stretched toward the sky, casting shades of purple and yellow over the area. Any other day, I would have thought the colors were beautiful, but today they reminded me of an enormous bruise. Oliver pulled me toward a bush on our side lawn, where he did his business. When he finished, I took him for a walk around the block, using the flashlight app on my phone to illuminate the way. Back on my street, two flashlights came at us from down the road. Soon I was even with the other early-morning walkers, Sarah and Kevin Linehan. Kyle told me he saw them every morning. I didn't understand why they were awake so early. They were retired and had the entire day to go for a walk, so why would they go before the sun fully rose?

Kevin pulled a dog treat from his pocket and tossed it to Oliver, who snatched it out of the air. The Linehans didn't have a dog of their own, so I suspected this was a part of the daily routine.

"Where's Kyle this morning?" Sarah asked.

I hadn't expected to have to explain Kyle's whereabouts before six o'clock in the morning. I hadn't expected to be awake until eight. "I was up, so I decided to take Oliver out. Let Kyle sleep for a change." I looked at Oliver as I spoke, wondering if Kyle was sleeping in today.

"But his truck is gone," she said.

Why did I even bother lying? Soon everyone would know. "I kicked him out," I blurted, yanking on Oliver's leash and making a beeline for my front door before she could ask me anything else.

Chapter 29

Ding-dong, ding-dong. The sounds woke me from a restless sleep on Saturday morning. Before I could move, the bed shook, and I felt Oliver's hot breath on the back of my neck. With his two front legs resting on the mattress, he stood over me, panting. Pound, pound, pound. I sat up, wondering who could be banging on my door so early. Oliver shifted his paws to my thighs, and I rubbed his head. The pounding stopped, but my phone started to ring.

"Are you still sleeping?" Dana's voice oozed judgment, as if it were two in the afternoon and not just before eight on a weekend morning. "We're waiting out front."

Waiting? Oh no. Today was June 2, Aunt Izzie's birthday. Every year we celebrated the day by hiking Lydia's Falls and sitting by the 140-foot waterfall with lunch and birthday cupcakes.

I lifted the shade and looked down on the driveway. Dana waved from the passenger seat of Aunt Izzie's Subaru.

My phone felt damp from my sweaty grip. "Go without me. I'm not feeling well." I was telling the truth. My entire body ached, probably because my muscles had been nonstop clenched since Kyle's bombshell.

"Nikki," Dana said. "Get your ass out here."

From the window, I watched her lean toward the steering wheel. She blared the horn until Aunt Izzie smacked her hand away.

Across the street, the Abramses' front door swung open. Mr. Abrams stepped onto the landing in a white T-shirt and red flannel pajama bottoms.

"Great, you woke my neighbors," I said into the phone.

Aunt Izzie's car backed out of the driveway and drove away.

Are they really going without me? A few minutes ago, I'd wanted nothing more than to crawl back under the covers and curl into the fetal position. Now, the thought of being alone all day with no one to talk to except Oliver had lost its appeal.

"We're going to get lunch to eat by the waterfall. We'll be back in twenty. You better be ready," Dana said.

As I showered, my phone pinged with a text. I assumed Dana was asking what kind of sandwich I wanted, but the message was from Kyle.

Kyle: I need to stop by to get a few things. Can we talk while I'm there?

Nikki: I won't be here, but make sure you take everything you need so you don't have to come back.

Kyle: All I need is you and Oliver. When can we talk?

Nikki: I don't have anything to say to you, and there's nothing you can say that I want to hear.

Three dots appeared as he typed his response. I shut off my phone before he finished.

~

"You're bringing the dog?" Aunt Izzie asked as Oliver jumped into the back seat.

"Do you mind? I don't want to leave him here by himself all day, and he loves hikes." I was also afraid that Kyle might take him and use him as leverage to make me talk with him.

"Where's Kyle?" she asked.

Heat crept up my neck to my face. I hadn't told anyone what had happened. I couldn't make myself say the words that Kyle had cheated and was having a baby with someone else. Voicing them would make his infidelity too real. Only the Linehans knew something was wrong, that I had kicked him out.

"He's working."

Dana turned from the front passenger seat to pet Oliver. "Your time with him is coming to an end."

I'd been in the process of buckling my seat belt, but I sat frozen, unable to move. *Does everyone already know? Did Kyle call her?* I tried to ask Dana how she'd found out, but I couldn't make my tongue move. Heat coursed through my body. I felt as if I might spontaneously combust. I wished I would. I didn't want to talk about this. I pulled my sweatshirt off and lowered the window. The protein bar I'd had for breakfast threatened to come back up.

Dana tousled the fur on the dog's head. "He's coming with me to the Cape."

What is she talking about? Who's going to the Cape with her? Kyle? "Coming with you?"

"Of course he's coming with me." Dana turned forward.

Aunt Izzie met my eyes in the rearview mirror. She flashed a sad smile.

All at once, I figured out what Dana meant. My stomach dropped. "You think you're taking Oliver with you to the Cape."

Dana looked at me over her shoulder. "Of course I'm taking him. He's my dog."

My hand rested on Oliver's spine in a proprietary way. "You had him all of two days before you gave him to me."

"I didn't give him to you. I asked you to watch him until I left for the summer."

Aunt Izzie turned onto Mountain Pass Road, and the car sped up.

"I've had him for three months. I trained him."

"And I appreciate that."

All the anger I'd bottled up over the past few days erupted. "You are so selfish. You can't just take him, rip him away from his family."

"You're not his family, Nikki. I am. He's my dog."

Aunt Izzie took the sharp corner at a fast speed. I swayed right with the car, my shoulder brushing against the door.

"I'm the only family he knows."

"Deeogee is mine."

"His name is Oliver."

My aunt's eyes met mine in the rearview mirror again. They were stormy this time.

"He's coming with me," Dana said.

"Enough!" Aunt Izzie slammed the brakes. The car skidded to a stop in the middle of the road. The momentum flung me forward. I bumped my head on the back of Dana's seat, clutching Oliver to keep him from being thrown to the car floor.

"Dana, your lifestyle, especially during the summer, isn't conducive to caring for a dog," Aunt Izzie said.

My sister's head snapped toward my aunt. "You always take her side."

A pickup truck came up behind us. The driver leaned on his horn.

Aunt Izzie stomped on the gas pedal. The car lurched forward. "You will not ruin my birthday. Not another word about that dog today."

We rode the rest of the way without speaking. Dana fiddled with her phone while I stared out the window, watching the tall pines pass and listening to the sound of the tires rolling over the gravelly mountain road.

In the parking lot at the bottom of the trail, Aunt Izzie pulled into a spot in the back corner, away from the dozen or so other vehicles. Dana leaped out of the car and raced toward the trail without waiting for us. Aunt Izzie and I watched my sister's back retreating into the woods.

The meandering dirt path shot straight up for about four hundred yards before taking a sharp left. Dana had already disappeared around the turn by the time we started the climb. Though it was a warm, sunny day, tree branches flush with leaves hung over the first part of the trail, keeping it dark and cool. Oliver kept tugging on his leash, pulling me to the side of the trail, burying his head in the brush to sniff or lifting his leg to mark a tree or bush.

As we made our ascent, gnats buzzed around our heads. I waved them away with my hand. We stopped, and Aunt Izzie sprayed on insect repellent, filling the air with a nasty chemical scent. She handed me the can, but I didn't take it, an aversion left over from when I was trying to get pregnant.

We started off again. Aunt Izzie walked a few steps ahead of Oliver and me, the distance between us growing as Oliver stopped to sniff. She looked back at us over her shoulder.

"We'll catch up at the top," I said.

Aunt Izzie nodded. "I want to find your sister. Talk to her so she doesn't feel like we were ganging up on her."

What we said was true, I thought, but I didn't want to get into another discussion about the dog, didn't want to think of Dana taking him away from me. "I doubt you'll catch her." Ever since we were kids, Dana raced up the trail while I took my time, observing the plants, trees, and rocks along the way.

Aunt Izzie took off, and soon she, too, disappeared from my view. Oliver and I trotted along. "It's just you and me, buddy," I said. "Better get used to it." He looked up at me with that golden retriever smile, and despite the sadness I felt, I couldn't help but smile back.

Soon there were voices and footsteps behind us, a man, woman, teenage boy, and preteen girl making their way up the trail. I pulled Oliver to the side so they could pass. The girl stopped too. "Aww," she said, bending to pat the dog. "What's her name?"

"His name is Oliver."

"He's really cute."

"Thank you," I said, as if I had something to do with the dog's beauty.

"Gianna," the girl's mother called.

A chill ran down my spine. "Your name's Gianna?"

The girl nodded.

"That was my mother's name."

"I don't really like it," she said. "People always mess up and call me Gina."

"I think it's beautiful."

Hearing my mother's name on this trail had to be some kind of sign. *You'll survive this blow from Kyle,* I imagined her saying. I wasn't so sure.

I continued on. Oliver pulled on his leash, leading the way as if he were walking me. Distracted by bright-purple flowers, I tripped over a knot of tree roots and fell. Oliver barked when I hit the ground and trotted back to my side. He nudged me with his nose and licked my face. "I'm fine," I told him as I struggled back to my feet. Was I? A quarter-inch gash ran across my knee, and blood trickled down my leg. I looked up the trail, hoping Aunt Izzie hadn't seen me trip. She was long gone, probably already at the waterfall with Dana.

I cleaned my cut with water and a tissue and fished through my backpack for a bandage. I found a box of Band-Aids at the bottom. They were decorated with an image of Bugs Bunny. Kyle had bought them shortly after we started IVF, and I had imagined placing the Looney Tunes bandage on a little boy's scraped elbow. *Does that Casey person really want to give the baby up for adoption? Will Kyle raise him or her?* Oliver lurched at a squirrel, yanking me from my thoughts, and I continued on my way.

At the top of the trail, Dana and Aunt Izzie sat on a long log by the waterfall. Dana wore red Oakleys, and her head was tilted toward the sun. Aunt Izzie rubbed sunscreen on her arms. The smell of coconut wafted in the air, reminding me of the beach.

"What are you going to do with Oliver when you're at work?" I imagined my sweet dog tied to Dana's lifeguard chair, getting scorched by the blazing sun and burning his paws on the hot sand.

I pulled a bowl from my knapsack and poured water for Oliver. He lapped it up. I refilled his dish before sitting.

"Let's talk about this later," Dana said. She extended a bag of her homemade trail mix toward me. The mixture consisted mostly of chocolate chips and flakes of coconut. I picked through it, pulling out a few almonds.

We sat there for a while, not talking, listening to the waterfall. A mosquito bit my leg, leaving a small smudge of blood. The family who had passed me scrambled up a rock face in front of us. Every now and then snippets of their conversation that didn't make sense drifted down to us, but then clearly: "Gianna, watch your footing."

Aunt Izzie's and Dana's heads both turned toward the family as if they expected to see my mother. In a way she was here with us. Just beyond the log we sat on was the spot we'd spread my parents' ashes.

"I miss her," my aunt said. "She was my best friend." She was drawing circles in the dirt with a stick, but she looked up and met my eyes and then glanced at Dana. "As sisters should be."

Dana gave me a sheepish look. "I'm sorry," she said. "I thought I was clear that I'd be taking Oliver back when I left for the summer."

"Kyle cheated on me." I hadn't known I was going to tell them, but once I had, the words kept coming. "Months ago, but he just told me." Aunt Izzie, Dana, and I sat side by side. Recounting the story without having to look at them made it easier to tell. As I spoke, Dana curled her arm around my waist. I leaned into her, her wiry frame giving me the strength I needed to share the story with the only family I had left. Aunt Izzie listened without interrupting, scraping the heel of her shoe through the dirt over and over again.

"The woman is pregnant. Someone he met at the Penalty Box." I wiped the sweat dripping down my forehead with the back of my hand.

"No, no, no." Aunt Izzie's face went slack. She stared into the distance with an unfocused gaze. The hole by her foot was several inches wide and deep now.

Dana unzipped the cooler and handed Aunt Izzie a sandwich. "You were probably having a better birthday when we were fighting about the dog," she said.

Chapter 30

The framed photos of me and Kyle had been on display in my office for so long that usually I didn't notice them. This morning, I couldn't turn away from them, one of me sitting on Kyle's shoulders in the water at Marconi Beach, another of us warming up by a fire and toasting each other with big mugs of hot cocoa after a day of snowboarding, and one of Kyle and me on the ice after one of his hockey games. All the photos had been taken before we started trying to have a baby. We looked insanely happy, big goofy grins on our faces and our bodies pressed so close together we looked like conjoined twins. Tears stung my eyes. We would never be happy together again. How could we be when he had fathered a baby with someone else?

In a frenzy, I raced around the room, snatching up each picture as if it were evidence of a crime I had committed. Stacked in my hands, the metal frames clanked against each other as I stared into the trash can, a pretzel bag crumpled in the corner its only contents. Boy, had my life changed since I'd eaten those pretzels last week. In the end, I couldn't make myself dump the pictures in the garbage, so I stuffed them in the back of my bottom desk drawer.

I settled in front of my computer, my hands poised on the keyboard, ready to write an article on the new yoga studio in town. Under Elizabeth's guidance, the entire magazine had turned into a multipage glossy advertising flyer. When she had given me my latest assignment, I'd asked why advertorial content outweighed editorial articles. "Think of the magazine as an activity guide for the region," she'd said. Her response made me question whether I wanted to continue working there, but where would I go?

For the first few hours of the day, I remained behind my closed office door, banging out a first draft. At lunchtime the occasional whispered chitchat in the hallway turned into a roar. A parade of coworkers marched by my office. Their laughter and voices drifted through the walls. "He's adorable," someone said.

"She looks just like you," Page said.

A few minutes later someone else said, "Oh, you have a smart one there."

Then there was the distinct sound of a baby crying. *A baby?* My heart clenched. Why would there be a baby in the office? Clearly, my imagination was playing tricks on me. My door cracked open, and Page popped her head in. "Elizabeth's nanny is here with the kids. They're adorable. Come see."

"I have a deadline," I lied.

Page licked her upper lip, looking around my office, her gaze lingering on the empty shelves. She stepped into the room and closed the door behind her. "What's going on? Why are you cleaning out your office?"

I swallowed the lump in my throat. "I just took down some pictures."

She studied my face as if it might reveal my reasons for doing so. "Is everything okay?"

The baby cried again, and I could feel my lips quivering.

Page raced around my desk and looked down at me. "Oh, honey, what is it?"

I wiped a tear from my face. "Nothing I'm ready to talk about yet."

She leaned down to hug me, her hair tickling my nose. The scent of her apricot shampoo filled my nostrils. "When you're ready to talk, I'm here for you. No matter when. Late at night, the butt crack of morning. I'm here for you."

"Thank you." As I watched her leave, I wondered why I hadn't confided in her about the trouble Kyle and I had trying to conceive. Maybe she would have been able to talk me out of withdrawing from my retirement fund. If I hadn't done that or if I had told Kyle the truth about where the money came from, he would have never been with Casey. That I was sure of.

After Page left, I couldn't focus. I kept reading the same line of an email over and over again. A bloodcurdling scream ricocheted down the hall. I imagined the poor baby getting passed from one of my coworkers to the next, each tickling his belly or pinching his cheek. I gave up trying to work and decided to go to lunch. Unfortunately, the only way out of the building required me to pass Elizabeth's office.

As I turned the corner, the party by her desk broke up. My coworkers streamed into the corridor, followed by a little girl and a twentysomething woman with long red hair cascading over her shoulders. She pushed a stroller with Elizabeth on her heels, barking in her ear. "You'll make sure to put him down for a nap when you get home. But don't let him sleep past three." The little girl dropped a doll she was carrying, and Elizabeth bent to retrieve it.

"I know," the red-haired woman said. We made eye contact. I could tell by her furrowed forehead and tight mouth that Elizabeth annoyed her as much as she sometimes did me.

"And you'll read to Hallie."

"Absolutely."

"One of the books I left on the dining room table." Elizabeth handed her daughter the doll.

The nanny rolled her eyes, and I smiled as I passed. "Of course," she said.

"Nikki," Elizabeth hollered. I thought about continuing down the hall without stopping, but she called my name again. "Come meet my kids."

She patted the girl's head. "This is Hallie." The little girl was a mini version of her mother, with dark hair and porcelain skin. The photographs in Elizabeth's office didn't do her justice.

"I'm Nikki," I said, waving.

The girl waved back.

"That's Danvers." Elizabeth pointed into the stroller, where the baby looked up at me with a toothless smile.

I didn't want to be a suck-up and tell Elizabeth that her children were beautiful, but they were indeed gorgeous. It figured. The damn woman got whatever the hell she wanted in life. "Your kids are adorable," I managed.

"Thank you," Elizabeth said. "You were supposed to send me a copy of the yoga story this morning. Why haven't I seen it yet?"

The nanny cleared her throat. "I'm going to get going before Danvers falls asleep."

Elizabeth placed her hand on the nanny's arm. "Wait—I'll walk out with you."

The nanny and I made eye contact again. Though no words passed between us, I knew she was telling me that Elizabeth was a huge pain in her ass too.

Elizabeth looked back at me as if she'd just remembered something. "My apologies," she said. "Nikki, this is the children's nanny, Casey."

Casey . . . My knees buckled, and I stumbled forward. *Casey? The name is a coincidence. Has to be. Casey is a common name, after all. Oh no, it really isn't.* My eyes flew to her abdomen. Her shirt ballooned over her waist, giving nothing away.

"Nikki, are you okay?" Elizabeth asked. "You've gone white."

I took a deep breath in. "You look familiar," I said to Casey. Though she really didn't. With her copper hair, fair skin, perfect cheekbones, and bright-green eyes, she was someone people remembered, I was sure.

"It's a small town," Casey said. "We've probably been at the same place at the same time before."

"The Penalty Box?" I asked.

"Yes! I'm there all the time. I sing there."

I felt light headed and reached toward the wall to steady myself.

"She has a lovely voice," Elizabeth said. "Sings to the kids all the time."

I didn't trust myself to speak, so I stood there staring at Casey, my mouth open. She was so young, a kid practically, somewhere in her early twenties, beautiful enough to attract any man she wanted. What would she see in a fortysomething married man?

"I, um, I should get the kids home." She turned her back to me and pushed the stroller toward the elevators, leaving Elizabeth and Hallie behind.

I wanted to shout after her. Ask her if she knew Kyle. If she really was pregnant. If she were sure Kyle was the baby's father. If he was, had they really only slept together one time? Maybe if I weren't at work or maybe if Elizabeth's kids weren't there, I would have grilled her. Instead, I raced toward the bathroom, sank to my knees on the grimy floor, and dry heaved into the toilet.

Chapter 31

Sharon didn't notice me moping in her backyard. I stood by an azalea bush bursting with purple flowers, watching her push Noah on a swing. Her horizontally striped shirt accentuated the bump in her belly. By the end of summer, she'd be a mother of three.

"You're flying," she cooed as Noah's swing swayed back and forth.

As I watched my best friend play with her son, memories of us teetering on a seesaw in the playground when we were eight or nine flashed through my mind. Our mothers had sat on a bench as they watched us. Dana slept in a stroller that my mom rocked back and forth as she spoke to Mrs. Driscoll. Sharon and I were trying to break our record for the most times going up and down, which was 503. We'd made it to 442 when Dana woke up, screaming. "We have to go, Nikki," my mother called.

"A few more minutes," I said.

"Right now." My mom's tone made it clear not to argue. I hopped off the seesaw.

"Babies ruin everything," Sharon said. "I don't like them."

She had come so far since then, created her own family, while I was about to be on my own again.

"Hey, what are you doing here?" Sharon called out. "Everything okay?"

My shoulders slumped as I shuffled toward the swing set. "I just met her."

Sharon raised an eyebrow. "Who?"

"Casey. Kyle's . . ." I'd been about to say *slut* but stopped myself because of Noah.

"You met Casey?"

"She's my manager's nanny. She brought the kids into the office today. She's young."

"Wait—she's your boss's nanny? Are you sure?"

"I mean, I didn't ask her if she slept with Kyle, but she said she sings at the Penalty Box."

"That's just wack," Sharon said. "What are the chances?" Noah's swing had come to a stop, and she gave it a shove. "I guess in this rinky-dink town anything's possible."

I lowered myself into the swing next to Noah's. "She's like twenty-three or twenty-four."

Sharon blinked fast but didn't say anything. A few nights ago, when I'd told her Kyle cheated on me with a woman at the Penalty Box, she hadn't seemed surprised, and she didn't curse him out, like I had expected. Instead, there was a long, uncomfortable silence on the phone. Finally, she'd said, "I'm sorry."

I didn't hear sympathy, though. I heard an accusation. *What did you think was going to happen? I told you to give the baby quest a rest.*

That blame I thought I heard made me defensive. "We were working things out. Things were good."

"But they weren't for a long time."

"You're blaming me?"

"Of course not," she'd said. "I'm trying to understand how Kyle could do something like that. It's so out of character."

She was right. Until he'd hooked up with Casey, Kyle was the most dependable man on the planet. So dependable, in fact, that he was boring. At least that was what I thought when we first started dating. Past boyfriends hadn't been reliable. I loved trying to tame them more than I loved them. Kyle was different. He called when he said he was going to call. He meant what he said. He didn't have cheating in him, or so I thought.

"How did you find out?" she'd asked.

"He told me."

"Couldn't live with the guilt. That sounds like Kyle."

I'd let her think that. Didn't tell her the part about Kyle getting Casey pregnant. Not because I was trying to protect him but because I was trying to protect myself. If I told her, she would know that Kyle's and my fertility issues were all my fault.

"Have you heard from him?" she asked now.

"He called a few times. I haven't answered." I pushed off the ground to move the swing.

She stopped pushing Noah. "You can't ignore him, Nikki."

I pumped my legs, trying to go higher and higher, like I had when I was a kid. Maybe if I pumped hard enough, I could soar through the sky, reach heaven, and talk to my mother. I wondered what advice she would give me. When I was a kid, I'd fallen off a swing and landed facedown in the grass. I lay there crying until my mother reached me. She helped me up and hugged me. "No crying. You're tougher than this swing." *You will be fine without Kyle,* I imagined her saying now.

"I'm not ready to talk to him."

"You can get past this."

I flung my feet to the ground. The heels of my shoes dug into the lawn. Grass, dirt, and pebbles flew through the air as the swing came to a screeching stop. "She's pregnant."

Sharon's eyebrows knit together. "Who's preg—" Her mouth gaped. "Casey?"

"Yes, she's having Kyle's baby, or so she claims."

"Oh, Nikki. I'm so sorry," Sharon muttered.

I knew what that apology meant, and it made me feel worse. She realized I was the reason Kyle and I couldn't have a baby together, and she felt sorry for me. I might as well acknowledge it. "So I guess it's clear. I was the reason we couldn't have a baby."

"That's not true. The doctors told you that you could have children."

"Clearly they were wrong."

Sharon looked at me with the same expression she'd had when she came to tell me about my parents' accident. She knew there was nothing she could say that would make me feel better. No words could fix this. Neither of us said anything. Somewhere down the street, a lawn mower roared. In the woods behind Sharon's house, leaves rustled as squirrels jumped from one tree limb to another. Above us, birds sang. Soon Noah's heavy breathing joined the surrounding sounds. He had fallen asleep, the top of his head resting on the swing's chain. I hadn't gotten more than two hours of sleep a night since Kyle left, and I envied Noah at that moment, wishing I could fall asleep no matter how uncomfortable I was. Sharon picked him up and carried him inside.

I pumped my legs until my swing started swaying again. I leaned back and looked up as it picked up momentum. The bright-blue sky made me want to cry. How could it be so beautiful when life was so ugly?

Chapter 32

I walked up and down the aisles of Hannaford with a lone carton of strawberries in my shopping basket, trying to decide what I wanted to eat. Pasta, chicken, soup. Nothing looked appealing. I didn't like cooking just for myself and had been living on deli sandwiches and yogurt for the past few weeks. Salads, I thought, and made my way across the store back toward the produce.

As I placed a head of romaine lettuce into a plastic bag, I started to feel self-conscious, as if someone was watching me. I scanned the area. Over by the fruit, two of the hockey wives, Missy Sullivan and Janet Cummings, whispered to one another, sneaking furtive glances at me.

Did you hear? Kyle knocked up the young singer at the Penalty Box, I imagined Janet saying.

Well, Nikki couldn't give him a baby, imaginary Missy replied.

A tingling sensation started in my chest and crept up my neck. Gossip spread like wildfire through this town. Before long, people would be whispering and pointing at me or casting sympathetic looks wherever I went. I'd have to walk through downtown wearing sunglasses and a baseball cap to disguise myself.

I closed my eyes to clear my mind. When I opened them again, both women were flat-out staring at me. Missy waved and Janet smiled. They each made their way around the bins of apples toward me. I swallowed hard and took a step backward, bumping my hip against a shopping cart.

"Nikki, how are you?" Missy asked. Her eyes were too wide for the question to be sincere.

"We haven't seen you at the games lately," Janet said. "Is everything all right?" She placed her hand on my forearm, as if by making physical contact she would be someone I would want to confide in.

I moved my arm so that her hand fell away. "Everything's fine. I've just been busy with work."

Missy and Janet exchanged a look. I broadened my stance and held my basket up by my chest as if it were a shield protecting my heart, waiting for them to come right out and ask what they really wanted to know.

"Kyle has been playing some of his best hockey," Missy said. "He's been a real scoring machine."

Did she smirk, or was I imagining the double meaning?

"We're having ladies' night next Saturday at the Penalty Box. You should join us," Janet said.

At the mention of the pub where Kyle had met Casey, I slouched against the shelf, knocking a plastic carton of spinach to the floor with my elbow. *Are they baiting me, or am I being paranoid?*

Missy leaned toward me and looked over her shoulder as if she were confirming no one could overhear what she was about to say. "There's a singer there who's supposed to be really good."

My face burned in embarrassment, and I was grateful for inheriting my mother's olive complexion, which camouflaged blushing. Never mind disguising myself—I'd have to leave this tiny community. I scanned the produce area, looking for the fastest way to escape.

"We're meeting at seven," Janet said. "Having dinner first."

"I—I—I have plans Saturday," I said, faltering. Missy started to say something else, but I was on the move, fleeing for the exit, where I ditched my basket with the romaine lettuce and strawberries and sprinted toward the parking lot.

~

I was kneeling in front of the flower bed, pulling weeds, when I heard Dana's car rumbling up the street. The noise was so loud that I could hear it with my headphones on. Still, the sound made me smile. *She's worried about me*, I thought, *stopping by to make sure I'm doing okay without Kyle.* I turned off the true-crime podcast I was listening to and slipped my earbuds into my pocket as she pulled into the driveway.

She wore an old DeMarco's Diner T-shirt that was the same shade of green as her eyes. Seeing the logo for my parents' restaurant made me picture them there: my mom leading customers to a table; my dad in the back whipping up orders; Dana and me sitting at the counter with plates of ravioli in front of us, watching him.

Dana held up a take-out bag from Declan's. "I got you a Waldorf salad." As she made her way down the walkway, the smell of fried food filled the air.

"Why do I smell french fries?" I asked.

"I'm having a Hawaiian burger," she said.

At the kitchen table, she opened a Styrofoam container, revealing a heaping pile of shoestring fries and a burger on a toasted brioche roll. Teriyaki sauce and pineapple chunks oozed from its sides. My stomach hurt just looking at it.

"Someday, all that's going to catch up with you." It probably wouldn't. Dana had been thin her entire life. It wasn't fair. We had the same genes. I took a bite of my salad. The sweet taste of a grape filled my mouth. "Thanks for bringing this."

"I came to talk about Deeogee."

At the mention of the puppy, I remembered he was penned in on the deck. I leaped to my feet to let him in. He moped inside without looking at me and slouched down at Dana's side. Oliver was a different dog without Kyle here. He wagged his tail less, slept more, and stood guard by the front door, staring out the window, as if he were waiting for Kyle to return.

Dana bent down and petted his head. The simple gesture was the most attention she'd paid the dog since the day she'd dropped him off. "You're going to be a Cape puppy."

Her passive-aggressive way of broaching the subject again by talking to the dog instead of me infuriated me. My jaw tensed. I took a deep breath to relax myself and decided to play along. I reached for Oliver. "You'd rather stay right here in Stapleton, wouldn't you, boy?"

"No, I'd rather go to the beach." Dana spoke in a low voice.

I did a better impersonation of my dog. "I'm not going anywhere without Nikki."

I shot up from the table and stalked across the room toward Oliver's food. I tossed a biscuit in his direction, and he scrambled to catch it. "What's he going to do when you're at work all day?" I snapped.

"Same thing he does when you're at work. Stay home."

That's not true. He goes to work with Kyle. The words rattled through my mind before I remembered they were no longer true. Since Kyle's confession, I'd been leaving Oliver alone while I was at the office. The headache I'd had since running into the hockey wives early this morning worsened. I sank back into my chair and massaged my temples. "Can we talk about this later?"

Dana's expression softened, and she slowly nodded. I had the distinct impression that she'd just now remembered what I'd told her on our hike. "Of course. I'm sorry." She hadn't said much that day, letting Aunt Izzie do all the talking. I wondered now what my sister thought of Kyle's cheating.

She leaned across the table toward me. "How are you doing with . . ." She stopped and looked up at the ceiling. "With the whole Kyle thing."

The whole Kyle thing.

"It's humiliating. I ran into two of the hockey wives this morning. I'm sure they know."

"You're being paranoid," Dana said. Behind her, sunlight poured in through the kitchen window.

I squinted when I answered, telling her everything Missy and Janet had said at the grocery store. When I told her the part about how the women had invited me to ladies' night at the Penalty Box, where Casey would be singing, Dana's eyes twinkled with mischief. "We should definitely go," she said.

"Are you out of your mind?"

"It will give us a chance to watch this Casey person, see what she's all about."

"How's that going to help?"

"You said you can't believe Kyle's the father. We'll find out if she's sleeping with anyone else."

"How are we going to do that?"

Dana picked up her burger. Pineapple chunks slipped out the sides and fell to the table. I reached for one and popped it in my mouth. "I'll talk to her, Nikki. Believe me, I'll get it out of her."

"I can't be there with her when all those hockey wives are there."

"I'll go without you." Dana's entire body vibrated with excitement, and I knew I wouldn't be able to talk her out of it. I imagined her at the Penalty Box interrogating Casey between sets with Janet, Missy, and the other hockey wives gawking while they shoveled the pub's complimentary popcorn into their mouths.

"I want to be there," I said. "But let's go when the hockey wives aren't there."

Chapter 33

Ever since I could remember, the Penalty Box had been a fixture in Stapleton. For years tourists had seemed to view the rickety, narrow wooden stairway leading to the entrance as a no-trespassing sign, and the place was frequented strictly by locals. A few years ago, the bar had changed ownership. The new proprietors made updates to capitalize on the tourist business, offering happy hour, food specials, and live entertainment and bringing in a fancy chef from the city. Tourists now referred to the pub as one of Mount Stapleton's hidden jewels.

Tonight was the first time I'd been there since the ownership turnover. To me, the bar looked almost the same as before. The wobbly staircase still led to the entrance, but now a big sign at the bottom read **All Welcome**. Also, the wiry railing that didn't offer much protection had been replaced with thick wooden banisters. Inside, a citrus scent masked the old stench of cigarettes and stale beer, the rustic oak floors had been resurfaced, and antique skis hung from the ceiling. The biggest difference was the addition of a stage in the far-right corner. I wished it had never been built, because then Kyle might not have ever met Casey.

Dana paused in the restaurant's entrance and scanned the room. She pointed to the corner of the stage, where Casey crouched, pulling a guitar from a case. Her long auburn hair was pulled back in a ponytail, but a few strands fell across her face.

"Is that her?" Dana's voice was higher than usual.

"Don't point," I whispered, pushing Dana's hand down.

Casey straightened to her full height. Dressed in loose-fitting black pants and a baggy blue shirt, she looked as innocent as she had when she visited the office with Elizabeth's kids.

"She really is young," Dana said, marching across the almost empty room toward Casey.

Paralyzed with fear, I stayed rooted to the spot where I'd entered. Coming here had been a bad idea, especially with Dana. Was she going to make a scene? Confront Casey? A framed poster of the Bruins' mascot hung on the wall next to me. Seeing it made me shiver. That damn bear looked vicious, like he was getting ready to pounce on me—again.

Dana plopped herself down at the table closest to the stage and motioned for me to join her. I didn't want to sit so close to Casey, but then again, this was why we'd come: to get to know her, to find out if there was anyone else she was sleeping with. There had to be. Slowly I made my way toward Dana, who watched Casey's every move. Luckily Casey had her back to my sister and didn't notice. I chose the chair kitty corner to the stage so that Casey would only be able to see my profile when she turned around.

"Not at all what I was expecting," Dana said.

"Shh." I hushed Dana and stole a glance at Casey to make sure she didn't hear Dana. Casey still had her back to us as she fiddled with a speaker.

"Like she would know what I'm talking about?" Dana said. "Chill."

"What were you expecting?"

Dana's eyes met mine. "A younger version of you, I guess."

My stomach twisted, and I blinked back tears. Before IVF and Dr. Evans telling me that newborns were usually adopted by younger couples, I'd considered myself old. Clearly Casey was a lot younger—young enough to get pregnant without any medical help.

The waiter, a muscular White guy with dreadlocks and a do-rag, bopped over to take our drink order.

Dana smiled, a wicked grin. "Redheaded Sluts for both of us." She caught my eye and tilted her head toward Casey, who was tuning her guitar.

I assumed Dana had made up that name and felt my face heating up at the veiled reference to Casey. I waited for the server to ask what the drink was. Instead he pumped his fist. "You ladies are out to have a good time tonight. That's what I like to see."

"It's a real drink?" I asked Dana after he left.

"A shot with peach schnapps, Jägermeister, and cranberry juice," she explained. "A perfect choice for our mission tonight."

"What is our mission tonight?"

"We're just going to keep an eye on her. See if there's any guy here who could be her boyfriend."

Sweat dripped down my back. "Please don't make a scene." Dana was so unpredictable. How had I let her talk me into coming here? "We should leave."

"You can call an Uber. I'm staying."

The waiter returned with our drinks. Dana ordered potato skins. "To the redheaded slut," she said. "May she be sleeping with many men." She clanked her glass against mine and laughed.

Cringing, I sneaked a look at the stage, but Casey was no longer there. Dana downed her shot in one swallow while I sipped mine.

"Haven't you ever done a shot before?" she asked.

"Not recently."

"Let's go. Toss it back."

I ignored her and continued to sip. "You're embarrassing me," she said.

When our potato skins arrived, Dana ordered another round of drinks, even though I still hadn't finished my first. By the time the waiter returned, the pub had filled up, and only a few tables remained empty.

Casey settled in behind the microphone. "I'm Casey Flanagan," she said. "Thank y'all for coming out to see me." She spoke with a drawl she hadn't had when I met her in the office a few weeks ago. This comforted me because the fact that she could be deceitful about an accent made me think she would have no trouble lying about who the father of her baby was.

She began her set with "Vice," a Miranda Lambert song. As I watched her, I tried to imagine what had happened the night Kyle met her. Had he approached her, or had she come on to him? On stage, she seamlessly moved from one song to the next, covering Kacey Musgraves, Sara Evans, and Carly Pearce. As she sang, she gyrated her hips, arched her back, and ran a hand across her chest. I decided she'd initiated things, and I hated her a little more.

Dana hadn't said a word since Casey began performing. With a big grin on her face, my sister sang along, seemingly oblivious that I was sitting next to her. When she caught me staring at her, her lips straightened. "She's super talented," she said.

Traitor, I thought as my chest tightened. I picked up the second shot, which until this point I hadn't touched. Casey finished the song, and the pub exploded with thunderous applause. I imagined Kyle here, dressed in his hockey shirt, leaping out of his seat to cheer her on. I tossed back my shot with one swallow.

Dana stared at me with a goofy grin. "Attagirl," she said.

The alcohol traveled down my throat, but about halfway down, it reversed course and came back up. I swallowed it down again and broke out in a coughing fit. At some point the waiter must have dropped off water, because Dana pushed a glass across the table toward me. I gulped large sips while Casey played the opening notes of "A Little Dive Bar in Dahlonega," by Ashley McBryde, a song that until that moment I'd liked but would always associate with Casey now.

Before Casey reached the end of the song, we made eye contact. She smiled and nodded. I thought about the way we had connected over Elizabeth in the office before I'd found out who Casey was. She was someone I would have liked in any other circumstance. By the time she finished her set, I had downed three shots. My vision blurred, my speech slowed, and sweat slicked my forehead. After a standing ovation, Casey hopped down from the stage and approached our table.

"Nikki, right? You work with Elizabeth?" She scrunched her nose at the mention of my manager.

Slouching in my chair, I cocked my head and narrowed my eyes, pretending to try to place her.

"We met last week," she said.

"Oh, right, Elizabeth's nanny." I sounded like I had a lisp.

"Redheaded slut," Dana hissed.

Instantly sober, I jolted upright and kicked Dana under the table. What the hell was she doing?

"Excuse me," Casey said. She and my sister locked eyes.

I shredded my napkin while they battled it out in a staring contest. This was not how I wanted tonight to go down.

Dana grinned. "It's what we're drinking. Join us." She summoned the waiter. "I'm Dana. Nikki's sister." She extended her hand toward Casey.

Casey's fists remained clenched, and the vertical furrow between her eyebrows remained.

"What are you doing in Stapleton, girl? Why aren't you in Nashville? You killed it up there," Dana said, laying it on thick.

It worked. Casey unclenched. "Thanks."

Dana used her feet to kick out a chair. Casey hesitated before sitting.

The waiter finally made it to our table. He caressed Casey's shoulder. "You rocked the joint tonight."

"I did, didn't I?" Casey beamed.

"Another round," Dana said. "One for the star too."

"No, no," Casey said.

"Oh, come on," Dana said. "Have one drink with us. A beer?"

"Ginger ale." Casey's hand dropped to her abdomen.

My stomach spasmed. She was protecting Kyle's baby. I jumped to my feet, wanting to flee.

"You okay?" Dana asked.

"Be right back." I wove my way across the bar to the restroom. A line snaked out the door down a long, narrow hallway. I took my place at the end. Most of the women waiting in front of me were almost half my age, like Casey. The contents in my stomach swirled. What the hell was I doing here? I wished I were home. Did it even matter if Kyle was the father? He'd slept with her.

When I got back to the table, Casey and Dana were laughing. "We're talking about the lack of good men in Stapleton," Dana said. "I just asked Casey if there are any cute, normal guys who come in here."

I eyed my sister, willing her to stop. I wanted to leave.

"Nikki's happily married. She has no idea," Dana said.

"We should go. It's getting late."

"I just ordered another drink," Dana said.

My leg bounced up and down under the table.

Dana turned back to Casey. "There must be some cute guys who come in here."

"There is this group of hockey players."

My throat went dry. I reached for my water. Casey had a dreamy look. She swirled the ice in her drink with a straw.

"One of them, he's older, but there's something so . . . I don't know." She paused and stared down into her glass. When she looked up again, she had a sultry grin on her face. "Something so scrumptious about him." Her cheeks reddened. "Me and the bartender call him Blake because he looks like Blake Shelton."

I picked up my fork, debating whether to stab Casey in the eye with it.

Dana twisted her mouth. "Did you say 'scrumptious'?"

"I just mean he's sexy," Casey said. "A man and not a boy like most guys my age."

I massaged my temples. "Are you dating him?" My voice quivered.

Dana shot me a warning look.

Casey bit down on her lip, and her eyes glazed over. "No. I—no. I shouldn't have even brought him up."

"You have a crush on him," Dana said.

Casey stood. "It's complicated."

"Complicated how?" I asked.

"I really have to go. It was nice talking to you both."

As she disappeared into a room behind the stage, I had a sick feeling that she was telling the truth about Kyle being the father of her baby.

Chapter 34

Oliver's whining woke me. He stood next to the bed with his two back legs on the ground and his front paws on the mattress, nudging me with his cold, wet nose. My head throbbed, and a sour taste filled my mouth. The putrid stench of sweat and alcohol filled the air.

Footsteps raced down the hall toward me. *Who's here? Kyle?* I shot up. The room spun. I closed my eyes, hoping the spinning would stop. It didn't.

Dana burst into the room. "Deeogee, get over here."

"What are you doing here?" My voice was hoarse.

Dana wrinkled her nose when she looked at me. "You look like shit. Get some sleep. I'll take him out." She grabbed the dog by his collar and rushed out the door, closing it behind her.

Blurry images came back to me: the red drinks; watching Casey sing; Casey sitting at our table, sipping a ginger ale with a protective hand resting on her abdomen; Casey talking about the guy she was into, an older man who looked like Blake Shelton. I tried to swallow, but my mouth was bone dry. I swung my legs over the side of the bed and stumbled toward the bathroom.

As I filled my glass with water, the image that stared back in the mirror terrified me. The whites of my eyes glowed neon red. Mascara streaked down my face, and a wrinkled, messy version of the blouse I'd worn yesterday hung from my body. What was I thinking, going to the Penalty Box last night? Why had I talked to Casey? I gulped from my cup. My stomach lurched as soon as the water hit it. I sank to my knees in front of the toilet and vomited. I stayed on the floor with my head resting against the edge of the toilet bowl until I felt hands sliding under my underarms and lifting me to my feet.

"You're in bad shape," Dana said. "You need to go back to bed."

I rotated my head to get a better look at her. The slight movement caused another wave of nausea to roll over me. I waited for it to pass. Dana curled her arm around my waist and guided me toward my bedroom. Her eyes were clear, and her skin radiated. The only thing off about her was her clothing. She wore a pair of my sweatpants, which fit her like capris, and one of Kyle's T-shirts with that damn Bruins mascot. God, how I hated that bear.

"Why aren't you hungover?" I asked.

"Hangovers are for amateurs."

If I hadn't felt so awful, I would have been worried about how much she drank to have such a high tolerance. My bed seemed a mile off the ground. I used all my strength to climb into it. "Casey's so young," I said.

Dana lifted the sheet and blanket over me. "She is." A hint of sadness tinged her voice. "Get some sleep."

Hours later, muffled shouts drifting up through the floorboards woke me. I lay perfectly still, trying to listen. "Don't go up there," Dana said.

"It's my house." A set of footsteps marched up the stairs.

"Not for long," Dana hissed. "Nikki will get it in the divorce, so don't get any ideas about living here with your baby mama."

I threw the covers off and scrambled into the bathroom, not wanting Kyle to see me in my current state. I eyed the window, wondering if I could jump. Maybe the boxwood bushes would break my fall. Probably not. I'd splatter on the flagstone patio. I imagined tomorrow's headline on the front page of the *Stapleton View*: *Woman Leaps to Death Trying to Avoid Her Cheating Husband.*

"Nikki." Kyle's voice called through the door.

"She has nothing to say to you," Dana said.

"We need to talk," Kyle said.

I turned on the shower to drown out their words. An urge to wash away last night and all that had happened during the past few months overwhelmed me. I tore off my clothes and jumped under the streaming water. I scrubbed my skin until it turned a fleshy red. Steam filled the room, loosening my muscles. I breathed in the rich scent of vanilla from my soap and felt my thoughts slowing.

By the time I dressed, the house was quiet. Downstairs, there was no sign of Kyle, Dana, or Oliver. As I poured a glass of seltzer, a squeaking sound came from the deck. Kyle slumped in an Adirondack chair, staring out at the mountains. I watched him through the screen door without saying anything. My heart ached. I so badly wanted to sit beside him, for things to be right between us, to have never tried IVF. Before everything went bad, we used to sit out there together every night, holding hands and watching the sun set or searching for shooting stars. When had we stopped doing that? Sometime after the first cycle. If only I had been able to get pregnant, we wouldn't be in this mess. I shook my head to clear my thoughts.

"I met Casey," I said through the screen door.

Kyle flinched at the sound of my voice. "Dana told me you went to the Penalty Box." He kept his back to me. "I don't understand why you went there."

"Did you know she works for my new boss? I actually met her at the office."

He swiveled so that he faced me. I swallowed hard. His hair, usually cropped close to his head, curled over his ears. Golden highlights and a deep tan made it clear he'd been working outdoors the past few weeks. Several days of stubble blanketed his face. "He looks like Blake Shelton," I remembered Casey saying. I'd never seen the resemblance before, but this unkempt version of my husband did remind me of the country music star.

Kyle set his jaw and studied me with a steady gaze. "She works for Elizabeth?"

I pushed the door open and stepped outside. The bright sunlight hurt my eyes. I squinted and tented my hand on my forehead. "She's Elizabeth's nanny. Came in with the kids last week."

His eyebrows furrowed together, and he turned back toward the mountain. "I didn't know."

"She's really young."

He hung his head, but he said nothing.

I eased into the chair next to him. "How did it happen?"

Kyle sighed. "Does it matter?"

"Yes, it does."

A rabbit scurried across the lawn as a hawk circled above. "Me and the guys. We always went to the Box after hockey, and her and I just started talking one night, and then every time I went there, she was so happy to see me." He scrubbed his hand over his jawline. "For the past two years, I'd been thinking of myself as a failure because I couldn't get you pregnant, and she had this way of looking at me like I was a hero. Because I scored a few goals." He shook his head. "Honestly, she provided an ego boost when I needed it."

A yellow jacket landed on the arm of my chair. I leaned away from it, toward Kyle.

"That day I found out you lied about the bonus. I was out of my mind with anger. Felt so betrayed. Casey sat down with us after her set and . . ."

I held up my hand, not wanting to hear any more. "I was out of my mind with worry that night, thinking something awful happened to you."

"I know. I felt so bad. I couldn't face you. That's why I left."

The insect crawled toward the backrest. I stood, moving away before it stung me, and looked down on Kyle. "The entire time you were gone, I blamed myself for driving you away, but what you did was worse."

I stepped toward the door, but Kyle grabbed me by the wrist. "Can we get past this?" His voice broke.

"I don't know."

"Can we try?"

"What about the baby?" Months ago, he had asked me to choose between him and a baby. Would I ask the same of him?

The yellow jacket circled my head. Kyle stood and shooed it away. "We can raise him or her together."

"You're asking me to raise a baby you had with another woman."

He inched close to me, but I stepped backward to create space between us. "I know we would have never planned it this way, but we've wanted a baby for so long."

I heard Oliver scampering across the kitchen floor. His head popped up in the door, and a second later Dana stood behind him, holding his leash. "Everything okay?" she asked.

Kyle brushed by me on his way inside. "I need to get more clothes. We'll finish this conversation another time."

After he left, Dana, Oliver, and I sat out on the deck. "What are you going to do?" she asked.

I stared off at Mount Stapleton as if it might have an answer. "I have no idea." I bent down to pat Oliver.

Dana watched for a few minutes, a pained expression on her face. "This probably isn't the best time to bring this up," she said. "But I'm leaving next week, and I'm taking Deeogee with me."

Chapter 35

As I carried the mail up my driveway, Dana pulled in, her entire life packed into her rusted-out Toyota Corolla. Duffel bags, cardboard boxes, coolers, and grocery bags crammed into the back seat obstructed the view out the rear window.

"You can't make a four-hour drive without being able to see out the back," I said. Sweat dripped down my neck as the hot sun beat down on me.

"Don't start, Nikki." She remained behind the steering wheel, pressing buttons on her phone.

I leaned into the driver's window. "Where's Oliver going to sit?"

Dana pointed to the empty passenger seat. Cases of water, twelve-packs of seltzer, and handles of rum and vodka cluttered the floor space below it.

I straightened. "He likes to lie down in the back seat."

"He'll be fine." She swung her legs out the door and stood. We faced each other without speaking. She looked healthy and fit in a purple sleeveless shirt and tan shorts that showcased her lean, muscular limbs. I envied her getting away from this town for the summer. Except for Aunt Izzie and me, Dana had no ties here. She didn't have to come back if she didn't want to. I thought about running into the house, packing my stuff, and following her. I pictured myself driving over the Bourne Bridge, living in a cottage on the beach, far away from all the gossip about me, Kyle, and Casey. A feeling of tranquility came over me that I hadn't felt since Kyle confessed his transgression.

I looked down at the stack of mail in my hand, the top envelope a bill from the IVF clinic. My mountain of debt and job at the magazine that helped chip away at it kept me rooted to Stapleton. Kyle and I would need years, decades even, to pay off all we owed. I couldn't go anywhere.

"Where's Deeogee? Is he ready?" Dana asked.

No, he's not ready. I'm not ready, I wanted to scream at her. "Are you sure you want to take him? Why not wait until fall, when you come back to Stapleton?"

"Come and visit. Anytime." She strolled up the walkway and into my house while I stayed planted to the pavement next to her car with the hot sun scorching the top of my head. I tried to take a calming breath, but the humidity made the air heavy, almost impossible to breathe.

The front screen squeaked open. An unleashed Oliver scampered down the walkway. Dana followed behind, carrying the box I had packed for him.

I swallowed down the lump in my throat.

Dana pulled open the passenger door. Usually, Oliver leaped right into my car, but he plopped down next to me, his tongue hanging from his mouth. "Come here, boy," Dana urged.

Oliver nudged my hand, but I didn't have the energy to move my arm to pet him.

"Come on, Deeogee. Get in the car," Dana said. The dog nudged me harder. Dana elbowed me. "Tell him to get in."

I sank to my knees, kneeling so that I could hug him. "Goodbye, buddy." He was still damp from the bath I had given him, and he smelled like the oatmeal shampoo I had used to wash him. He curled his leg around my shin as if he were trying to hug me back.

Dana scooped him up and deposited him in the passenger seat. Oliver whimpered as she slammed the door. He jumped up so that his front legs rested against the window. His nose twitched.

"I love you, little guy." My voice cracked.

Dana pulled me into an embrace. "Oh, Nikki, I didn't realize how attached to him you are." My heart leaped; I was sure she wouldn't take him now that she understood how much the little red fur ball meant to me. "I'll call Marie. See when her next litter is due so you can get a puppy of your own, or better yet, you can swing by the rescue center. There are plenty of dogs who need love and a good home."

I wasn't going to explain this to her again. She would never understand. "Promise you'll take good care of him."

"Count on it."

"Where's his water bowl for the ride? Biscuits? Does he have a chew toy?"

"I've got it covered." Dana slid into the driver's seat, and the car roared to life.

"You need to stop on the way. Walk him. Let him go to the bathroom. Get some . . ."

Dana's window shot up before I finished speaking, and the Corolla backed out of the driveway. *She'll call me within a week to come and get him,* I thought.

Oliver circled in his seat, yelping. I imagined he was calling out to me. *Don't let her take me.* I stood where I was, tears rolling down my face, watching until they disappeared from view.

～

More than a week after Dana left for the Cape with Oliver, I still wasn't used to the silence of the house. When I came home from work, I expected him to leap up on me at the front door and bathe my face in soggy dog kisses. Every time I entered the kitchen, I waited to hear him trotting down the hallway after me. At bedtime, I listened for the tap, tap, tap of his nails on the hardwood behind me. Before I went to sleep, I texted Dana, asking her to send pictures, and Oliver's furry little red face was always the last thing I looked at before falling asleep.

Sometimes I didn't know whom I missed more, the dog or Kyle. Their absences fed off each other, making my loneliness grow.

Aunt Izzie took pity on me and invited me to her house for dinner on a hot Thursday night in July, a few weeks after Dana had left. We sat at the table on her deck surrounded by her flower beds, which were blooming with orange daylilies, white daisies, and yellow sunflowers. I thought back to the day Dana and I had carried the table outside. Back then, spring had still been fighting to knock out winter, Aunt Izzie's yard lacked color, and Kyle and I were in a good place. At least I'd thought we were.

"So much has changed since Dana and I set the furniture up out here back in the spring," I said.

Aunt Izzie scooped a heap of salad out of the serving bowl and transferred it to her plate. A cherry tomato rolled onto the table. I caught it as it fell over the edge.

"Good catch," Aunt Izzie said. "Have you spoken to Kyle?"

"Not since before Dana left."

"You can't go on in limbo. You two need to figure out how you're going to move past this bump."

Bump. Her word choice infuriated me. It minimized what Kyle had done. I imagined venting to my sister and Dana making a joke. *It is a bump. A belly bump.*

"Do you want to work things out, save your marriage?" Aunt Izzie pointed to the bottle of balsamic. "Pass that to me."

"I just don't see how I can with the baby."

"The baby will be the easy part. You'll fall in love with it." I didn't know if I was more surprised by what she said or by the confidence with which she said it.

"I'm afraid I'll resent the baby." I hated admitting this, but it was the truth.

"The poor baby didn't do anything."

"No, but it will be a constant reminder of what Kyle did."

"Only if you let it."

"How could it not be?"

Aunt Izzie sighed.

"Also, I'll be an outsider in my own house."

Aunt Izzie laid her fork down on her plate. "Whatever do you mean?"

"Kyle will always have a more meaningful connection because he and the baby share the same blood."

Aunt Izzie bit down on her lip. Otherwise, she didn't move.

"What?" I asked.

"What if you change the way you think about this?"

"What do you mean?"

"Think about how much you'll love the baby and how much she or he will love you. Focus on the bond the two of you will make. I'd be willing to bet your connection will be equally as strong as Kyle's." She paused and looked off toward the mountains. I had the sense that she was weighing her next words. "You don't need to have the same blood to have a strong bond."

Chapter 36

I scrolled with my right hand and reached for my ringing phone with my left. "I'm back," a deep, booming voice said. *Hank.* "Have you given any thought to what we talked about before I left? Do you want to know what happened when I came back to Stapleton?" I hadn't heard from him in so long I'd assumed he'd forgotten all about the conversation he wanted to have with me. That his call came the day after my dinner with Aunt Izzie didn't come as a surprise.

"It's not really my business."

Hank sighed. "I want to tell you."

My stomach twisted. Why was he so intent on telling me this story? "It's not a good time. Things are crazy."

Hank didn't say anything. I heard the sound of gushing air and a door closing. "Your aunt told me about what's going on with Kyle. I'm sorry, Nikki."

My grip on the phone tightened, and I jumped to my feet. "She told you?"

"She's worried about you."

"So worried that she's helping to fuel the gossip."

"It's not like that," Hank said. "She thought it might help you to talk to me."

I remembered that night back in March when Kyle and I had gone to the restaurant, the odd way Hank had spoken to Kyle and Kyle's nervous reaction. *They have some good live entertainment. That girl, she can really sing. What's her name? I'll keep an eye out for you . . .* "You knew."

Hank cleared his throat. "I suspected."

My face felt like it was on fire. "Am I the only one who didn't know?"

"Why don't you come over for dinner tomorrow. We'll talk."

"No offense, but you're the last person I'd want to talk to about this." The words flew from my mouth, and I immediately regretted them. I was mad at Aunt Izzie for telling him and taking it out on him. "I'm sorry. I just wish my aunt hadn't said anything."

"I've known you since you were a kid, Nikki. I've helped you through rough patches before. I might be able to offer advice now. At the very least, I can be a sounding board."

For a split second, I felt as if I were talking to the old Uncle Hank, the one who used to make me and Dana laugh at the diner, the man who was our rock in the days immediately after my parents' accident.

"If you don't want to come to the house, stop by the restaurant."

The restaurant. Just like that, he was back to being the man who'd reneged on his promise to preserve my parents' legacy.

My computer pinged with a new email, Elizabeth reminding me that the article I was working on was due tonight.

"I have to run," I said. "I'm working on deadline."

∼

As I left work that night, my phone vibrated with a text from Dana. It was a picture of Oliver perched high in a lifeguard chair overlooking the Atlantic Ocean, a bright-orange life vest strapped around his chest and a crowd of kids gathered below him. Dana's message read: **Deeogee's fast become the favorite lifeguard on the National Seashore.**

I smiled at the image, but at the same time, my shoulders tightened. *How long has he been out in the hot sun? Does he have water? Would he hurt himself if he jumped off the chair?*

A car door slammed, and I looked up from my phone. Kyle stood next to his Jeep, his hands jammed into the pockets of his jeans. Seeing him at my office surprised me so much that I started to smile. The slight uptick of the corners of my lips gave him all the encouragement he needed. He strode toward me with a determined expression until we came face to face at the bottom of the stairs. He'd had his hair cut since I'd seen him last, and the stubble around his mouth had grown into a mustache and goatee. I'd never seen him with facial hair. I didn't like it. I imagined he'd grown it because he thought it made him look younger. It didn't. The gray specks gave away his age.

"You're working late," he said.

"How long have you been waiting out here?"

He shrugged. "Forty-five minutes, an hour."

Annoyance replaced the momentary joy I had felt at seeing him. How could he think showing up at my place of employment was a good idea? "You shouldn't be here."

"I was hoping we could grab something to eat and talk."

I pictured us walking into a restaurant and all the other customers whispering to one another, pointing at us, and eavesdropping as we discussed how we would deal with Kyle's illegitimate child. "That's not a good idea."

"We need to talk, Nikki." The unfamiliar pleading in his voice made me soften toward him.

"Another time. I've had a long day." I stepped toward my car, but Kyle shuffled to the right, blocking me from reaching the driver's door.

"It's been a few months. You can't ignore me forever."

Elizabeth's Range Rover turned in to the parking lot. My brain did gymnastics, trying to make sense of this. Elizabeth had been sitting in her office, talking on the phone, when I left. Who was driving her car? *Oh no.* My hands started to shake. I had to get out of there.

Elizabeth's vehicle pulled into a spot a few spaces in front of where Kyle and I stood. There were footsteps on the stairs behind us and then

Elizabeth's voice. "The story on the bike shop needs to be rewritten and on my desk by the end of the day tomorrow," she said.

The door to the Range Rover clicked open. Casey stepped out, humming along to a Zac Brown song on the radio. She smiled at me, but her smile faded as her eyes landed on Kyle. Her entire body went still.

Kyle rotated his head side to side as if he were trying to work out a crick in his neck.

Elizabeth reached the spot on the pavement where Kyle and I stood. She extended her hand toward him. "Elizabeth Sanders."

He blinked twice and swallowed hard. "Kyle Sebastian."

"I'm sorry I kept Nikki working so late," she said.

"It's fine," Kyle said, his voice so soft that Elizabeth leaned toward him.

As they spoke, Casey tiptoed her way around the back of the Range Rover toward the passenger side. She'd just about made it there when Elizabeth called out to her. "Casey, I have an email I need to answer, so you can drive back to the house."

Casey froze and looked toward us. Her yellow short-sleeved tunic hung loosely over her belly. Seeing her wearing that baggy shirt to conceal her baby bump made her pregnancy real to me in a way it hadn't been before. My insides twisted into a knot.

Still talking to Casey, Elizabeth nodded in my direction. "You remember Nikki, and this is her husband, Kyle."

Casey's cheeks burned a crimson red. "Your husband?" Her chin trembled.

I saw her then for who she really was, not a villain but a young, vulnerable girl who hadn't thought about the consequences of her actions.

Our eyes locked. She crossed her arms over her stomach and looked away. "I didn't know," she said. Her knees went weak, and she crumpled to the pavement.

Elizabeth, Kyle, and I raced toward her. "I didn't know," Casey repeated, burying her head in her hands. "I didn't know."

Kyle reached down to help her up, but she batted his arm away. "Leave me alone."

He stepped away from her without saying anything.

"Are you okay?" I asked Casey.

She lifted herself from the ground. Her wet eyes met mine. "I'm sorry. Truly sorry."

My chest burned, and my head swam. It was so much easier thinking of Casey as a shameless home-wrecker and not as a victim whose life had been thrown wildly off course by a single reckless decision. I looked away from her toward the mountains. They seemed to be creeping closer, pinning me in this tiny parking lot with Casey, Kyle, and Elizabeth.

"What's going on here?" Elizabeth asked.

I wished the pavement would open and swallow me whole.

"Casey? Nikki? Is there a problem?"

She was going to find out. The entire office would know. The entire town would know. We'd be the talk of the town, more than we already were.

A baby's teary sobs broke the silence. For a moment, I imagined the sound came from Casey and Kyle's unborn child, sensing the mess he or she would be born into.

"Mommy? Casey?" a tiny voice called.

Elizabeth's head snapped toward the back passenger window of the Range Rover. "I need to get Hallie and Danvers home," she said. Casey shuffled toward the driver's side. Elizabeth shook her head and pointed to the passenger door. "I'll drive." She turned to me. "I'll see you tomorrow."

Instead of answering, I tried to figure out how I would ever face her again.

Chapter 37

"You'll never believe what happened when I left work today." Still keyed up from the encounter with Kyle and Casey in the parking lot, I paced the length of my deck, holding my cell phone to my ear and wishing I could remember where I had put my headphones.

On the other end of the line, voices murmured and a can snapped open before Dana spoke. "No idea." She made a loud gulping sound.

"What are you drinking?"

"Seltzer," Dana said. "It may or may not be spiked."

I sank into one of the chairs that faced west. The sun had already dipped behind the mountains, leaving a burnt-orange glow in its place. "I'm betting it's spiked."

"You would be correct." She gulped again. "Cape Cod cranberry—it's delicious." The voices in the background grew louder, and someone started to play a guitar.

"Is this a bad time?"

"We have people over."

I pictured a smiling, tanned Dana in a living room crowded with happy people, celebrating summer. Then I thought about me helping Kyle's distressed mistress to her feet in my employer's parking lot and coming home to an empty house. For the first time that I could remember, I envied my sister's carefree life.

"Hold on," Dana said. There was a whooshing noise and the sound of a door banging shut. "I'm outside now. Tell me what happened."

Now I imagined her sitting how I was, alone on a deck in an Adirondack chair. I wished I hadn't pulled her away from her friends to complain about my miserable existence. "Why don't you call me after everyone's gone."

Dana laughed. "There are always people here. Just tell me what happened."

"Is Oliver outside with you?"

The phone clicked before Dana answered. "I just put you on speaker. Say something to him."

If Oliver still lived with me, he would be sitting in front of me with a paw on my thigh and his tongue hanging out of his mouth. I could almost feel his hot dog breath on my leg. "I miss you, little buddy." My chest burned as I spoke the words.

"He says he misses you too. Now, tell me what happened."

"Am I off speaker?"

"No, you're on Instagram Live," Dana deadpanned.

"Funny." I inhaled sharply before launching into the story of what had happened when I left work today.

As I spoke, Dana's breathing grew louder. From time to time she gasped, but she refrained from saying anything until I finished.

"That asshole! He has no right to just show up at the magazine after what he did."

My phone vibrated in my hand. For a second, I thought the force of Dana's angry words had caused the vibration, but there was an incoming text from Elizabeth.

My throat went dry as I read her words. I'd been holding out hope that Casey would be too ashamed to tell Elizabeth that Kyle was the baby's father, but clearly Casey had told her.

"Great," I said. "Just got a text from my boss. She knows what happened between Kyle and Casey."

"What did the text say?" Dana asked. "'Hey, I heard your cheating, no-good husband knocked up my kids' nanny.'"

"It said, 'Just checking to see if you're okay?'"

"And from that you think she knows what happened?" Dana laughed.

Her infectious giggle had the same effect on me as a good massage. My back muscles, which had been wound tight since seeing Kyle, all relaxed. "Why else would she be checking on me? She's never texted me before."

"First off, my version of the text is much more interesting. Second, she might not know, but even if she does, you can hold your head high. You didn't do anything wrong. Kyle did."

I twisted my wedding ring, thinking about the vows Kyle and I had made the day he slid it on my finger. "I still can't believe he cheated."

Dana sighed. "One of my roommates, her mom is a hotshot attorney at a big family law practice. She specializes in divorce. I'll text you her contact info."

My back felt tight again. "I'm not sure . . ."

"You don't have to decide anything now," Dana said. "But it won't hurt to know how to contact her if you want to later."

"I feel like it's partially my fault. Like I pushed him to it."

"Unless you pushed him on top of Casey and told him to . . ." Her voice trailed off. The line was silent for a few seconds. "It's not even the tiniest bit your fault, Nikki. I would tell you if it were."

I felt myself smile because I knew she would. Instead of blaming myself, maybe I had to accept that this was Kyle's doing and try to find a way to forgive him.

There was a commotion on Dana's end, and then someone said, "There you are."

"I should let you get back to the party. Thanks for listening."

"Am I a better listener than Sharon?" Dana laughed, but I cringed, feeling guilty for keeping so much from her through the years. "Don't answer that," she said. "I was joking."

After we said goodbye, I stayed outside, watching fireflies light up the dark sky and listening to the crickets chirp. I felt as if they were trying to tell me something, but I had no idea what, just like I had no idea how to forgive Kyle.

Chapter 38

The scent of coffee became stronger as I walked down the hall toward the conference room. My coworkers all stood around a credenza in the back corner with bagels and a tub of cream cheese set up on top of it. The sound of their laughter bounced off the walls.

"Elizabeth brought breakfast." Page tossed a crumb-ridden paper plate into the trash. "Why do you think she's being nice to us?"

Because she feels sorry for me.

Today was the first time in the five months that Elizabeth had worked at the magazine that she'd done something nice for the staff. She sat at the head of the table, scrolling through her phone. I couldn't help but think her kindness was directed at me because Casey had told her that Kyle was the father of the baby.

Elizabeth looked up from her phone and scanned the room. When she spotted me, her eyebrows rose slightly, and she nodded. *I'm right. She knows.* I reached for the wall to steady myself, wishing it would slide open to reveal a secret tunnel leading far away from Stapleton.

Elizabeth cleared her throat. "This was a good way to start the day, but we have lots to do. Let's all get to work."

One by one, my coworkers filed past her on the way out of the room. As I got closer to the exit, Elizabeth tapped my shoulder. "Can I talk with you for a moment?" Excuses floated through my head. *I'm on deadline. I have a dentist appointment. I have to bring my car to the shop.*

Sooner or later, though, I'd have to face her, so I decided to get it over with. She pointed to the chair next to her. "Have a seat."

Page stood statue-like in the hallway, looking back at me. She thought I was in trouble. I wished I were.

Elizabeth reached behind her and pushed the door closed. We were alone. "I'm not going to beat around the bush," she said. "Casey told me everything."

I slumped in my seat as if I'd been shot.

"It's none of my business. But I wanted to see how you're doing and tell you I'm here if you need to talk."

Other than discussing my parents' restaurant on the day we'd driven to Pendleton 88 for Hank's interview, Elizabeth and I had never talked about anything personal. Why did she think I'd confide in her now?

"Thank you. I'm good."

She leaned toward me and spoke in a low voice. "I have some experience being caught up in scandals not of my own making."

Of course I wanted to ask her about her experience, but then she'd expect me to confide in her. I didn't want to do that. I looked away from her toward the whiteboard. Someone had used it to brainstorm advertorial ideas. I read through the list of ideas: *New zipline park, downtown painting place (Sip and Strokes?), bed and breakfast (leaf peeping season).*

"My husband." She stopped and cleared her throat. "My ex-husband. Still not used to saying that. He was the mastermind of a Ponzi scheme. Stole from all our friends. They all thought I was involved."

My gaze shot back to her. Even after confessing this, she looked as confident as ever, with her shoulders back and chin high.

"It's how I ended up here."

"I'm sorry." My words seemed inadequate.

"I tell you this only because I know what it's like to be the talk of the town, fodder for gossip."

"You moved to get away from it." I tried to think where I could go. I'd lived here my entire life.

She nodded. "Can't outrun it, though."

"What do you mean?"

"Social media follows you everywhere."

I rarely used Facebook and didn't have a Twitter or Instagram account.

"You can't control what people say, Nikki, only the way you react to it."

"Are people talking? Outside of Casey, have you heard things, seen things on Facebook?"

"I haven't heard anything yet, but it's only a matter of time."

∼

Back in my office, my desk phone blinked, indicating I had a voice mail. The first message was a hang-up from a restricted number. In the second, the owner of the bike shop asked when the photographer would stop by. In the third message, also from a restricted number, I heard wind noise in the background, but again no one spoke. I set down the phone and started to work on my article. Not five minutes later the phone rang with *Restricted* flashing across the caller ID screen.

There was a long silence after my first hello, but I heard the same wind sound in the background, like someone was outside walking or driving with the window down. "Hello." My voice conveyed my annoyance with all the hang-ups in my messages.

"Nikki?" The female caller's voice shook.

"Yes?"

"It's . . ." She spoke softly and her voice trailed off. I heard a loud breath, and she started again, louder. "It's Casey Flanagan."

My hand tightened on the receiver.

"I know I'm probably the last person you want to talk to." I thought about hanging up, but I couldn't make myself move. "I have so much I want to say to you, starting with I'm so—"

I cut her off. "This is a really bad time."

"No, I understand. Sun—Sunday, will you meet me at Cast—Castleton Lake?" she stammered. "I know it's a lot to ask, but it's . . . it's important."

"I don't have anything to say to you."

"You don't have to say anything. Just hear me out. Please."

I wanted to say no, but something about that quake in her voice got to me. I imagined her summoning all her courage to make the call. The groveling way she'd said *please,* as if she were down on her knees.

"What time?"

"One o'clock? Will that work? I'll meet you on the benches by the walking path."

"I'll think about it."

She sniffed, and I wondered if she was crying. "Well, I'll be there," she said. "If you decide to come."

Fat chance, I thought as I hung up the phone.

Chapter 39

"You need to talk to Kyle," Sharon said. She poured a jar of salsa into a bowl and placed it on the table in front of me with a bag of chips. Her due date loomed a mere two weeks away, and she looked as if she had swallowed one of those stability balls from the gym. Honestly, I didn't understand how her rail-thin legs were capable of supporting her bulky midsection and wouldn't have been surprised if her knees buckled and she crumpled to the kitchen floor.

"What do you want to drink?" she asked.

I pulled a chair away from the table and pointed to it. "Sit. I'll get it."

As she eased herself down into the cushion, she winced and placed a hand on the small of her back. She had looked more uncomfortable throughout this entire pregnancy than her others. I wondered if it was because she was older or because she was having a girl this time.

"Just meet him for lunch. Hear what he has to say," she said.

The scent of curry hung in the air, a dead giveaway that Kyle had been there the night before. The only time Sharon cooked with the Indian spice blend was when he came for dinner. I waited for her to tell me that he'd been to see her and asked her to talk to me, but she said nothing more. We sat without speaking, sipping strawberry-infused water and listening to the whirring sound coming from the window fan. Rick and the boys were at Cameron's T-ball game. The house didn't feel like Sharon's without their little feet running around and their tiny voices and contagious giggles coming from the next room. It felt barren, like mine.

"You're still wearing your rings, and you haven't talked to an attorney about divorce, so a part of you must want to work things out," Sharon said.

I imagined Kyle with bloodshot eyes and his gray-speckled goatee sitting in the same chair I sat in now. I could see him burying his head in his hands when he talked about Casey and the baby. I had no doubt that he was ashamed of himself and embarrassed by his transgression. It was so not Kyle. He prided himself on being one of the good guys. I bet he'd even had tears rolling down his cheeks when he talked about me.

"Did you have curry-coconut shrimp for supper last night?" I asked.

At the mention of a dish she only made for Kyle, she blinked fast and nodded. "Kyle came for dinner," she admitted.

"Whose side are you on?"

"Always yours, Nikki, but so is Kyle."

It hit me then: Sharon's and Kyle's babies would be born within a few months of each other. They'd grow up together in this tiny town and become the best of friends. I thought back to all the times through the years that Sharon and I had talked about raising our kids together and joked that if one of us had a boy and the other a girl, we would insist they marry.

"Do you think you and Casey will become friends?" I asked.

Sharon cocked her head. "I've never even met her."

"Yeah, but you're going to have kids around the same age. I bet she'll become one of your mom friends."

"Kyle said she doesn't want to raise the baby. She's moving to Nashville right after it's born."

"She won't be able to go through with that." I'd only spoken to Casey a few times, but I felt certain that once she saw the baby she wouldn't be able to give it up.

"You need to talk to Kyle. She said she'll renounce her parental rights."

I pictured Casey cowering by Elizabeth's car in the magazine's parking lot and heard her sorrowful voice saying *I'm sorry*. I shook my head. "He can't let her do that. She'll regret it."

"You can't possibly know that. You're projecting," Sharon said.

"She asked me to meet her. To talk."

Sharon's eyes doubled in size. "Ballsy. Did you agree?"

I sipped my water, still trying to decide. "I told her I'd think about it. She's going to be at Castleton Lake tomorrow at one o'clock." I tapped the toe of my shoe on the floor, imagining Casey sitting on the bench by herself, waiting for me. If I wasn't going to show up, I had to let her know. "I mean, what are we going to talk about?"

"Compare notes on Kyle?" Sharon laughed, but I glared at her. "Sorry, so not funny," she said.

"Dana thinks I should talk to an attorney about a divorce. She gave me the name and contact info for one."

Sharon rolled her eyes. "Dana, please. Since when do you take advice from your sister? She's a disaster."

My back muscles stiffened. I was already annoyed with Sharon for hosting Kyle last night for dinner, and now she was throwing shade at my sister. While I had no problem making unflattering remarks about Dana, Sharon had no right to do the same. They weren't blood. I dunked a chip into the salsa without responding.

"The person you should talk to is Kyle," Sharon said.

"How did he seem to you?"

The corners of Sharon's mouth ticked upward. She thought I was softening toward Kyle because I'd asked about his well-being. "He's a mess, Nikki."

This brought me momentary joy. I hung my head, not liking myself for the feeling.

Sharon reached across the table and placed her hand over mine. "Just hear what he has to say. That's all I'm asking."

I pulled my hand out from under hers. "It doesn't matter what he has to say. It won't change anything. He's having a child with another woman." My voice sounded so bitter that I almost didn't recognize it as my own.

Sharon rested a hand on her belly. I imagined she was trying to shield Baby Sharon from my soap opera–like life. "You were going through a rough time. I mean, really, you were separated."

I pushed the salsa and chips away from me. "We weren't separated. We had a huge fight, and he slept with someone else. And then he felt so guilty that he left."

Sharon did that thing where she lowered her chin to her chest so I knew she was about to say something inappropriate. "You both hurt each other in ways that were equally bad."

"You can't compare me withdrawing money from my own retirement fund to his cheating."

"I can," she said. "Because both of you betrayed each other's trust."

Chapter 40

Casey and I sat side by side on a bench overlooking Castleton Lake. Sunbathers on towels and beach chairs reading, talking, and eating crowded the beach in front of us. Two boys tossed a football back and forth. A mother played Wiffle ball with her son. Swimmers frolicked in the shallow end, and out deeper, sailboats, kayaks, and paddleboards glided across the water. In the distance, Mount Stapleton stretched toward the sky.

"This is my favorite spot in town," Casey said. Her folded hands rested on her protruding belly.

When I'd woken up this morning, I'd had no intention of coming here today, but Sharon's voice telling me Casey planned to renounce her parental rights played on an endless loop in my mind like a jingle in an annoying commercial. I wanted to talk sense into Casey. Make her understand that she'd regret this decision for the rest of her life. Now that she was sitting next to me, I wished I hadn't come. I didn't owe this girl anything.

She took in a deep, ragged breath, and her hand moved to the arch of her back. I froze, fearing she was going into early labor. She was still only in her second trimester, but that would be my luck, being here with her when she gave birth to my husband's baby.

"Are you okay?" I asked.

"The baby just kicked. This kid's either going to be a Rockette or an amazing soccer player."

Hockey. Kyle's son or daughter will play hockey. I pictured Kyle in the stands cheering on a boy who looked like him, and then I changed the image to him sitting on the bench, coaching the team. He looked happier than I'd ever seen him.

"Thank you for meeting me," Casey said. "I know this can't be easy."

Since I'd arrived and sat down next to her, I'd avoided looking at her by staring out at the lake. Now I turned to face her. As always when I saw her, her baby face gutted me. How could Kyle have been with someone so young? Did he find my aging body repulsive? Part of me hated Casey, but there was another part that wanted to protect her, the part of me that had felt it was important to come here today.

She licked her lower lip. "I just want you to know that I didn't know he was married. Not until after. I would never . . ." Her trembling chin dropped to her chest. "I'm so sorry."

I turned back to the lake. A man on a paddleboard lost his balance and fell into the water. He disappeared below the surface, and I waited with my breath held until he popped up again. Casey and I sat quietly, watching him struggle to pull himself onto his board. Eventually, he gave up and swam back to shore, pushing the board out in front of him.

"I don't blame you," I said.

"I wasn't even going to tell him. I planned to have the baby, put it up for adoption, and move on." She shook her head. "But somehow that just didn't seem fair to him or the baby."

I wish you'd never told him. I squirmed on the bench, uncomfortable with how selfish my thinking was, but the thought was true. Kyle and I had finally been happy before he'd found out, and now we'd never be happy together again.

"Kyle told me your story. I mean, about how you guys tried to have a baby."

Her words stung like a sudden slap to my face. Kyle telling her about our problems felt like another of his betrayals, worse than sleeping with her. It suggested an emotional intimacy between them. How much had he confided in this girl? Why had he told her? To earn her sympathy before seducing her?

"I mean, he told me after, when I told him about the pregnancy."

An image of his shocked face popped into my head, and I heard his bewildered voice. *You're pregnant? My wife had a miscarriage shortly after we got married, and couldn't get pregnant again. We tried for years, spent tens of thousands of dollars.* Had he felt relieved to know our fertility problems were my fault, not his? I stretched my arm, trying to release the tension building in my shoulders.

"I think you'd be a great mom," Casey said.

I turned to look at her again. "Why would you say that? You don't even know me."

She swung her legs back and forth. "I can just tell, and you know, you did so much because you wanted to be a mom."

Did so much. Withdrew from my retirement fund and lied about it. Had Kyle told her that? The late-July sun beat down on me, and I was sure that somehow it had scorched my heart.

"A baby has never been in my plans," she said. "All I want to do is sing."

I closed my eyes, picturing crispy, burnt pieces of my heart breaking off.

"I was on the pill but was taking antibiotics because I was recovering from strep."

I swallowed hard, thinking about how hard it was to get pregnant. When we were deciding whether to try IVF, our doctor at the time had reminded me that I was fast approaching forty, as if I didn't know. "Well, by age forty, women have only a five percent chance of getting pregnant each month," she'd said. When we met Dr. Evans and she explained all that had to go right for IVF to work and a woman to get pregnant, Kyle had joked, "It's a wonder humans don't become extinct with those odds." Casey had made getting pregnant even less likely by taking precautions against it. God loved to play practical jokes.

"I'm sure Kyle told you. I don't want this baby, but I could never, you know, get rid of it, have an abortion." As her leg swung out in front of her, her flip-flop flew off and soared through the air. "I believe women have a right to choose; don't get me wrong. It's just not my choice."

I couldn't listen to another word of this. "I should have never come here." I stood, retrieved her shoe, and stepped toward the dirt path leading back to the parking lot.

"No, please. Just let me finish." Casey jumped to her feet. Her momentum caused her to stumble forward. I caught her before she fell and could feel her trembling. "I know you would never have planned it this way, but this . . ." She pointed to her belly. "This can be the baby you wanted. I'll sign away all my rights." She spoke faster than she had been, and her voice was two octaves higher than usual. "I've already talked to a lawyer, a friend of Elizabeth's."

Sweat dripped down my back. I felt dizzy. My legs wobbled.

"You don't look good," Casey said.

I had to sit before I lost my balance. I teetered back to the bench. Casey eased herself down next to me. She reached into her bag and handed me a bottle of water.

I gulped it down without looking at her. "You can't sign away your rights, Casey. You'll regret it."

She shook her head. "I don't even like kids."

"What are you talking about? You're a nanny, and from what Elizabeth says, you're great with Danvers and Hallie."

"I'm a nanny because taking care of Elizabeth's kids pays a lot more than my last job as a barista. If anything, the last few months have convinced me that I definitely don't want children. I mean, I can't even go to the bathroom in peace. They won't leave me alone long enough to send a text. It's overwhelming. All I want to do is get out of this hick town and sing in Nashville."

I stared at Casey, wondering what type of vetting Elizabeth had done before hiring her.

"Kyle's going to be a great dad," she said. "But I'd feel better knowing this baby has two parents. She's going to need a mother."

She. "You're having a girl?"

"Kyle didn't tell you?"

"We don't exactly talk about the baby. We don't really talk much these days."

Casey's cheeks flamed red. "She's due November eighteenth." She placed her hand on my arm. "Can't you just think of me as a surrogate?"

My mouth gaped. "No. What you and Kyle did . . ." I shook my head. "That's not how surrogacy works."

Casey cleared her throat. We sat without speaking. Music from an ice cream truck drifted toward us from the parking lot. A group of boys, around twelve years old, ran past us toward the sound. "I want an Italian ice," one of them screamed.

An image of me standing in front of the truck with a little girl came to mind. She had Casey's copper hair and Kyle's blue-gray eyes. I could feel the weight of her hand in mine as we waited in line for our turn. Somehow I knew she'd order a grape Popsicle. I could even see purple streaks running down her chin.

I stood. "I should go."

Casey reached for my arm. "I really didn't know he was married." Her green eyes watered, and I couldn't tell if the bright sun bothered them or if she was fighting off tears. "My dad left when I was fourteen. Married the skimpy-dressing neighbor across the hall. Destroyed my mother. I never wanted to do that to someone."

I pushed my shoulders back. "Kyle's cheating hasn't destroyed me. I'm fine."

Tears rolled down her cheeks. I pictured her as a young girl trying to comfort an older woman, listless on the couch. I thought about my own mother, smiling and making everyone at DeMarco's Diner laugh.

"I just mean I never wanted to ruin someone's marriage," Casey said.

"You didn't. Kyle did."

As I rushed toward the parking lot, I heard her calling out to me. "Please, think about it."

Chapter 41

"I've been cooped up inside for days," Aunt Izzie said. "I thought we could hike up to the waterfall and eat lunch there." She grabbed a small cooler sitting on the counter, and we headed out the door.

Ninety minutes later we sat on a rock beside Lydia's Falls. The waterfall always managed to surprise me. I never knew what to expect when I came here. Today, the water merely trickled over the rocks. The local meteorologists had been talking about drought conditions for weeks, but I had been skeptical. To me, every day this summer had seemed like a dismal gray rainy day.

A White couple and a girl about six or seven who looked like she might be Asian meandered past us. "Daddy, why isn't the water flowing?" the girl asked.

"There hasn't been any rain, sweetie," the man answered.

I wondered if the couple had adopted the girl. Had they had trouble conceiving? Would Kyle and I have avoided all our problems if we had adopted?

Maybe the girl wasn't adopted. Maybe, like Kyle, this man had fathered a child outside his marriage or with a former partner, and now his wife was helping to raise her. If I asked, she could offer me advice on raising Casey's daughter. Or more likely, I was desperate to believe my and Kyle's situation was more common than I thought.

"Beautiful day," the woman said to me, and I realized I had been staring.

Aunt Izzie handed me a bottle of iced tea and a chicken-parm panini wrapped in white butcher paper. She kept the meatball-and-provolone sandwich for herself. A memory of my father trying to teach her how to make meatballs popped into my mind. "You, Izzie, are the only Italian woman on the planet who doesn't know how to cook," he'd joked.

Her voice interrupted my memory. "This is delicious." She swiped her tongue across a smear of tomato sauce above her upper lip.

"Do you remember when my dad taught you how to make meatballs?" I asked.

My aunt flexed her foot. "Right before Hank returned."

It was the last time I could remember that my aunt and father had gotten along. After that, there was always tension between the two of them.

"What happened between you and my dad?"

Aunt Izzie bit into her sandwich.

"You were so close, and then you weren't."

Aunt Izzie took her time chewing, exaggerating the movement of her jaw. An eagle landed in a tree across from us, and she pointed at it. "Would you look at that." She stood and approached the tree, taking picture after picture with her phone. After the eagle flew off, she examined the photos. "I'm going to send this to . . ." She seemed to lose her train of thought, but then she said, "Dana," and busied herself swiping at her screen.

I took another bite of my sandwich, coming to terms with the fact that I'd never find out what had caused the falling-out between my aunt and father.

"No signal. I'll have to send this later," Aunt Izzie said. "I spoke with her last night. She's making out well with the dog. Her roommate is helping out."

"She got lucky with that. Imagine if she had to do it all herself."

"Maybe we don't give Dana enough credit."

I rolled my eyes. "She should never have taken Oliver away from me. I still miss him."

Aunt Izzie wiped her mouth with a napkin. "Well, he was her dog first, Nikki."

I picked up a stone and threw it toward the waterfall. "Let's not talk about Oliver."

"Have you made any decisions about Kyle? Are you going to try to work things out? I won't pretend to know what you should do, but you should make a decision."

"From one bad topic to the next. This is a fun lunch."

Aunt Izzie laughed. "I don't want you to live in limbo for too long. You could get stuck there and never move out. Weigh your options, make a decision, and run with it." Her voice had a wistful tone, and I wondered if she was giving me advice she wished someone had given her long ago.

"I met with Casey last week."

Aunt Izzie's jaw dropped open. "Good grief, why would you meet with her?" She snapped open a ginger ale. The can exploded, and the amber-colored liquid sprayed all over her shirt. She laughed as she mopped it up. "Sixty-one years old, and I still can't remember not to bring carbonated drinks on my hikes because I jostle the cooler too much on the way up."

I handed her more napkins. "Casey doesn't want to keep the baby. She asked me to raise h—" I stopped. "She's having a girl. She wants me to reconcile with Kyle so we can raise her together." I looked toward the waterfall, shading my eyes with my hand. "She said she'd sign away all her rights." A chill ran down my spine as I said the words, because I couldn't believe someone could give up their baby so easily.

"The Lord works in mysterious ways. You wanted a baby, and now she's offering you one."

I dropped my hand and squinted against the bright sun. "I wanted a baby of my own." I let out a sarcastic laugh. "She said I should consider her a surrogate mother."

"That would be a way to put a positive spin on this."

"Do you think it could work?"

Aunt Izzie looked toward the sky as if she were looking for divine inspiration. "If you want it to work, then yes, I think it would work. And you certainly have nothing to lose by trying."

"I have everything to lose."

"How so?" Aunt Izzie asked.

I watched the family climbing on the rocks. The girl rode piggyback-style on her father's back, giggling while the mother watched with a huge grin. "What if Kyle and I reconcile and I fall in love with the baby and everything is going great, but then Casey changes her mind and takes the baby away. Just like Dana took Oliver away." It was all I could think about since talking to Casey at Castleton Lake.

"Love doesn't come without risk, Nikki." Aunt Izzie picked up a stick and doodled in the dirt. "But you just told me Casey said she would renounce her parental rights. If she does that, you can adopt the baby, and Casey won't be able to take her away. The law will be on your side."

"She's twenty-four. Too young to make such an important decision."

"Your mother had you when she was eighteen. She never once thought about giving you away."

"She wasn't afraid when she found out she was pregnant?"

Aunt Izzie smiled. For a moment she looked so much like my mother that my heart hurt. "Oh, she was plenty scared. Scared to tell our parents, but determined to raise you from the moment she found out."

"How did Nonna and Nonno react when she told them?"

Aunt Izzie picked up a stone and stared down at it as if it were a screen replaying a memory. "She waited to tell them until after she eloped with Dom. They were more worried about the marriage than the pregnancy."

"Because she was so young?"

"They were concerned." Aunt Izzie stopped speaking and tossed the stone to the ground. "I was concerned."

I had a feeling she was debating whether to tell me more. "What were you concerned about?"

Aunt Izzie took a deep breath. "We all wondered if she married him for the right reasons."

"You thought they only got married because she was pregnant."

She opened her mouth but then snapped it shut without answering.

"You worried for nothing. If it hadn't been for the accident, they would have celebrated their thirty-fifth anniversary and who knows how many more."

Aunt Izzie shook her head. "I still have trouble believing she's gone. Just now when I saw that eagle, the first thing I thought was, *I have to send this picture to Gianna.*" Her eyes misted over.

"You were a great sister to her. You must really miss her." For five years my parents' accident had been about Dana and me losing our parents. From day one, Aunt Izzie had stepped up to be there for us, but neither Dana nor I had ever tried to console her over the loss of her sister. My face burned with shame. I wrapped my arm around my aunt's shoulder and pulled her to me. "You've been so strong for me and Dana, but we haven't been there for you. If you ever want to talk about her, I'm here."

"We've all been there for each other," Aunt Izzie said. "Dinners, paint night, hikes. We're all doing the best we can, and I know your mom would be proud." She pulled away from me and wiped her eyes. "How did we get on that topic? What were we talking about?"

I reminded her that we'd been talking about my meeting with Casey.

She nodded. "You're uncomfortable with her signing away her parental rights, but lots of people give up babies for adoption."

"I don't think it would be fair to keep her away from the baby if she changes her mind, and shouldn't the baby have a right to meet her biological mom, know where she comes from?"

Aunt Izzie picked up her sandwich and stared at me for several seconds without biting into it or speaking. "You're worrying about things that may never happen. Take it one day at a time. Do you love Kyle? Do you want to be with him? If so, you owe it to yourself to give your marriage another chance."

"It's not about loving him or wanting to be with him. I don't know if we can work our way through this."

"Nonsense. If you want it bad enough, you'll put in the effort to work it out." With that she took a big bite of her sandwich, and we ate the rest of our lunch in silence.

By the time we'd finished eating and hiked back to the parking lot, a thick coat of pollen along with dust from the unpaved road we had driven over to get here covered Aunt Izzie's Subaru.

"Oh, Greta," Aunt Izzie said, looking at her car. "You need a bath."

I laughed. "What she needs is to be put out of her misery." Aunt Izzie had been driving around in that rust box for the last fourteen years. When she backed out of the parking space, I knew the pavement would be slick with oil. That was if the car even started.

"She doesn't mean that, Greta." Aunt Izzie patted the dashboard before turning the key in the ignition. Three times the car sputtered without starting.

"I knew we should have taken my car."

Aunt Izzie patted the dashboard again. "Don't let me down, Greta." This time when she tried, the car started. Aunt Izzie smiled at me. "Greta and I have a long history together. I'm not going to get rid of her at the first sign of trouble."

I knew she wasn't talking about the car, but I wasn't going to bite. We sat in silence as she navigated the bumpy dirt road to town. Back on the paved streets, Aunt Izzie flipped on her blinker in front of the car wash. Lines five cars deep waited in front of each of the bays. "Do you have to do this now?" I asked. I'd been afraid of car washes since I was a little kid.

A pickup truck stopped to let us go, and Aunt Izzie turned across the lane of traffic. As we waited, I wondered if I'd end up like Aunt Izzie, alone and naming my car as if it were a loved family member instead of a means of transportation. I wouldn't even have nieces to keep me company.

When it was finally our turn, Aunt Izzie pulled into the bay and put the car in park. The door behind us shut, trapping us. Sprayers on the ends of long arms moved toward us, as if they were getting ready to attack. I took a deep breath. Jets moved over and around the station wagon, blasting it with soapy water. Suds covered all the windows so I couldn't see out. My pulse throbbed in my neck.

Slowly the windows cleared, and my breathing returned to a normal pace. On all sides, blowers moved toward the car. Even though we were sitting still, I felt like the car was moving. I closed my eyes, hoping the feeling would pass.

A buzzer sounded. The door in front of us rose. Aunt Izzie pulled out of the bay. She parked to inspect Greta, and I jumped out for fresh air. The vehicle shone a sun-faded shade of green with no signs of the grime from the trees and dusty trail. Nobody looking at it would know what a mess the car had been minutes before.

"Greta was a bit roughed up, but with a little love, she's as good as new," Aunt Izzie said.

Chapter 42

The phone rang in the dead of the night, waking me from a restless sleep. Scared, I reached toward my nightstand, fumbling for my phone. A box of tissues and the book I'd been reading at bedtime crashed to the floor.

The name and picture lighting up my screen confused me: Sharon. My hands shook. *Why is she calling me at two in the morning? Did something happen to Rick or one of the boys?*

"I need you to come here quickly. Watch Cam and Noah." Rick's words came at me in a rush of nervous energy. A high-pitched squeal in the background drowned out whatever he said next.

I jumped out of bed. "What's wrong?"

"Sharon's in labor, and her parents are in Maine. I have to get her to the hospital."

"I'll be right there."

Fifteen minutes later, Rick's vehicle whizzed past me, traveling in the opposite direction on a street around the corner from theirs. I brought the gas pedal all the way to the floor, and my car lurched forward. Sharon's driveway was dark, but light poured out the living room window. I let myself in the unlocked front door and took the stairway two steps at a time. In the boys' dark room, I could make out the outlines of their small bodies. Cameron flipped from his stomach to his side. "Mom?" he said, his voice groggy.

I backed out of the room into the hallway and listened. No other sounds came.

Downstairs on the couch, I texted Rick that I was with the boys and not to worry. A half hour later he replied, Sharon Driscoll Grey born at 2:57 am on August 10, weighing 7 pounds, two ounces. My phone vibrated with another message, an image this time, Sharon in a tranquil green johnny in her hospital bed, cradling a baby swaddled in a pink blanket. Baby Sharon's red wrinkled face reminded me of the shrunken apple heads we used to make in elementary school in art class. My friend Sharon looked down at her daughter with shiny eyes and the most genuine smile I'd ever seen. My stomach twisted as my mind replayed our lunch at Stapleton Tavern, when I had questioned if she enjoyed being a mother. Would I ever stop regretting the things I'd said and done when Kyle and I were trying to have a baby?

My phone shook with another text; this one was from Kyle. Congrats, man. She's a beauty!

I looked closer at Rick's original message and realized that he'd included Kyle. In a few months, Kyle's daughter would be born in that same hospital. My pulse quickened. Would he be in the delivery room with Casey? Would seeing the baby change Casey's mind about walking away from her? Would she and Kyle raise the baby together? Would he marry her?

That same part of me that was embarrassed by my behavior with Sharon that day at the Stapleton Tavern scolded me again. *If you hadn't lied about the 401(k), none of this would be happening.*

~

Someone tapped my shoulder. "Auntie Nikki," a small voice said. I forced my eyes open. My face was smooshed into blue sofa cushions. A small hot hand pulled my arm. "Where's Mommy and Daddy? Why are you here?"

I flipped over so that I faced the room and not the back of the couch. Cameron, light-brown hair sticking straight up in the air and lines from his pillow on the side of his face, stared down at me. "I want Mommy."

I pushed myself up to a sitting position. "Your mom and dad went to the hospital to have the baby."

Cameron tilted his head. "Baby Sharon's here?"

I held up my phone. "Want to see a picture?"

He plopped down on the sofa next to me. "Why's she so wrinkly?" he asked.

"The wrinkles will go away."

"I'm going to be the best big brother to Baby Sharon," he said. "I'm already a great big brother to Noah."

"I know you are." I patted his hair, trying to flatten the pieces that stuck up near his forehead. "What do you say we go get Noah and make some breakfast?"

~

With Noah strapped into his booster seat and Cameron standing next to me, I pulled the pancake mix from the cabinet. "Mommy lets me help," Cameron said.

I placed the box on the table so he could reach it and handed him a stainless steel measuring cup. "Fill this to the top."

He dug his spoon in and scooped out some of the powder. When he transferred it to the measuring cup, most of it landed on the floor or table. I flashed back to my father teaching me how to make pasta at DeMarco's Diner. I was about the same age as Cameron then. My dad had pointed to the mound of flour on the butcher's table. "We're going to dig a volcano right in the center of it." I stood on a chair with his arm curled around my waist so that I wouldn't fall. The silky powder slipped through my fingers as I dug a hole in the middle of the pile. By the time I finished, there was more flour on me and my dad than on the wooden table. "You'll get the hang of it," my dad had said. Eventually, I had, but I never loved cooking like my parents did. Maybe if I had, I wouldn't have sold the restaurant to Hank.

I showed Cameron how to scoop the pancake mix out of the box with the measuring cup, and he did it perfectly. "Quick learner," I said, tousling his hair.

"Mommy never lets me do that part because I'm messy, and Dad gets mad."

A layer of powdery dust covered the floor. "That's what brooms are for," I said.

While I measured the water, he pulled a wire whisk from a drawer. "This is the part Mommy lets me do." He blended the mix together. Something about the way his little tongue poked out of the corner of his mouth as he concentrated on his task undid me. A collage of everything I would never experience with a child played through my mind—first words, first steps, first day of school, teaching him or her to drive, first date.

I shook my head to clear my thoughts. This wasn't the time for a pity party. I made goofy faces at Noah until he started laughing while Cameron finished mixing the batter.

I had him sit down next to Noah while I cooked the pancakes, shaping them like a bear. "What do you think this is?" I asked.

"Pancakes."

"Does it look like anything?"

"Three circles." He sounded proud of himself.

I laughed. "Any other guesses?"

He studied his plate. His tongue slipped out of his mouth again. "Oh, I know, a snowman."

I smiled at him. "It's supposed to be a bear!"

"That doesn't look like a bear."

The doorbell rang. Kyle stood on the front stairs, shifting his weight from one leg to another. "Rick told me you came over in the middle of the night. I figured you might need to grab some sleep."

Cameron ran up behind me. "Uncle Kyle." He pushed past me and opened his arms. Kyle scooped him up. Noah started to cry, so I left the two of them at the door and ran back to the kitchen. Kyle and Cameron came in a few minutes later, and Cameron insisted on making more pancakes for Kyle.

After he finished eating, Kyle took the boys into the backyard to play. I went up to the guest room to nap.

Kyle's voice drifted in through the open window. "You're doing great, Cameron." A few minutes later: "Noah's flying."

I peeked outside. Kyle stood in the middle of Sharon's two sons, alternating between pushing Noah on a swing and tossing a ball to Cameron. Even from the second floor, watching him through a window, I could sense his joy. His body easily swayed from left to right as he turned to face Noah and then Cameron. His shoulders hung loosely, free of all tension. His forehead was smooth, with none of the rigid lines that were there when he spoke to me, and his lips curled upward. He looked happier than I'd seen him in months. *He's going to be an amazing dad,* I thought. For a split second, an overwhelming sense of joy filled me. I was glad he was going to be a dad, knew his daughter would be getting a wonderful father. The good feeling was short lived, replaced by an all-consuming rage directed at my own body for betraying me, preventing me from giving him a child. My anger switched course and landed on Kyle for his infidelity, and with it came a feeling of envy toward Casey and her fertile, young body that so easily made Kyle a father.

Kyle glanced up at the window. Our eyes locked. His softened, and he smiled. A collage of memories played through my mind: his grin in the chairlift when he handed me the flask, the shy kiss he gave me at the end of our first date, the tears in his eyes as I walked down the aisle toward him on our wedding day, the way he held me and wouldn't let go the night of my parents' accident, his booming laugh when Cole jumped up on our bed and licked his face, singing duets while we cooked dinner together.

For months, I'd been afraid he would never look at me with soft eyes and a smile again. Now that he was, I felt as if my heart had been jump-started. I knew then that I still loved him. My knees buckled, thinking of all we had lost and all we could still have.

~

Kyle and I spent the rest of the morning playing games with Cameron and Noah. In the afternoon, the four of us sat around the picnic table on the patio, eating hot dogs that Kyle had grilled. After lunch, the boys changed into their bathing suits and ran through the sprinkler, filling the backyard with shouts of joy and uninhibited laughter. Kyle and I kept smiling at each other as we watched them play. As my eyes met his, I imagined the two of us in our own backyard playing with an auburn-haired little girl. I could feel her small hand in mine and hear her calling me Mommy.

"Come on, Uncle Kyle, Auntie Nikki." Cameron beckoned from under the sprinkler.

Kyle grinned at me. "What do you say?"

"I'm going to stay here where it's dry, but go ahead."

Not bothering to remove his work boots or T-shirt, he stepped toward the sprinkler. He glanced back over his shoulder, and in one fluid motion that seemed choreographed, he whirled around and grabbed me at the waist.

"No," I yelled.

He lifted me off the ground with Cameron cheering him on and marched toward the sprinkler. As the spray of water moved toward us, I buried my head in his shoulder, taking in his familiar cedar scent. God, how I had missed that smell, missed him. The pellets of icy water pummeling my sweaty skin shocked me. I tightened my grip on Kyle's arms and shifted so I could see his face. He pulled me so close I could feel his warm breath on my mouth. As his eyes met mine, the gray specks in his blue irises sparkled. I couldn't remember ever feeling so giddy about the way he looked at me.

Sharon's parents arrived in the late afternoon to take over babysitting duty. As Kyle and I said goodbye to the kids and got ready to head to our separate homes, the light, spacey air I'd been floating on since he rang the doorbell early this morning turned heavy and thick. I slogged down the driveway to my car, hoping he'd ask me if he could come home. He climbed into his Jeep. "Have a good night." As he closed the car door, I could feel a vibration in my chest, and I imagined more pieces of my heart splintering off.

Chapter 43

At the end of Sharon's road, Kyle turned right, and I took a left, dreading returning to my quiet, empty house. Out on the main street, I eased up on the gas. There had to be somewhere else I could go. The driver behind me beeped. I sped up and steered toward Aunt Izzie's. Her car was parked in the garage. The front door and all the windows were open. Inside, fans whirled at full speed, providing no relief to the stifling heat. The house felt like a sauna. The smell of tuna fish lingered in the air.

"Aunt Izzie," I called. No one answered.

I sat down at her card table and began to work on her latest puzzle, one thousand pieces that when slotted together would be an image of the Golden Gate Bridge. I'd been to San Francisco once with Sharon. We took the trip to the West Coast shortly after I'd met Kyle. While riding the cable cars, I told her he was the one. I'd been so sure about him from the beginning.

After a few minutes, the heat and number of puzzle pieces all painted varying shades of blue frustrated me. I struggled to figure out which made up the ocean and which were for the sky.

I gulped down an ice-cold glass of water, sat down on the couch, and sent Aunt Izzie a text telling her I was at her house. She told me to wait; she was talking to the neighbor down the street and would be home in a few minutes.

The TV remote control rested on the coffee table next to a photo album with a light-blue cover and the word *Memories* stenciled in black across the top. Dana and I had found a green one just like it the day we carried the patio furniture up from Aunt Izzie's basement to her deck. I could still hear the panic in my aunt's voice as she shouted at us to stop looking at the pictures. Would she be mad if I looked at the photos in this blue memory book? After several seconds, I convinced myself she would have no objections. I picked up the photo album and glanced toward the door. A bang echoed through the house. I dropped the book back down on the coffee table. A second bang sounded and then a third. *The ice maker.*

I reached for the photo album again and flipped to the first page. An image of Dana at four or five years old stared back at me. She wore wide-legged blue jeans and a shirt with Yogi Bear on it, clothes that seemed all wrong. Dana used to be afraid of Yogi Bear, and the pants looked like something from the seventies. I leaned closer to the picture and gasped. It wasn't Dana. It was my mother. I felt a prick of jealousy toward my sister for inheriting all my mother's beautiful features.

More pictures of my toddler mother filled the next few pages. Some had been taken on the same sofa I sat on now when the house belonged to my grandparents. In one of the photos, my mother sat on my grandfather's lap. He'd died shortly after I was born. Although I'd seen photos of him, I'd never before realized he had been the one to pass on those distinct green eyes that I felt cheated out of.

In the next picture, my mom and Aunt Izzie stood side by side in front of a woodstove. My aunt's expression reminded me of Cameron's face this morning when he'd told me he was going to be a good big brother to Baby Sharon. Aunt Izzie had always been protective of her little sister.

"Nicole."

I jumped at the sound of Aunt Izzie's voice. "I didn't hear you come in."

"Put that down. Right now." Her icy tone cooled the room better than central air could have.

I tightened my grip on the photo album and pulled it toward my chest. "They're pictures of my mom as a kid. Why don't you want me to see them?"

My aunt stared at me with an intense gaze and a piqued expression. She leaned sideways against the room divider as if she needed it for support. "Put it down."

I flipped to another page. A picture of my mother riding on a bicycle with training wheels slipped out from under the protective plastic and fluttered to the floor.

Aunt Izzie strode across the room. I thought she was going to pick up the picture. Instead, she ripped the photo album away from me.

"They're pictures of my mother. I want to see them."

"I said no."

"I don't understand."

Aunt Izzie sighed as she bent to retrieve the photograph that had come loose. She stared at the image of my mother on the bike while she paced the room. I could see my aunt's mouth moving, but no words came out. I imagined she was having an imaginary conversation with my mother, asking if she could show me the photos. She stopped pacing and stared out the window, her back straight and her shoulders rigid. She seemed to decide something and turned on her heel, striding back across the living room toward me.

"I always look through this near your mother's birthday. I meant to bring it back downstairs but got distracted."

I felt a tightness in my chest at the mention of my mother's birthday and the thought of my aunt looking at old pictures to commemorate the day. Next year, I'd make a point of spending time with her so she wouldn't be alone with her memories.

"Maybe it's good that I didn't. Maybe it's time for you to see this." Her voice sounded too timid to be my aunt's.

I nodded, not sure if she expected an answer.

Aunt Izzie sat down so close to me that our arms touched. She slid the photo album onto my thighs with the care of an explosive expert deactivating a bomb. "Have you seen any of the high school pictures yet?"

"No, just baby and toddler pictures."

Aunt Izzie swiped her tongue over her upper lip, something my mother used to do when she was nervous. The photo album couldn't have weighed a pound, but it felt heavy enough to crush not only my legs but my life. I was no longer sure I wanted to look inside.

Aunt Izzie watched me with her lips folded inside her mouth. I started at the beginning of the book again, taking in the toddler pictures. Photo after photo, my mother's smiling face looked back at me. In some of the pictures, she was with her parents. In others, she posed with Aunt Izzie. My favorites were the ones of the four of them together.

Halfway through the album, my mother's friends began to appear. At first the pictures were from elementary school. I recognized my mother's best friend, Rosemary, but none of the other girls.

As I turned the pages, my mother aged before me. Soon, I was watching her get ready for the prom. Next to me, Aunt Izzie scooted toward the front of the sofa cushion as if she were preparing to bolt.

My mom and Rosemary starred in the first prom photos, wearing their taffeta gowns with the big hoops, Mom's dress pink, Rosemary's blue. Mom looked radiant. Her olive skin darker than usual with a spring tan and her eyes as bright as I'd ever seen them. God, I missed her. In the next picture two teenage boys held white corsages. I recognized my father right away; even then his thick eyebrows had dominated his forehead. It took me a moment to figure out the second boy was Hank.

I turned the page. Aunt Izzie sat up straighter. Hank posed with his arm curled around my mother's waist. My mother leaned all her weight against him. I bent closer to the photo album, not understanding what I saw. My mother stared adoringly at Hank, seemingly unaware that anyone else was in the room with them. He, on the other hand, looked right into the camera lens with a huge smile. From the photograph, teenage Hank appeared to be looking right at me, making me as uncomfortable as the grown man did in real life. His eyebrow was slightly raised, and I had the feeling the boy in the picture was about to let me in on a joke.

Aunt Izzie put a hand on my arm.

"I don't understand. Why is Mom posing with Hank and not Dad?" My question came out angry.

"Nicole," Aunt Izzie said. "You can stop looking if you want to."

The next several pages were more pictures of Mom and Hank. There were shots of them in their graduation gowns, at a party reclining in lawn chairs by a keg, sitting shoulder to shoulder on a beach blanket by the water at Castleton Lake. The last picture was under a banner that read *Good Luck*. Hank held my mother in a tight embrace, her face buried in his shoulder. A New York Rangers hockey shirt with Hank's last name and the number eighty-eight embroidered on the sleeve hung on the wall behind them. I pulled the photo out from underneath the plastic. On the back, in my mother's large loopy handwriting in purple ink, was the date, August 17, 1980, eight and a half months before I was born.

"So Mom cheated on Hank with Dad." That was it. It had to be. My voice betrayed the calm I tried to project. "So what. They weren't married, and Hank was leaving anyway."

Aunt Izzie squeezed my hand. I looked up at her. She wore a sorrowful expression. "Hank should tell you what happened. It's his story to tell, not mine."

Chapter 44

Hank led me through his house to a wraparound deck in the back overlooking Mount Stapleton. The ski lifts were running, carrying tourists over the lush green pine trees to the summit to take pictures or ride the alpine slide down. In the distance, mountain bikers in bright shirts whizzed across trails carved through trees and rocks. I took it all in, watching these people enjoying their lives while fearing everything I thought I knew about my own life was about to be blown apart.

Hank pointed to a large sectional wicker couch arranged in a U around a table. I ignored him and settled in a hanging swing chair shaped like an egg.

He leaned against the railing with his back to the spectacular view so that we were face to face. I couldn't see his eyes beneath his dark sunglasses, and his impassive expression gave nothing away. When I'd called him yesterday to tell him I needed to speak with him, he had agreed without asking any questions about what I wanted to talk about and suggested we meet at his house. I'd assumed my aunt had warned him that I'd seen pictures of him and my mother. Had Hank and Aunt Izzie conspired about what story he would tell me today?

"Your aunt told me you found your mother's old photo album. I wish you had brought it with you."

"My aunt has it. She's very protective of it. Didn't want me or Dana to see it."

Hank flexed his hands. "Well, there are some things that your mother didn't want you to know, and I . . ." He trailed off and turned to face the mountains. A few seconds later, he continued in a soft voice. "I reluctantly went along with her, kept her secrets."

Secrets. His use of that word made my stomach twist. I pushed against the floor deck with my feet so that my chair swayed. If only it would break free and soar into the sky so I could fly away from Hank's house and whatever he was about to reveal, away from Kyle, Casey, and the baby, and away from this tiny town, where everyone knew what had happened.

Behind me, the glass door slid open, and footsteps crossed the deck. "It's hot out here. I thought you might want some iced tea," Arianna said. She placed a pitcher and two glasses filled with ice cubes and mint leaves on the table.

My mother had always sneered when she'd come across photos of Arianna, which were everywhere when I was a kid. I could never understand my mother's dislike of the woman because my mom loved everyone, and all the articles I'd ever read about Arianna proclaimed how down to earth she was, how likable. The supermodel who could be your best friend.

"Call me if you need anything," Arianna said, squeezing Hank's arm. He watched her as she cut across the deck and slid the door closed behind her.

Hank took off his sunglasses and looked me in the eye. "Tell me about the pictures you saw that have piqued your curiosity."

"The prom pictures. My mother in a dress and you in a tux with a matching cummerbund. A bunch of other photos of the two of you looking cozy together, one from eight months before I was born."

He slumped and moved to sit on the wicker couch so we no longer faced each other. "What did your aunt tell you?"

"Not much. She said it was your story to tell."

Hank massaged his temple. "It's your mother's and my story." He filled both glasses and took a long sip.

The silence weighed down on me, crushing my chest and squeezing all the air from my lungs. "How long did you date?"

He returned his glass to the table with a thud. "We met in junior high. At the eighth-grade Halloween dance. She went as the Bionic Woman. I was the Six Million Dollar Man. They were popular shows at the time." He smiled at the memory, and I could almost see the little boy he had been, stocky, with his dark curls falling into his eyes. "We were pretty much inseparable after that."

"Until you left Stapleton."

"Until I left for New York." He reached for his glass again. "I needed to focus on hockey and only hockey, so I didn't want her to come."

"And she got back at you by sleeping with my dad?"

The vein in Hank's forehead pulsated. "He wasted no time moving in, always had a thing for her."

"Did you love her?" I had never suspected Hank had feelings toward my mother, but the pained expression on his face told me I'd missed something.

He picked at the wicker on his chair. "We were kids. What did we know about love? I thought wearing the number eighty-eight on my sleeve was love."

His words confused me. Their meaning snapped into place as I watched a cart race down the mountain. "August eighth, my mother's birthday."

"I never quite mastered the romantic gesture."

I thought his choosing my mother's birthday as his hockey number was sweet, but I didn't offer my opinion.

"A mutual friend told me she married Dom. Neither of them bothered to tell me themselves."

He stood to bring me my iced tea. The glass felt cold and wet in my hand. Condensation dripped onto my leg.

Back at the couch, Hank adjusted the tilt of the umbrella. I had the feeling he was weighing his next words.

Leave now, before it's too late, a voice in my head commanded. I pictured myself running down the deck stairs and around the house to the driveway, cruising down the mountain, my life exactly as it had been when I woke up this morning.

Hank's voice, like a sledgehammer, broke through my thoughts. "She never told me she was pregnant."

Get up and run.

"Things were different back then. No cell phones. No internet; no Facebook, Instagram, or Snapchat where people posted pictures and status updates." He leaned forward so his elbows rested on his knees. "I didn't piece together what happened until I came back here years later."

A mosquito landed on my knee. I shooed it away before it could bite me, but my leg still felt itchy; my entire body itched.

"You were ten by then, almost eleven, and I knew the moment I saw you."

Here it comes, I thought. *The moment my life blows apart.* I put the glass down on the table next to me and tightened my grip on the chair's chains.

"Your dimples, your curly hair, your dark eyes."

All three were the things that made me stand out from my family. "Knew what?" I hadn't meant to ask, but the words slipped out.

"Knew you were mine."

A buzzing sound echoed through my head, making it hard to think. "No."

"I'm your father, Nikki."

I closed my eyes and imagined my dad, could feel the tightness of his hugs and remembered how I'd believed he could protect me from anything. I saw him racing into my room to comfort me after a nightmare, always a few steps ahead of my mother. I could hear Dana whining, *You're his favorite.* I felt his arm hooked through mine as he walked me down the aisle.

"You are not my father." My voice cracked, and tears threatened to spill from my eyes. I blinked hard to get rid of them.

"Your biological father. I didn't get a chance to be more. Dom stole that from me." His tone reminded me of Oliver's growl.

"Stole it from you how?" My entire body shook. I stood and paced the deck, trying to expel some of this energy that felt like gasoline searching for a flame.

Hank cleared his throat. "You don't need to know."

"Don't you dare tell me what I need to know."

He took a loud breath in and exhaled. "First, let me tell you about how I broke up with your mom." He patted the couch. I sat down next to him, sure to leave plenty of space between the two of us.

"For months, most of senior year really, I'd let her believe that once I got settled in New York, I'd send for her. She couldn't wait, kept talking about how she was going to decorate our home, started to look for a job out there, inviting her friends to visit, picking out plays she was going to see on Broadway. The night before I left, I told her I didn't want her coming with me." Hank picked up his glass and shook it so that ice cubes clanked against the sides. "She was devastated. For her, the breakup came out of the blue, but I'd been planning it for months, working up the courage to tell her."

My chest burned as I thought of my mom as the teenage girl I'd seen in the photo album and remembered the way she'd looked at Hank as if he were a deity she worshipped. I wished I had a time machine to go back and hug her or, better yet, warn her to stay away from him.

"Why did you lead her on like that?"

"I was an asshole, full of myself, had no use for the little town of Stapleton or the people in it."

Hank isn't the villain you've cast him to be. Give him a chance. Have dinner with him. My aunt's words, which had always made me angry when she spoke them, made me angrier now. I'd been right to stay away from Hank. He was even more of a prick than I'd thought he was.

"So then why do you blame my father?"

"Dominic let Gianna believe he told me about the baby, about you, and that I said, 'Tell her to get rid of it.'" Hank shook his head. "We never talked about the baby. I didn't know anything about you. He asked me for a loan to get the restaurant started, and then he told her I gave him that money as a way to clear my conscience."

I jumped to my feet. "He wouldn't do that."

"He did it, Nikki." Hank's voice was barely a whisper.

"I don't believe you. My dad, he wouldn't. No."

Hank shrugged.

You're a liar, Dominic.

I was so in love with you. That's why I did it. Do you really think he would have given up his hockey career for you?

Memories of my parents screaming at each other after Hank moved back flooded my head. Hank was telling the truth. My vision blurred. I grabbed onto the railing.

"Are you okay, Nikki?" Hank asked. "Sit down."

Sitting was the last thing I wanted to do. On the mountain, the lifts still chugged uphill, and bikes and carts raced down. I closed my eyes and saw crowded sidewalks, skyscrapers, neon signs, and yellow cabs zigzagging through bumper-to-bumper traffic. I could even hear the obnoxious horns. My life would have been so different if my mom and Hank had raised me in New York City. I would have had an entirely different lifestyle if my father had been a famous hockey player and not a struggling restaurateur. Part of me felt sad for this version of myself that had never gotten to be.

"Why didn't you tell me before? Why didn't they tell me?"

"I wanted to tell you, but I didn't want to blow apart your family. Your mother and father, Dom, didn't want you to know. They were worried about how both you and Dana would react. I'd already hurt your mom enough, so I went along with what she wanted."

At the mention of my sister's name, I collapsed against the railing. Not only was my father not my father, but Dana was no longer my full sister. This felt like the bigger loss because she was all that remained of my childhood family. She was the only other person in the world who knew what it was like to grow up in DeMarco's Diner.

"I went along with it on the condition that I could be a part of your life. So I bought this house, lived here a few months during the year, and did some part-time work at the restaurant so I could watch you grow up, get to know you."

Customers had always questioned why Hank worked at the diner. "What are you doing here?" they would ask. "You could have a sports talk show or announce the games. Be in New York with that gorgeous wife of yours."

Hank always smiled when responding. "Helping out friends. I'm good for their business." He would wink and walk away.

"I don't understand why my mother didn't tell you she was pregnant."

Hank wrung his hands. "Gianna hated me after what I did. I can't blame her."

"Weren't you angry when you found out?"

"I was, but I understood why Dom did it. He was trying to protect Gianna. My ego exploded after I got drafted. All this money started coming in, and women, groupies—I guess you call them puck bunnies now—they threw themselves at me. In every city I played, they'd hang out by the locker room after the game, just waiting for us. It was a crazy time."

The glass door slid open, and Arianna walked across the deck carrying a platter of pita bread and hummus. "I thought you might be hungry."

Hank watched her with an expression similar to the one my mother had in the photo when she was looking at him. "My life changed when I met Arianna," he said. "She tamed me."

"Tamed and trained." She winked.

Hank waited until she stepped back inside and closed the door behind her. "I'd like to think I would have done right by your mother, but the punk kid that I was, who knows? I just wish Gianna had told me and I'd had the chance to do the right thing."

"I don't understand how you all worked at the restaurant together. How could you be around my dad after what he did?"

"At first, it wasn't easy, but it was important to me to be around you. Make sure you were okay. Arianna didn't want kids, and I never pushed her, but I wanted them. So when I found out about you, that I had a daughter, I was ecstatic."

Hank Pendleton is my father. The realization hit me all at once. My head spun as I tried to make sense of it. Exhausted, I sank to the couch next to him and felt tears in my eyes. I wasn't sure if they were for Hank or me.

"I didn't want to stay mad. Anger eats you up, Nikki. It will destroy you if you let it. Forgiveness is where the power is." He leaned toward me as he spoke. I felt as if he was giving me advice to forgive my parents for the secret they had kept from me.

"It's a lot to take in," I said.

"I've always wanted to tell you. I'm glad you know now." He sat up straighter, as if a huge weight had been lifted from his shoulders. "After what happened with your mom and Dom, the accident, it seemed more important that you know."

Guilt over the way I'd treated Hank these past years bubbled up in my throat. I'd cast him as the bad guy, but he was also a victim. My father and my mother had stolen so much from him, taken his chance to be a parent.

"I know I can never replace your dad, but I hope we can have a meaningful relationship. That someday you won't think of me as the asshole who shut down DeMarco's Diner."

"I'm sorry, Un—" I stopped because it didn't feel right to call him Uncle Hank anymore. "I'm sorry for the way I treated you about the restaurant. I so badly wanted to keep the diner running because it was the only way I could carry on a piece of my parents."

Hank shifted so that he faced me. "You and Dana, the kind young women you've become. The people you touch through love and caring. That's their legacy, not the restaurant."

Chapter 45

Aunt Izzie stood in her foyer, staring out the screen door, as if she had been expecting me. She stepped onto her front landing before I slid out of my car. The late-afternoon sun cast a shadow on half her face, or maybe I was just seeing the dark and light sides of her. For my entire life, she'd always been there for me. She was the caretaker when my parents were busy at the restaurant and the anchor who kept me moored after their accident. Looking at her now, though, I felt like she had betrayed me, and I didn't know if I could trust her.

"How did it go with Hank?" Her voice vibrated with nervous energy.

"How do you think it went?" She recoiled as if my harsh tone had landed like a puck to the face. I marched up the walkway, pointing my finger at her. "How could you have kept that secret from me? I had a right to know."

She widened her stance and placed her hands on her hips. "It wasn't my secret to tell."

"You lied to me for my entire life."

Across the street, the garage door rumbled open. Aunt Izzie's twentysomething neighbors walked bicycles out onto their driveway and stared our way while adjusting their helmets.

"Let's talk about this inside," my aunt said in a hushed whisper. She turned on her heel, letting the screen door slam behind her.

I stormed up the stairs after her. Inside, she showed none of the defiance she had displayed outside. Cowering in the corner of the living room, she seemed like a version of herself that someone had unplugged. Her green eyes had lost their sparkle, and her olive complexion had been muted to a dull yellow. She slumped on the arm of the sofa as if she didn't have the energy to lower herself all the way to the cushions.

I took pity on her, realizing that my parents had put her in an untenable position. They had been the ones who decided to live a lie, and she hadn't wanted to expose it. I softened my voice. "Is it true that Hank's my father?" I knew the answer, but I had to ask, hoping for a last-ditch miracle, like a hockey player making a desperate slap shot from behind his goal line in the final seconds of the game.

"Your biological father, yes, but Dom is your father in every way that matters." Her voice shook, and I realized she'd been dreading this conversation since I'd found the photo album, if not for my entire life.

"You're defending my da—you're defending him now?"

"One thing I can say with certainty about Dominic is that he loved you, Dana, and your mother."

I'd never questioned my father's love for my mother, but now I thought if he had really loved her, he wouldn't have lied about Hank saying he didn't want the baby. Hank had told me my father wanted to protect my mother, but I wondered if my father had lied as a way to worm his way into her life. That, to me, certainly wasn't love. Love was putting the other person's happiness above yours, not sabotaging it to get what you wanted. My shoulders stiffened. Hadn't I put my happiness above Kyle's and potentially sabotaged his future by withdrawing from our retirement fund? I had no right to judge my father. Still, I couldn't picture the man I had known and loved my entire life telling such an outrageous lie.

"Did my father really tell Mom that Hank wanted her to get rid of me?"

Aunt Izzie chewed on her lower lip. As I watched her struggle to answer, the reason for her falling-out with my father became crystal clear. "You found out about my father's lie. It's why your relationship with him soured."

She sighed. "I'm not convinced that Hank would have done right by you and your mom, but he never had the chance."

I sank to the sofa. The photo album still sat on the coffee table. I thumbed through it until I reached the page with the prom pictures. The teenage boy my dad had been when he told his lie looked back at me. That awkward kid with his lanky body and nose too big for his face bore only a tiny resemblance to the sturdy man I remembered. The unkempt eyebrows that he'd never learned to tame were the same, and seeing them made me smile. I used to tease him about them all the time. "Thank God I didn't inherit those from you," I would joke.

"No, instead you got my nose hair." He could never get through his response without laughing.

While he'd had fun with my comment, I wondered now if my words ever caused him angst. Was he ever tempted to tell me the truth?

"Dom stepped up in Hank's absence. Though, honestly, your mom would have been fine on her own," Aunt Izzie said. "I would have helped."

"He never treated me any differently than he treated Dana."

Aunt Izzie smiled. "He loved you as if you were his own. No doubt about that."

"I guess I never knew him, because the man I thought he was could never have told such an awful lie."

"Don't be so hard on him, Nikki. He made a bad decision and did a bad thing. That doesn't make him a bad person." My aunt's complexion had returned to its normal color, and her eyes shone brighter. "Sometimes when we want something so badly, we do things we're not proud of to get them."

I flinched, thinking she was talking about me lying to Kyle about getting a bonus so he would do another round of IVF, but then I remembered Aunt Izzie didn't know I had lied about that. The hot, steaming mound of anger I'd been feeling toward my dad shrank. He was a man with faults like all of us. I wondered what my sister would think when she found out. *Does she already know?* The thought of her knowing made me queasy. I couldn't take another person keeping secrets from me.

"Does Dana know?" I heard the terror in my voice.

Aunt Izzie shook her head. "I was the only other person who knew."

"Why didn't they tell me?"

Aunt Izzie looked at the ceiling. "I don't know. It wasn't a decision I agreed with."

"How am I going to tell Dana?"

"You're going to use your words. Simple as that." She fiddled with a button on her blouse. "Nikki, Hank's your father, but that doesn't change anything about who you are. You're still the same person Dana has known and loved her entire life."

I didn't feel like the same person. If I was being honest, I hadn't felt like myself since I'd lied to Kyle. I needed to find a way to move past my lie, past Kyle's mistake, and on with our lives. Knowing that my parents had survived my father's lie gave me hope for me and Kyle.

"When my dad married my mom, did everyone know the baby—that I—wasn't his?"

"There was some talk in town. People love to gossip, but your parents didn't care. They were happy together, and they weren't going to let anyone stand in the way of their happiness." She pointed a bony finger at me. "You have to do what makes you happy."

Chapter 46

On Sunday morning, I awoke to the sound of the doorbell ringing. I glanced at the clock, surprised to see it was after ten. I expected to find Aunt Izzie at the door with a bag of bagels or box of donuts, coming to check on me after yesterday's revelation. Instead, Kyle leaned against the iron railing. He wore a gray T-shirt with the words *Marconi Beach* across his chest. Seeing it made me think of Dana. I had called her last night, intending to tell her the news about Hank, but I couldn't make myself say the words. I'd decided I would tell her in person when she came home after Labor Day, which was only a few weeks away.

"Were you sleeping?" Kyle asked.

I tugged at my pajama top, wishing I'd thrown on real clothes before coming downstairs. "Why didn't you use your key?" The fact that he no longer felt comfortable walking into his own house made me wonder if we had waited too long to try to work things out. *Start now,* a voice inside my head screamed.

Kyle shrugged. "I don't know. I just . . ." He trailed off without finishing his thought and glanced across the street. "Mr. Abrams called this morning. Has a water stain on the living room ceiling and wanted me to take a look." He pointed to our front lawn. "Noticed the grass needed mowing, so I figured I'd do it while I was here."

"I actually had that on my list of things to do today." By that I meant calling the high school kid around the corner who had been cutting my lawn all summer.

Kyle grinned. The cleft in his chin appeared. I'd forgotten just how handsome he was when he smiled. "Sure you did."

～

The house smelled like bacon and eggs. I'd set the table for two and changed into my most flattering sundress. Kyle leaned against the doorframe with an expression I couldn't read. Sweat soaked through his shirt, and his face glowed a bright red. He pointed toward the stove. "What's all this?"

"I figured you worked up an appetite."

He glanced toward the clock, and my muscles stiffened. *He has plans. He can't stay.* I pictured him at Castleton Lake in a canoe with Casey.

He strode across the room and pulled open the refrigerator. *He's thinking of a way to tell me that he has to go.*

"It's fine if you don't have time to eat. I'll pack you a to-go container."

He twisted open a bottle of water and gulped it down. "You look so nice. I thought maybe you had a date coming. Luke told me he saw you driving up toward the mansions in the sky yesterday."

My stomach fluttered. He was jealous. "I just went to see Hank."

Kyle tilted his head. "You went to Hank's?"

My fluttery, happy feeling morphed into a jittery nervousness. I wasn't ready to tell anyone what I had learned yesterday.

Kyle fiddled with the cap of his water bottle. "Why did you go to Hank's?"

Sunlight poured in through the back door. I squinted into it as I looked at Kyle, trying to decide whether to tell him. "We can talk over breakfast." I pulled out a chair.

He sniffed and made a face. "I can't stand the smell of myself. Do you mind if I take a shower?"

I bristled at the question. "You don't have to ask. It's your house."

Kyle opened his mouth as if he were about to say something, but before any words came out, he snapped it shut and marched toward the bathroom. A few minutes later, I could hear him singing over the running water, a Luke Combs song about beer never breaking his heart. With a huge grin, I sang along from the stove.

Fifteen minutes later, he returned to the kitchen with damp hair. "There's enough food for a feast here." He snatched a piece of bacon from the frying pan while I scooped scrambled eggs and hash browns into his dish.

We began eating, both of us concentrating on our breakfast and not speaking. I had so much I wanted to talk to him about, but I didn't know where to start. Kyle glanced around the kitchen. His gaze landed on the spot where the dog bowls used to be.

"It's weird here without Oliver," he said.

Now was my chance. *It's weird here without you.* Even though I wanted to, I couldn't say it. What if he told me he was never coming home? "I miss him. Dana sends pictures all the time." I reached across the table to where my phone sat and scrolled through it until I found the latest texts my sister had sent.

Kyle smiled as he looked at them. "He looks bigger."

"Yeah, he's definitely not a puppy anymore."

My Samsung whistled, indicating I had a text. Kyle frowned as he looked at the screen. He slid the phone across the table toward me. I saw right away that the message was from Hank. My mouth went dry, hoping he hadn't written anything about being my father.

I felt Kyle watching me as I read the message. Hope you're okay after yesterday. I know it must have been a shock. Let's have dinner soon.

"What happened yesterday?" Kyle asked.

I waved the question away. "Nothing worth talking about."

Disappointment flashed across his face, and I knew I'd let him down by not confiding in him. The person I'd been before lying about the bonus would have told him everything. If we were going to work things out, we needed to get back to that. I had to tell him about Hank.

"Listen, Nikki." He went to the refrigerator and spoke with his back to me. "I can't stay at Luke's forever." He returned to the table with a bottle of hot sauce. "We have to figure out what we're going to do. Work things out or . . ."

The unfinished thought hung in the air between us. My eggs caught in my throat. I chugged my iced tea, trying to push them down. We'd never talked about divorce. Was that what he wanted? I forced myself to look at him. He studied me with a cool gaze. "We need to make some decisions. Casey told me she talked to you, so you know she doesn't want to be in the baby's life."

"She'll change her mind when she sees her."

"I don't think so. She's already met with a lawyer." He pushed the potatoes around his plate with his fork. "Whatever Casey decides, I need to be out of Luke's place before the baby comes."

I shifted in my seat. *Just be honest with him,* an insistent voice shouted in my head, a voice that might not have spoken up if I hadn't learned yesterday that my entire childhood had been a lie. "I want you to come home, but before you do, I need to be certain I can raise the baby." I'd had months to figure this out, but I felt no closer to an answer than I had back in May. "Can I just have more time to think about it? And in the meantime, we can start spending time together again. See how things go."

"I want you to be sure. So take the time you need. I can find someplace with a month-to-month lease until you decide. I know it's a big decision."

After breakfast, we drove to Castleton Lake. Young families sat on the beach under umbrellas or in tents. A group of women Aunt Izzie's age stood knee deep in the water, talking. In the grass behind the sand, a group of college kids played cornhole. Kyle and I rented kayaks and paddled out beyond the swimming area. The waves gently lifted and lowered our boats as we floated side by side, staring off into the mountains. Since I was a kid, being out on the water had always relaxed me. A light feeling came over me, and I knew I was ready to tell Kyle about Hank.

"I found a photo album at my aunt's with pictures of my mom and Hank," I said. "Turns out they dated in high school, from eighth grade until senior year." My kayak started to drift away from Kyle's. He reached out with his paddle and pulled it back toward him. "He broke up with her before he left for the NHL."

The midday sun beat down on my bare shoulders, and I wished I had worn a shirt over my bathing suit.

"Right after he left, she found out she was pregnant, but she never told him." Realizing too late that voices carried over the water, I turned toward the beach to see if anyone was looking at us. One woman in a red bikini looked our way, but she might have been watching the paddleboarder just behind us.

"Are you saying—"

I cut Kyle off. "Yes."

He dipped his hand into the water and stirred it around. A school of fish scurried off.

"Hank didn't find out about me until his career ended, and he didn't want to destroy my family, so he never told anyone."

"Why wouldn't your mother tell him?" Judgment laced his voice, and I feared he would never again think of my mother in the same positive light he always had.

The sun slipped behind a puffy white cloud. "Doesn't that look like a rabbit?" I pointed toward the sky.

Kyle glanced upward and shook his head. "What do you make of all this?"

I pointed at the cloud. "Those are the floppy ears. That's his cotton tail."

Kyle tilted his head. "It looks a little like Mickey Mouse."

I frowned, trying to see how he saw the Disney character, but I couldn't. "I'm angry at my parents for lying. I feel bad I've been so hard on Hank, and I'm wondering how Dana will react when she finds out."

We were both quiet for a few minutes. Sounds of laughter from the beach drifted toward us. I started to paddle in toward the shore. Kyle followed behind, slowly at first, but then he quickened his pace, splashing me with his oars as he zoomed by me. The sudden coldness of the water shocked me. I let out a startled yelp. Kyle looked back at me, grinning. I hurried to catch up to him, and we raced to shore. He beat me by several boat lengths and helped me drag my kayak out of the water.

As we walked back toward his Jeep, Kyle took my hand in his. The gesture bolstered me. I felt as if he were giving me the strength I needed to handle the news about Hank being my father. "I'm glad Casey told you. I'm glad you get to be a dad to this baby," I said.

"I hope you'll be a mom to her," he answered.

Chapter 47

From my living room window, I watched Dana pull into the driveway. She parked and beeped the horn in a celebratory blast. As I raced outside and around her Corolla, I noticed too late that she stood by the driver's side with her arms spread, ready for a hug. I thought about turning back to her, but Oliver had started spinning in circles in the passenger seat when he saw me. I opened the car door, and he leaped out, wagging his tail and barking. He jumped up on his hind legs and rested his front paws just below my shoulders. He'd grown over the summer, and standing on his back legs, he was almost as tall as I was. I patted his red fur, taking him in. He wore a bright-blue bandanna with the words *Cape Cod* around his neck and a new dog tag that read *Deeogee* with Dana's phone number under his name.

"Welcome home, buddy. I missed you so much." I could tell he was excited to see me too. He tilted his head, looking at my face and panting hard with his tongue hanging out of his mouth. He moved his paw back and forth across my chest as if he were petting me. I felt myself breaking out in a smile as I scratched behind his ears.

The horn beeped again. Both Oliver and I startled. "What about me?" Dana was leaning into the car with her hand on the steering wheel. She'd been home for over a week, staying with Aunt Izzie, but I'd been avoiding her. I knew when I saw her, I'd have to tell her about Hank, and I feared our relationship would change, that she would think of me as Hank's daughter and not her sister.

"Did you miss me or just Deeogee?" There was a combination of hurt and resentment in her voice.

"I missed both you and Oliver."

"Don't start with that Oliver bullshit. His name is Deeogee."

"Fine." I sprinted to the other side of the car. Deeogee trotted behind me as if he didn't want to let me out of his sight.

Dana folded her arms across her chest. "I haven't seen you in months, and you greet the dog before me."

"I'm the worst." I pulled her into an embrace. After a few seconds, she wrapped her arms around me too. "I can't believe you didn't come to visit all summer. You love the Cape."

"I meant to, but time got away from me." I held her closer, thinking of our shared history, the hours we'd spent giggling at the counter of DeMarco's Diner, the competitive games of Connect Four we'd play, even the way we fought over who would ride shotgun when we drove around town with my mother. Everything about my sister was so familiar: the scent of the coconut-lime shampoo that she'd been using since high school, the diamond stud she'd worn in her right ear since college graduation, the feel of her lean, muscular arms around my shoulders, and the way she would never be the one to end a hug first.

"I was hoping you and Kyle would have worked things out by now," Dana said.

"We're working on it." Pointing with my head, I indicated she should follow me inside. We made peanut-butter-and-jelly sandwiches. Dana slipped potato chips inside hers, just like she used to do when we were kids.

We took our lunch outside and ate on the Adirondack chairs. Deeogee rested at our feet, gnawing on a toy bone. It was a warm September day, but the cool breeze whispered that we'd better enjoy our time outdoors while we could.

After we finished eating, Dana asked about Kyle again. I was glad for the question because it allowed me to put off talking about Hank.

"We're seeing a lot of each other, but I can't let him move in unless I know with certainty that I can be a good mother to the baby."

"You absolutely can," Dana said.

I stared off toward the mountain. Some of the leaves on the trees at the top had turned an orangey red. Despite the beauty of fall in New England, this time of year always made me sad. Everything was dying.

"How do you know that?"

"Because I know you."

Not as well as you think you do, I thought. I took a deep breath and squared my shoulders, preparing to tell her about the enormous secret our parents had kept from us. "I have to tell you something."

"Okay." She responded without thinking. I wondered if after I told her this information that would ruin everything she believed about our family, she would wish I'd kept the secret to myself.

Below me, Deeogee had fallen asleep. He was lying on his back with his four legs sticking up in the air. He looked as uncomfortable as I felt.

"It's about Hank."

"Nikki, you have to let it go. Really."

"He . . . he's my father."

Dana smirked. "Very funny."

"It's why Aunt Izzie didn't want us going through those boxes with the old photo albums. There were pictures of him and Mom together. They dated all through high school."

Dana's posture straightened. "You're serious."

My head felt like it weighed two hundred pounds as I nodded.

"Mom and Hank were a couple?"

"From eighth grade until they graduated high school."

"So why did she marry Dad?"

I told her the story about how Hank had left for New York and our mother never told him she was pregnant because she wanted him to focus on his hockey career. I didn't tell her about the lie our father told because I didn't want to make him look bad.

She listened without speaking or moving. I wasn't even sure she was breathing. When I finished, she hunched down to pat Deeogee. He got up and sat down in front of her. She wrapped him up in a hug. After a minute or so, a slow smile spread across her face. "So you're my sista from another mista." She elbowed me. "Mom and Hank, doing the nasty. Can you imagine?"

I blocked my eyes with my hands. "Stop."

We both burst out laughing.

"You have to admit Hank is hot. Certainly hotter than Dad."

After all that time I'd worried about telling her, she was making a joke about it. I should have known.

"Do you think they ever hooked up after?"

"Dana!"

Her expression turned serious, and she sat up straight. "I don't think it's a coincidence that you saw that photo album now and learned that Hank's your father."

"I don't think Aunt Izzie left it out on purpose, if that's what you mean. She was really mad when she caught me going through it."

"It was Mom and Dad letting you know that you can raise Casey's baby just like Dad raised Hank's baby."

Chapter 48

"Nice place you have here, Nikki," Hank said. Two months had passed since the warm August day when he'd told me he was my father. Since then, we'd gotten together twice. Both those times, Aunt Izzie and Arianna had been with us. Tonight, we were alone.

He handed me a bouquet of red sunflowers. Last month, when we'd had dinner together at Declan's, I'd told him they were my favorite. I was touched he'd remembered.

His gaze rotated around the room, taking in each object as if he were looking for clues to my personality in the paintings on the walls, books in my bookshelf, and knickknacks on the end tables. When his eyes landed on a set of shiny black coasters designed to look like hockey pucks with the NHL logo in the center, he smiled. "I have these in the condo in New York. See, we have some things in common." He looked so pleased that I didn't bother to tell him Kyle had bought them.

As I made my way to the kitchen to put the flowers in a vase and pop dinner in the oven, Hank slid into Kyle's recliner. Seeing him sitting there made me twitchy. I fought an urge to ask him to move to the couch. Kyle should have been sitting in that chair. He should have been here with me, getting to know Hank.

When I returned to the living room, Hank was holding a Polaroid. He studied it with a pained expression that turned to a smile as his eyes met mine. He extended the picture toward me. The white borders had turned yellow with age, and there was a pinhole in the top center as if the picture had hung on a bulletin board for years.

I expected the image to be of him and my mom, but I was wrong. A ten-year-old version of myself smiled up at me. A younger Hank had his arm wrapped around my shoulder and a big cheesy smile on his face.

"That was taken at the Stapleton County Fair," he said.

"You took me on a ride."

Hank smiled. "You remember that?"

My parents, Dana, and I had spent the day at the fair. Hank had been there in a charity booth, taking pictures with fans and selling autographed photographs of himself. Right before this picture was taken, my father and I had ridden the Tilt-A-Whirl while my mother, holding two-year-old Dana, looked on. By the time the ride ended, she and Hank sat on a bench together. I wanted to ride again, but my father said he was too dizzy, so Hank took me. When the teenage ticket taker saw Hank, the boy's face had turned bright red, and his hands had shaken so much he dropped the ticket. "You're Hank Pendleton," he'd said.

Hank nodded. "I am."

"You were my favorite. Sorry about the knee."

Hank winked at me. "You're riding with a celebrity, kid."

My father had originally refused to let Hank take me on the ride. The two had words. My mother had intervened, and my father begrudgingly agreed. Had that really happened, or was I making it up based on what I knew now?

Either way, in that moment in my living room, as I saw that tattered Polaroid that Hank had treasured for three decades, my entire perception of him changed. I saw him as a man who had been betrayed by his best friend and made an unthinkable sacrifice for a woman he had once loved. The familiar feeling of guilt over the horrible way I had treated him for the past five years bubbled up in me.

"You kept this picture all those years."

"I actually have a painting of it hanging in the office in the place in New York. Your aunt painted it for me."

A wave of sadness rolled over me. Tears flooded my eyes, and I fled the room to check on the chicken before they broke free. Hank followed me into the kitchen and eased himself into a chair. "You okay?"

I sat down across from him. "I'm still trying to wrap my head around how you were able to forgive my parents."

He cocked his head. "Well, like I told you, I didn't treat Gianna right at the end. It wasn't easy, but forgiveness is a choice. I had to forgive them and myself."

"But why did you choose it?" *And why can't I?*

Hank's eyes locked with mine. "Are you and Sebastian still trying to work things out?"

I fidgeted in my seat, wondering if I was easy to see through or if he knew me better than I thought he did.

The timer buzzed. I jumped out of the chair and pulled dinner from the oven.

"Smells delicious," Hank said.

"Chicken rollups. I hope you like goat cheese and sun-dried tomatoes."

"You can never go wrong with either."

I served the food and poured us both big glasses of wine. Hank told me he and Arianna had visited the vineyard in Oregon where the pinot noir originated. Throughout dinner, he entertained me with stories of all the places they had traveled. New Zealand was his favorite. He showed me pictures on his phone from a hike he'd done on the Abel Tasman Coast Track. The beauty of the blue-green water made me want to jump on a plane and see it in person.

As we ate dessert, a key lime cheesecake that Sharon had baked and dropped off earlier in the day, Hank steered the conversation back to Kyle. "You never answered me about Sebastian."

I took a deep breath in and slowly let it out. "I want to forgive him. I really do." Since the Sunday afternoon we'd gone kayaking, we'd spoken every day and seen each other several times a week. We were getting along great, but I was still questioning whether I could raise Casey's baby.

Hank leaned forward in his chair. "What's stopping you?" I felt as if he was willing me to make amends with Kyle and give my marriage another chance.

"I don't know."

He sliced a second piece of cheesecake. "Are you afraid he'll do something like that again?"

"No." I was surer of that than of anything else in my life right then. Even after what had happened with Casey, I still trusted Kyle. Our struggles with IVF had pushed him into being a person he wasn't, just like they had changed me. The situation had brought out the worst in each of us.

"Then what's the problem?" Hank spoke softer than usual so that the question didn't come off as impatient.

"What kind of woman helps her husband raise a child he had outside of their marriage?"

Hank steepled his fingers together and cocked his head. After several seconds, he answered. "What kind of man stands by and watches another man raise his daughter?"

I took in his slumped shoulders and slack jaw and saw what his decision had cost him. My neck itched as I thought about the assumptions I had made and the way that I had treated him since my parents' death. I cleared my throat, trying to wipe away my shame.

"A man who tried to do the right thing," I said.

He reached across the table and put his hand over mine. "Maybe for you, forgiving Kyle and being a mother to his baby is the right thing."

Chapter 49

Kyle moved home a week before Halloween. He spent his first day in the house painting the office a seafoam green. After work two nights later, he lugged a crib he had built at Luke's into the house. I could tell by the detail that making it had been a labor of love. Painted a weathered gray, the crib included four drawers, three shelves, and a changing table that folded down.

"It's not quite done." He pointed to the backboard. "I want to paint her name there."

"I guess you'll have to decide on one, then."

Kyle shook his head. "I want it to be our decision." He stepped closer. "The first of many we make together about her."

I imagined us picking out a preschool for her, discussing what type of activities we wanted her to participate in, arguing over her curfew, and debating at what age she'd be allowed to date. I looked forward to all of it.

"Do you have anything in mind?" I asked.

I waited for him to say Jasmine. That had been the name he'd wanted before I had the miscarriage. He'd planned to call her Jazz.

He rocked back and forth on his heels. "Gianna."

"Gianna." My voice cracked as I said the name. "You want to name her after my mom?"

He hesitated. "And my mom for her middle name. Gianna Kathryn Sebastian." He folded his arms across his chest. "What do you think?"

"Why Gianna?"

"It's a way to carry on a piece of your mother and make you feel more connected to the baby."

I glanced at the crib and imagined my mother's name painted in seafoam green across the backboard. The image made me smile. "It's perfect."

~

I stood in the hallway outside Elizabeth's office, about to knock. She sat behind her desk, squinting and leaning closer to her monitor. Whatever she was reading caused her to scowl. I slowly backed away from the door. I wanted to talk to her about taking time off when Gianna was born, but seeing her expression made me think this wasn't the right time.

"What do you need, Nikki?" she asked without looking away from her screen.

Her voice startled me. She'd given no indication that she had seen me standing there.

"I can come back when you're not busy."

"When would that be?" She looked up and motioned for me to come in.

I pushed my shoulders back and stuck out my chest, trying to radiate confidence as I crossed the carpet to Elizabeth's guest chair. She could refuse to let me take time off. State law didn't require employers to provide parenting leave, and the magazine was too small for the Family and Medical Leave Act to apply.

As I sat, Elizabeth slid her top desk drawer open and pulled out a bottle of ibuprofen. She popped two in her mouth and swallowed them with a large gulp of water. "I hiked to Lydia's Falls with the kids yesterday," she said. "I carried Danvers and am paying for it today."

This time of year, looking down on Stapleton from high on the mountain was like watching a fireworks show. The leaves on the trees were brilliant shades of red, orange, and yellow. "At least the view from the top made it worthwhile."

Elizabeth gave me a sheepish grin. "We didn't make it to the top. Danvers got too heavy for me with the steep inclines."

An image of my boss cradling her son against her chest while holding her daughter's hand as they climbed to the waterfall popped into my head. A heavy backpack hung from Elizabeth's shoulder. Of course she needed help. "If you decide to try again, I can come along and help with the kids." The words came out before I had time to think about what I was saying. I wished I hadn't said them, because once I asked for time off, she might think my offer had been a way to butter her up.

She smiled. "I might take you up on that."

The phone on her desk rang. I looked at it and started to stand.

"Voice mail can get it. What did you need?"

I took a deep breath. Maybe I should wait until after the baby was born to broach this subject. After all, there was still a chance Casey would change her mind about giving her up. Then again, I had to know what my options were. "I'd like to take an extended leave after Casey has the baby."

Elizabeth's face tensed. She picked up the bottle of Motrin and rolled it between her hands. The rattling of the pills frayed my nerves. "What exactly do you mean by 'extended'?"

Sharon had told me to ask for six months so that I would have room to negotiate. I couldn't ask for that much time. Elizabeth was the poster child for a single mom with a thriving career. She would laugh me out of the room. "How much time did you take after you had Hallie and Danvers?"

"I returned to work exactly one month after Hallie was born." She said it with pride, as if it were one of her greatest accomplishments.

I swallowed hard. "One month?" I prayed my voice didn't sound as disgusted out loud as it did in my head.

She leaned back in her chair. "Well, the truth is I was diagnosed with preeclampsia and confined to bed rest for several weeks before she was born, so I couldn't wait to get back."

"And with Danvers?"

"Different circumstances. My life was falling apart when I was pregnant with him. After he was born, I focused on moving away from New York."

"Are you glad you came here?"

She sighed. "I miss the city, but this is a great place for my kids to grow up."

Staying in Stapleton for her children, comforting me when she'd found out about Kyle and Casey, and connecting Casey with an attorney to talk through her options. Elizabeth might be a difficult boss, but she was a good person. She would understand that I needed time. "Five months."

She smiled. "Four. I'll talk to Andrew about making sure you're paid for some of it, but you have to promise you're coming back."

"Not coming back isn't an option," I said.

"Who will take care of the baby when you return?"

I smiled. "My aunt said she would watch her a few days, and believe it or not, Hank and Arianna also volunteered. What will you do if Casey leaves?"

Elizabeth reached across the desk and patted my hand. The gesture was so unexpected that I flinched. "Casey is leaving. By herself." Her voice was as gentle as I had ever heard it. "She already rented a place in Nashville, found a job, and lined up gigs. She's not going to change her mind."

I blinked back tears. Casey and Kyle had repeatedly told me the same thing, but still I wasn't convinced. Elizabeth's effort to reassure me made me warm to her further. "I hope you're right."

"I am. I've been interviewing nannies and have it narrowed down to two. I'm meeting with them both again later this week."

Her phone rang again. This time when I stood, she didn't stop me. When I reached her doorframe, I turned back toward her. "Thanks for agreeing to the time off, and good luck choosing Casey's replacement."

"Your baby will be close in age to Danvers," she said. "Maybe they'll be friends."

~

Gianna arrived on a blustery December day, two weeks after her due date. On the day we took her home from the hospital, Casey boarded a plane for Nashville. I had told Casey I wanted to wait six months before officially adopting Gianna because I wanted Casey to be sure of her decision. She reluctantly agreed. The time dragged. Every time the phone rang, I was sure the caller would be Casey saying she had changed her mind. She never did.

On an unseasonably cool June day, I officially became Gianna's mother. Kyle, Gianna, and I celebrated with Aunt Izzie and Dana at Pendleton 88. Hank carried the baby around the restaurant all night, introducing her to the other customers as his great-niece.

She had dark hair, and some people commented she looked like me. The comments always made me smile. I would thank the person and say nothing more. Like Kyle, Gianna had blue-gray eyes, and I saw more of him than Casey in her, but maybe I was only seeing what I wanted to.

On the way home from dinner that night, Kyle and I listened to *The Highway* on satellite radio. The DJ announced a song as the latest "Highway Find," a program that identified up-and-comers in country music. The song was called "Doing Good with My Bad" and was written and performed by a new singer named Casey Flanagan. I swear, Gianna smiled as we listened.

Chapter 50

Seven Years Later

A crowd of small children with paintbrushes in their hands sat around easels at Sip and Strokes, listening to Aunt Izzie's instructions on how to paint a unicorn. "Find the shapes with the number nine on your drawing and use your pink paint to fill them in." She had been teaching at the studio for almost five years. Under her guidance, the place had become a favorite destination for kids on Saturday and Sunday afternoons.

Gianna especially loved painting there with her great-aunt. Today, Kyle and I had invited our little girl's entire first-grade class and a few other friends to celebrate her seventh birthday.

"Gigi looks like she's having fun," Dana said. My sister had started calling Gianna Gigi shortly after her birth. Despite my objections, the nickname had stuck.

"She always does," I said. My girl's most defining characteristic was her huge smile.

She sat at a table with Baby Sharon, who everyone called Sharra these days, and Elizabeth's daughter, Hallie. Twelve now, Hallie was five years older than the other two girls and treated them like little sisters, always watching out for them. We'd even let her babysit a handful of times when we went out for a quick dinner.

Now Hallie pointed at her painting and said something that made Sharra and Gianna burst out in laughter. Gianna leaned closer to

Hallie's easel, holding her brush high in the air. Pink paint dripped onto her smock. She'd even managed to get some in her hair, which was the same chocolate-brown color as her dad's. At this early stage in her life, she resembled Kyle, with the same oval face, puffy lips, and cleft chin. She definitely had some of her biological mother in her too, though. She'd recently played Ariel in the school's performance of *The Little Mermaid*. Seeing her singing on that stage with the red wig reminded me so much of Casey that I had felt goose bumps on the back of my neck.

Gianna must have sensed that I was watching her, because she turned toward the bar where I sat and blew me a kiss. Love surged through my body as I reached out with my hand, pretending to catch the kiss.

Kyle dropped his arm over my shoulder and whispered in my ear, "She's such a mommy's girl." It was true. All the worrying I'd done that Gianna and I wouldn't connect was for naught. I was the one she always asked to tuck her in and read her a story at bedtime. I was the one she cuddled with on family movie night. I was the one she wanted in the snow tube with her when we went sledding.

At the front of the shop a bell rang, pulling me from my thoughts. The door opened, and Sharon stepped inside, carrying a large teal bakery box with her maiden name and logo embossed in the bottom corner. She set the box down on the bar in front of me and slowly lifted the cover, watching me closely as she did so.

Driscoll's Bakery had officially opened five days ago. Gianna's was the first birthday cake Sharon had baked for her new business. It was shaped and decorated like the unicorn the kids were painting.

I bounced on the balls of my feet as I took in all the details. The body was purple, Gianna's favorite color. "This is amazing." One of my favorite touches was the sugar-cone horn. I pulled Sharon into a hug. "You are going to be so successful."

She laughed. "You should wait until you taste it before saying that."

Elizabeth snapped a few photos of the cake with her phone. *Mountain Views Magazine* was featuring Driscoll's Bakery in the March issue.

"Who's ready for cake?" I asked.

Everyone gathered around the bar. I lit the candles and stood behind Gianna as we all sang to her. When the time came for her to blow out the candles, she leaned closer to the cake with her tongue hanging out of the corner of her mouth. I knew she was thinking about what to wish for. She'd been trying to decide for weeks between a bicycle and a puppy. She loved Deeogee and wanted a dog of her own. "I'm going to make two wishes," she said. I smiled, knowing both would come true. Earlier in the month, Hank had asked if we minded if he gave her a bike, and after the party, Kyle and I were picking up a two-year-old black Lab from the animal shelter.

As everyone sat around the tables eating cake, which tasted as good as it looked, Dana synced her phone with the wireless speakers to play music. A Taylor Swift song came on. "This is my favorite," Sharra said. She jumped out of her chair to dance, pulling Gianna up with her. The two sang along.

The song ended. As the girls sat down again, the opening chords of Casey's latest began to play: "Knowing My Baby's Happy Makes Me Happy."

"This is Mommy's favorite song, isn't it, Mommy?" Gianna said.

I smiled at her. "It sure is."

Someday soon I would tell her why.

ACKNOWLEDGMENTS

My most heartfelt appreciation to you, the reader. There are so many great books to choose from; thank you for reading mine.

Thank you, too, to everyone who takes the time to leave a review, including book bloggers who go the extra mile by posting beautiful pictures and have helped promote my previous novels.

This book started as a writing prompt Elizabeth Berg gave me in a workshop several years ago. Thank you to Elizabeth and all the other writers in the workshop who reacted so positively to what I wrote.

Most of the first draft for this book was written in GrubStreet's Novel Generator program, taught by Annie Hartnett. Thank you, Annie, for your guidance. I learned so much from your critiques. My book is so much better than it would have been without your advice.

Thank you to all the writers in the Generator program who commented on my work. A special thank-you to my critique partners, Joanne Barahona, Lee Hoffman, and Ben Cotton. I miss our evenings at Flatbread! I so enjoyed reading your pages, and I hope someday I have the opportunity to read your complete novels.

Lauren Hughes, your enthusiasm for my manuscript came at exactly the right time and meant the world to me. Your suggestions made the book stronger, especially the ending. Thank you, too, for the great title!

Thank you to the Women's Fiction Writers Association (WFWA), which matched me with critique partners, and to everyone who read a part of this story in its many iterations. Michele Lugiai, thank you for staying with me to the end of this story and reading the same scenes over and over again. Donna Carbone, thank you for beta reading. Lidija Hilje, thank you for your critique of the first chapters and for teaching me the inside outline, which was instrumental in my revisions.

Julie Peterson, thank you for reading a complete draft and pushing me to do better.

My writing group at the Hudson Public Library! I'm so glad Zoom allowed us to keep working together through the pandemic. You have been with me from my debut, and I can't imagine writing a book without you.

Susan Timmerman and Susan Devane, thank you for reading and commenting on several drafts. And thank you for your unwavering support for everything I write.

Alicia Clancy, thank you for believing in this story and for your insightful comments on the manuscript. Your edits strengthened Nikki's character and the overall book. Riam, you are a superstar! Thank you for your keen eye and incredible attention to detail. Elyse, thank you for your sharp eye and gentle suggestions. I am grateful to everyone at Lake Union who has worked on this book. It's been a wonderful experience.

Liza Fleissig, superagent and friend, I gush about you so much that I'm sure by now you know how much I admire, respect, and adore you. Thank you for standing by me, encouraging me, and looking out for me and even for the tough love. To everyone at Liza Royce Agency who reads my manuscripts, thank you for your input.

Jack, I hope you are with Shirley now, smiling down on us. I get my best writing done at the lake, and I have you both to thank for that.

Mom and Dad, thank you for everything you have done and continue to do for me. I wouldn't be a writer or have an interest in books if you hadn't encouraged me to read. Love you to the moon and back.

Steve, last in my acknowledgments, first in my heart. Always. Thank you for making our life such a fun adventure, and thank you for insisting I step away from my computer and take the life-changing drive to New York to meet the red dog.

ABOUT THE AUTHOR

Diane Barnes is the author of *More Than*, *Waiting for Ethan*, and *Mixed Signals*. She is also a marketing and corporate communication writer in the health-care industry. When she's not writing, she's at the gym, running, or playing tennis, trying to burn off the ridiculous amounts of chocolate and ice cream she eats. She and her husband, Steven, live in New England with Oakley, their handsome golden retriever. She hopes you enjoy reading her books as much as she enjoyed writing them.